The

067
9456774

Brian McCabe

For Mary Berford

Foreword

Brian McCabe's gripping novel is set in Dublin in the years between 1900 and 1922 — a turbulent period in Irish history which encompasses the lock-out, the 1916 Rising, the War of Independence and the disastrous civil war which ushered in the new Free State. This unfolding drama is seen through the eyes of the Berford and McNeill families in their respective enclaves in Dublin's teeming north inner city.

The author has set himself an ambitious project but he acquits himself with distinction. He brings to the task an intimate knowledge of the geography and history of his native city and makes it come vividly alive for the reader. As a result we see these historic events through the eyes of the participants, mainly Dublin working-class people. Many readers will be shocked to learn of the poverty, hunger and social deprivation which were widespread in Dublin a mere century ago and the gulf which separated rich and poor.

The novel is a tour de force in which McCabe accomplishes a remarkable feat in writing. He has produced strong characters who grip the reader's imagination and he has welded these to a riveting plot which makes the story gallop along at a cracking pace from the very first sentence. *The Stoney Road* is compassionate and humane and combines those rare talents of skilled storytelling and fine writing which is a pleasure to read.

Brian McCabe has produced a novel which bears comparison with James Plunkett's masterpiece *Strumpet City.*

Eugene McEldowney
(Novelist and journalist)

Author's Note

Stoneybatter derives from "stoney *bóthar*" (*bóthar* being the Irish for road). It was part of the Slí Chualann — an ancient road connecting Royal Tara with the monastic settlements in Glendalough.

PART 1

Chapter 1

Golden calf

(Dublin 1900)

Bamma Berford, black-clad in her awesome widowhood, hovered behind the kitchen curtains staring in disbelief. Coiled within her widow's weeds of twenty years, watching the hedgerows surrounding the Berfords' piece of ground called 'Mooney's Field'. Ready to pounce.

One minute she was sure she had glimpsed Fenian McNeill through the gaps in the briary whitethorn. At the next, she sensed that the luminous May blossom was deceiving her. Spectres of her daughter's suitor everywhere. And there it was again. There was no mistaking the sloping, bull shoulders and short legs of James McNeill driving his cow towards Cabra Cottage. Would he have the audacity?

She continued to knead the dough for bread way past necessity. Her adult son and daughters, sitting around the table behind her, smelt the air heavy with things impending. And still her pummelling grew more urgent.

"Mary," she said, so low it was just audible.

"What is it Bamma?"

"Has that ageing illiterate you're consorting with taken leave of his senses?"

"Is it James you're referring to Bamma?"

"Yes madam. And he's driving a dumb beast up to the house! I sincerely hope you did not give him permission to come here."

Her grown children continued to sit around the well-scrubbed pine table trying to concentrate on being productive. Bamma asked for no help around the house but she would not tolerate idleness. They could sit while they waited for their meals but they would do something useful while they did. Even with the storm brewing,

1

Philip's slide rule continued working at the same problem over and over without the answer penetrating to his brain. Lena was stitching a third line of thread to the already secure cerise lily on the hat she was making. Nelly began to blubber into the hem of a half-made mantle. Gypsy continued marking the school papers she and Mary had earlier begun.

The air continued to fracture.

Mary folded the copybook she was marking and rose from the table. "Give him a hearing, that's all I ask."

"This is an educated family. I will not have the Berford line sullied by an illiterate cattle jobber with a house full of urchins and a wife in the grave. And that he should have the effrontery to pay court to one of my daughters without first seeking my permission!"

"Courting did not come into it. We were both working for the cause. You know perfectly well that I'm on the anti-enlistment committee. So is James and he's had the decency to walk me home from town at night. He's coming to the house to talk to you now. Please give him a hearing."

"He's just looking for someone to mind his children. He'd make a skivvy of you given half the chance, but I'll put a stop to that."

"He's kind, gentle and generous Bamma. I'm thirty years of age for God's sake. How many more chances will I get?"

"You'll have time in plenty before I'll allow a daughter of mine disgrace this family."

With that she removed her apron, secured her hair bun with a rapier of a hatpin and set out to meet James in the middle of the field.

The grass around her darkened as the broad frame of James McNeill cut out the sun.

"Good evening mam. I'm James McNeill, son of the Fenian McNeill," he said showing her the respect of tipping his cap though not the deference of removing it. "I hope you will forgive the impertinence of calling on you unannounced but I have certain matters I need to discuss with you."

Standing upright, she answered in a voice so measured it was almost devoid of inflection. "I know who you are. And to what do I owe this unexpected honour?"

"I've often passed Cabra Cottage mam and admired your lovely field — good grass and little enough weed or moss. You know I believe it to be one of the best in the parish if not the whole county. I mind that in the days when your dear lamented husband was alive, light of heaven shine upon him, an animal's grazing always cropped that field. It's a shame to see it going for hay to feed another's stock."

"You were only a boy then."

"I was to be sure. But I remember admiring this field even then and I driving cattle down from Mulhuddart at six in the morning. How lush it looked in the early light and always a healthy-looking beast in it grazing away. I remember too, attending Mr Berford's funeral with my mother. God Almighty spare them both, him passing away so soon after my own father fell at Tallaght. They were two great Fenians, God be good to their immortal souls."

Bamma smoothed down her frock front, flicked a white ginny-joe off her sleeve and watched it float off on the wind. "Mr McNeill, my husband, like myself, was a teacher who believed that resistance alone was not enough. It was our belief that Ireland would never become a nation again until we became an educated people once more. Education makes a nation, Mr McNeill. He died, not of a lead ball like your own dear father, but of the plague trying to bring learning to the poor of Dublin. I have seen to it that our children were brought up to be educated people despite having to do it on my own. I hope to see our grandchildren carry on in the same mould. Now, I'd dearly love to continue reminiscing but it's suppertime"

"Suppertime is bad time to call and my apologies for the inconvenience, Mrs Berford. I won't take but a minute of your time. Look at this beauty. Isn't she the loveliest milch cow in Ireland?"

Bamma watched in silence as James stroked the haunches of the young cow talking to her all the while. "Haven't you the grandest flanks ever seen in three counties and the sweetest milk ever tasted. Don't fret now for your beautiful calf. I've seen her safely to the lush meadows of County Meath this very morning. And you'll be well cared for here with all Mooney's Field at your disposal."

He stood upright and turning to Bamma said, "'Tis true for you Mrs Berford. Education will be the making of our nation. However, it's the likes of me who'll see to it that that nation grows strong-boned on good meat and milk and not waste away like the bread and tea terriers we see skulking the city streets today."

3

Then playing gently with the cow's ear he said, "Mind her now and she'll take care of you. It will be a fine thing always to have fresh, safe milk for yourself and the family."

He took the halter off the cow's neck and coiled it as he began to walk back across the field, turning momentarily to say, "And by the way, Mary and I are walking out together … with your permission of course."

Chapter 2

Night of the Big Wind

(Dublin 1903)

In the Phoenix Park saplings of chestnut and elder were being torn from the earth, and in the stables behind the shops and houses, cattle gathered into corners, as Mary McNeill made her way from her home in Stoneybatter to her homeplace on the Old Cabra Road. She pulled her cloak hood down in front to shield her eyes from the heavy rain that drove in sheets with the rising wind. With her other hand, she gathered the garment in front to keep out the cold and mask her condition.

Passing 46 Prussia Street, she saw the slates of Mrs Trench's roof rise in a black flutter that scattered, then gathered again before dashing themselves to smithereens against Gavin Lowe's high wall right in front of her very face. Mary stiffened with fright and began to reconsider the wisdom of setting out at all on such a night. It wasn't so bad as she was leaving the dairy in Stoneybatter just before eight o'clock, but the wind was getting up for a gale and there wasn't another soul out.

Mary would have slipped into her sister's house in number 46 but knew Gypsy would already be at Bamma's. Besides, she couldn't wait to get to Cabra Cottage to tell Bamma and the girls all about her near escape.

The pulsating lightning ceased and the world became a dark, quiet place as she bent herself into the rising gale, driven by a terror that struck deeper than even the howls of wind and frightened animals. She would be with her mother and her sisters and the thought made her feel easier in her mind.

Her James was usually so practical … whatever's got into him now over the confinement. Holy Mother, I know that if I go into one of those hospitals I might never come out!

A bolt of lightning cracked the sky, followed by a bang so loud and so soon, she knew it was getting closer and closer. How she wished at that moment James was with her. She'd never feel frightened when he's around. He was such a good man really … no longer young, she'd concede that, but he was temperate and could be very gentle and considerate for all that he had no education. They'd have been married in 1900 if she'd had her way. Bamma was so slow to give her blessing it was a worry as to whether there'd be a wedding at all or not.

Mary couldn't wait to be sitting with her sisters in front of the glowing range once more. They'd help Lena fill her private orders for Easter bonnets by stitching silk roses onto the brims. They'd toast bread on a long-handled fork and it would be lovely and cosy watching the butter melt into the browned honeycombs of the freshly carved turnover.

It was coming to the end of February already and her confinement was set for the first week of March. If it's a boy, she'd call him Philip, after her only brother. If it's a girl they'd name her after Lena, not that it'd make any difference if the Berford strain comes out in the child's complexion … everyone would call her Gypsy anyway.

Forked lightning crackled deltas of light towards the earth. In her confusion Mary could not remember whether sheet or forked lightning was the most dangerous and said a fervent prayer that she and her unborn child might be protected from it all.

As the high wall of St Joseph's Institution loomed, she began to relax. Mooney's Field was only across the road from the Deaf and Dumb and she'd be in Cabra Cottage, home and dry in no time.

Philip was most likely out, paying court to young Molly Wilson … wasting his time … Bamma would never give her blessing to a Berford marrying into a 'Bluecoat' family. Poor Philip wearing his Fenian heart on his sleeve for the picking.

Bamma had also been against James for a long while because he couldn't read or write, never mind that he was a hard-working man who understood animals better than most vets. Mary was proud that the milk sold in McNeill's dairy in Stoneybatter was the finest you could get in the city of Dublin. She didn't know what the Cowkeepers Association would think if they saw her James putting linseed oil into the feed for the pregnant heifer to make her hide glisten like coal and her nearly bursting out of her skin.

She thought it quite amusing that no sooner was she, herself, in the family way, than everyone was remarking on her blooming health. Even Gypsy was envious of the sheen on her jet-black hair. And Gypsy still made heads turn when she walked past the cattle markets.

As she walked past the institution's high walls, sheet lightening lit up the night. Mary could see Mooney's Field just across the road with Cabra Cottage glowing by its edge. The huge chestnut trees stood in a line along the inside of the wall, swaying violently in the wind. They were the familiar giants of her childhood. And while she loved the trees themselves, she was always uneasy about the way their exposed roots dug into the earth like gnarled fingers forcing their way down towards the high boundary wall that bulged pregnantly as they insinuated their way into its very fabric.

Lilly Kerrigan was breathless. She had been trying to catch up with Mary McNeill since first seeing her cloak flapping wildly across the yellow light of Hanlon's window. Lilly was a nurse in Grangegorman Lunatic Asylum, so the storm didn't frighten her any more than the screaming of the demented patients cowering under their blankets. She wanted to chat to her friend about the preparations for the confinement.

When she was within earshot of her friend she called her name out loud above the storm. Mary turned in time to see the institution's great wall yield to wind and intruding roots as the huge, black blocks fell in a tumble of cascading masonry, burying the young nurse beneath the newly created cairn. Mary felt her legs become pleasantly warm and wondered whether she was wetting herself or if it was her waters breaking before she passed out.

Chapter 3

A bad Good Friday

Felim Mooney was in the dissecting theatre of the Mater Hospital wondering about the ethics of cutting up a cadaver that was once a near neighbour and childhood friend. There would be an inquest when death was sudden and violent … someone had to do the autopsy; luck of the draw that he happened to be on duty. Besides, he needed the experience and it was as well that he kept an eye on that big, bog-trotting senior houseman. Ryan was crouching over the slab in font of him, wielding his scalpel like a number seven shovel … the worse for a weekend's drinking.

The Irish Times usually had little in the way of big headlines but the morning's edition of 27 February had five concerning the gales. Felim Mooney didn't need the papers to tell him that the storm, foreshadowed by driving rain at eight o'clock on Thursday night, had manifested into a full-scale cyclone by midnight that raged until six o'clock on Friday morning. An emergency ward littered with lacerated faces and broken limbs was testament to the destruction visited upon the city.

The *Times* report spoke of viaducts falling down and estate walls collapsing but didn't mention Lilly Kerrigan of Cabra Lodge and how her bustling frame lay crushed beneath an institution's long-neglected walls.

There was great coverage of the disruption wreaked on the tramlines with all the papers dramatising the danger posed by fallen electric cables. Telegraph communications were said to have ceased in a tangle of wires. But none reported on the fire brigade freeing Lilly's lovely body from the black masonry, or how it was by pure chance that they stumbled upon the crumbled figure of her friend, Mary McNeill, lying on the ground a mere ten feet away in arrested childbirth. Felim thought it ironic that the hurricane had blown all three childhood friends together — Lilly in the dissecting theatre, Mary in the emergency ward and he there with them.

As it was in the beginning, so shall it ever be. Yes it was indeed peculiar, thought Felim Mooney, that they should all be as contiguous during the great storm as they had been most of their lives — just across Mooney's Field from each other — Cabra Cottage on one corner, Cabra Lodge at the other and Springfield back in behind the trees. Funny the way even his own family had come to call it Mooney's Field despite it being in the Berfords' name since his grandfather's time.

Felim's attention turned to the matron who burst into the dissecting theatre and snapped at his senior to immediately stop whatever it was that he was doing and to direct his energies towards Mrs McNeill who was having 'complications'.

As matron's beefy hips disappeared out the swinging doors, Ryan laid the scalpel on the kidney tray and wiped his hands on his apron.

"Dr Ryan, you finish off here if you like and I'll go to Mrs McNeill. She's a neighbour of mine and I'd like to see to her if I may."

"Love to oblige you old chap, but matron would tear out our scrotums with her bare kneecaps if we don't do exactly as she ordered. I'll tell her you were asking for her."

In the afternoon, they brought Mary's baby to her and though she was weaker, more confused than at any time since she could remember, she took so much pleasure from all the compliments being showered on him it felt almost sinful. It was the general view of the community of hospital staff, patients and visitors that her Philip was the most beautiful baby boy they had ever seen — dark and olive-skinned — real foreign looking, they said. Everyone agreed that he was going to be a heartbreaker some day. He had his mother's colouring, his father's large eyes and neat ears along with the finest shock of black hair they had ever seen on a newborn infant.

But so much as they were all pleased by the new arrival, it was nothing to the pride James displayed in his new son. Mary smiled at the incongruity of her husband with his thick, short neck and sloping muscular shoulders holding the baby in his huge hands as though it were made of delicate china.

The day wore her out. By evening time, she began to feel hot and wasted from all her travails and couldn't help drifting from consciousness to dreams. Then she woke from a nightmare in which she was held bound and motionless by malignant roots covered by tail-less rats, as a massive stone wall hurled its black masonry on top of her. Opening her eyes, she was relieved to see that James was still there, mopping her brow with a cold compress he had obviously made himself. But the room had changed. The walls were no longer painted cream and brown but covered with floral wallpaper. She was at home in Stoneybatter in her own bedroom. She also noticed that sitting on the dresser was an Easter bonnet with golden apples on the brim. It was champagne in colour. James moistened her lips with a thin, milky liquid and she slipped back to sleep again.

James sat for hours, watching his second chance at happiness fall to the same fever that had taken his first. He was transfixed by her lovely face and thought how captivating she had looked on that day in October '99 coming towards him through the huge gathering in Beresford Place, distributing anti-enlistment handbills among the crowd.

He had been amazed at how confident and strong her voice had sounded when she remarked on his separatist pin: "Why don't you come and join us on the Transvaal Committee? Irishmen shouldn't be fighting 'England's Robber War'," she had said to him. And of course he would be honoured. Wasn't England's trouble Ireland's opportunity after all and weren't the Boers giving the Tommies a right pasting out in Africa? And good luck to them. He would join her in the association — he would join with her forever if she would let him.

They were wonderful months, filled with the excitement of her company and the expectation that something was at last moving in the separatist direction. They were bitterly disappointed when the recruitment figures came out showing that more Dubliners had joined the British Army between 1899 and 1901 than at any time in history. But still he felt lucky for having the companionship of a beautiful, cultured woman and he no more than a cattle jobber from Blackhall Place.

He hadn't been looking for a second wife. True, he had three children under ten years of age but he had a childless, married daughter eager to mother her young brother and two little sisters.

He loved accompanying Mary on the long walk from the mass meetings in Beresford Place to her home in Cabra Cottage. Then one evening, as they strolled along Stoneybatter, she brought his attention to a notice board advertising premises to let in number 23 with a shop in front, spacious rooms above and a good byre at the side.

They would marry and spend their whole lives together. She would leave her teaching post in the Loreto Convent and they would set up a dairy together in number 23. He could continue with his cattle dealing and she would look after the shop and the little ones. Between them they would ensure that the children that were, and were to be, would grow up to be the kind of people who would build the Irish nation.

James began to despair when he could no longer get her to take even a drop of the two-milk whey that his father said had protected the McNeills against the famine fever. On Holy Thursday, Bamma and the rest of the Berford girls came to the rooms above the dairy and told James it was no longer safe to have an infant in the house with the fever still raging. They would take the baby to Cabra Cottage where Bamma would mind it by day and Lena in the evening after work. Gypsy would take Mary to 46 Prussia Street where she could be nursed day and night by a woman.

On Good Friday, James took three of the children on the tram to the Pro-Cathedral for the Stations of the Cross. The Auxiliary Bishop of Dublin did the 'Sorrowful Mysteries'. In number 46, Gypsy couldn't find any compress cold enough to still the fire bursting from her sister's head.

James and the three children got off the tram at the junction of Blackhall Place and Ellis Quay. Holding hands crossing the busy thoroughfare, they walked up Stoneybatter — the once paved road to Royal Tara. As they approached the dairy, the church bells began ringing out all over the city that it was three o'clock, and Christ was dead on the cross.

Up the road, in 46 Prussia Street, Mary McNeill slipped into her final sleep.

In Cabra Cottage, Bamma boiled the milk she had taken from the young milch cow she kept in Mooney's Field and after allowing it to cool, poured it into a glass bottle.

Then having stopped the bottle with a cork into which she had forced a hollow tube, Bamma cradled Philip McNeill and let the life-giving liquid trickle into his hungry mouth.

Chapter 4

After burial

Felim took in every last detail as he walked across the flagstone kitchen floor. For although he played with the Berford children all of his boyhood, he was never inside Cabra Cottage or any other cotter's house for that matter. His parents were happy enough to see the Berford and Kerrigan children in Springfield or gallivanting with them in Mooney's Field, but he was absolutely forbidden to cross the threshold of a cottage door.

He placed a placating hand on the slouched shoulders of Nelly Berford sobbing softly into the dark inglenook below.

"I'll go down to the bedroom and tell Bamma you're here," said Lena, all watery and red-eyed as she ushered him into the parlour.

The 'room', as the parlour was more usually called, was mostly for special occasions or for visitors of high status such as priests, undertakers and, Felim supposed, doctors. It gleamed with varnished wallpaper and bees-waxed ball-and-claw furniture that offered final proof that the Berfords were city people of the educated, Catholic, middleclass.

If furniture validated the family's social position, wall hangings confirmed its political allegiance.

Full-length lithographs of great Irish heroes flared from gilded rococo frames — Robert Emmet, Wolfe Tone and Lord Edward Fitzgerald. There were many he could not identify but noted the absence from the pantheon of the pacifist liberator Daniel O'Connell and the constitutionalist Charles Stewart Parnell.

Lena returned and led him back through the kitchen and up the stairs to Bamma's bedroom without saying a word. Knocking on the door and opening it in one movement, she announced, "Dr Mooney is here to see you mother." She closed the door behind him, then ran back down the stairs to comfort her sister.

"I've cried so much, I've hardly a tear left to cry," Lena said, stroking the long, black hair of her sister Nelly. But Nelly couldn't stop and continued to sob uncontrollably as she absent-mindedly rocked the wickerwork cradle bearing her dead sister's baby.

"I don't think Bamma is going to survive this. I think she's just going to lie down and die ... so she is," Lena said and the saying brought on a fresh bout of sobbing from her younger sister. Then with sudden resolution, "I'm going to hand in my notice to Pims first thing in the morning."

The shock announcement brought Nelly's crying to a sudden stop.

"Oh! Lena, don't even think of saying things like that. You'll never get another position. What would we all do then?"

"We'll do well enough and don't you worry. As things stand, I have my ladies beating a track to the door, night, noon and morning, begging me to make them an exclusive. I have it worked out to a tee. Working forty-eight hours a week and spending nearly half as much time again travelling across town on trams ... it'd never pay you. I'll have more time to devote to my own work and I can be here to look after Mary's baby, God rest her ... and mind Bamma too, if needs be." Then leaning into the cradle, she stroked her nephew's chubby cheeks with her little finger. The action made the infant smile and gurgle milky bubbles. Lena's face filled with an enormous joy. "Isn't he only gorgeous? He's so like his Uncle Philip."

"And his mother, Lord have mercy on our lovely Mary," said Nelly and bursts out crying again.

"What if you didn't get enough work to keep us Lena?" she said when the tears subsided. "An apprentice's wages hardly keeps me in tram fares and I've nearly two more years to go."

"I don't know, Nelly, but I do know this, if something drastic isn't done and done soon, that infant will be joining his mother in the clay before any of us are very much older."

"What will Bamma say? She'll never allow you give up your good position in Pims, no matter what."

"That's why I'm going to do it immediately before she's in a position to say anything. I'll give them a month's notice so as they'll have plenty of time to find a replacement ... give them no excuse but to give me a good reference ... just in case I need one ... at some time in the future."

But as the conversation faded, Lena became concerned about how the news would be received by Fachtna Harford. There wouldn't be many more chances at her age. If a girl wasn't chosen by twenty, she may as well content herself with spinsterhood or

16

catching a man on the second turn of the merry-go-round like Mary with James McNeill. Bamma couldn't stand James on account of his illiteracy.

She had no complaints in that department with Fachtna. Never even mentioned that his teeth were so prominent he was in danger of splitting the palm of his hand in half every time he sneezed. Lena giggled at the thought and immediately felt guilty for her moment's levity in a house of mourning. A national schoolteacher and the same Norse-Gael mix as the Berfords — it would make no difference to Bamma if his buckteeth sliced her nose off with the first kiss.

Nelly would have even less of a problem with Dunny Kerrigan, him being out of the same mould as the Berfords — Fenians by seed, breed and generation ... even if his sister had a child by a Dublin Fusilier. She knew Dunny would be making his move as soon as Nelly was out of black.

"What will Fachtna say when you tell him about handing in your notice?"

"Can't say for certain Nelly. He says so little at the best of times ..." Indeed, marriage had not been mentioned but it was taken that they would tie the knot in due course. But she wondered might he be frightened off by the prospect of taking on the responsibility of an infant that was not his own flesh and blood.

"I'll invite him over to tea on Monday night, after I've handed in my notice ... I'll make a nice, rice pudding ... real creamy with a big blob of jam in the middle ... strawberry is his favourite."

Felim sat at the edge off the bed, held Bamma's wrist and proceeded to take her pulse while looking out the window.

"Dublin is changing rapidly and I'd love to think it was for the better. Did you ever see anything like the world of new houses they're building in what's left of Sallcock's Wood? Knocking down all those lovely trees ... people have to live somewhere, I suppose, but it seems a terrible shame, doesn't it Mrs Berford? God, it was a whole world to itself when we were all kids."

"A great place indeed, when you were all small ... wouldn't see sight nor hair of you from morning to night."

"This is a sphygmomanometer, Mrs Berford. Very effective in measuring blood pressure. Blood pressure, Mrs Berford, is one of the hidden killers in Ireland today. You'll feel it tighten a little around your upper arm. It won't do any harm."

Felim pumped air into the cuff of the apparatus and released it by turn, listening to Bamma's pulse through the cold metal of his stethoscope. He busied himself with removing the straps while gathering as much *gravitas* as he could muster.

"I suppose, Mrs Berford, you have made all the necessary arrangements."

Emboldened by her silence, he continued. "You have suffered a great loss, God only knows, but you still have two single daughters, one not finished her training yet, and a son. I need not remind a good woman like yourself, Mrs Berford, that Mary's infant will need a lot of care. What arrangements have you made for when you are gone?"

"Is it my heart?"

"No your heart is as sound as a pound … blood pressure up a bit but nothing to be concerned about as yet. No … physically I'd say you are as fine a specimen of womanhood as can be found in a lady your age."

"Then what is it?"

"Melancholy, Mrs Berford, melancholy — a condition only you yourself can cure."

Bamma wondered when it was that Felim Mooney got so big in himself. What would the Mooneys know of people like the Berfords?

"Lean forward and I'll check your lungs. Deep breaths please." And as her chest rose and fell, Felim said softly, "My father always says that the Berfords are a model for the whole community and a credit to their parents."

"Who sent for a doctor?"

"The girls … they were concerned for your health."

"Did all three arrive at your door together or did they approach you one at a time?"

"I bumped into Lena at the Lodge and she said that …"

"Lena … who would have thought … Lena … Did you notice any other monumental changes in the household on your way in?"

"Only that your family is very concerned for your health. I'll give you a little something to help you sleep. I'm confining you to bed for one more week. You'll be needing a tonic … I'll tell the girls what to get … I'll call back to see how you are doing next week."

Is there a tonic for a heart lost in fathoms of sorrow, Bamma wondered, then closed her eyes to the doctor and the world.

Downstairs, the babble of conversation between the sisters paused to pepper Felim with questions.

"What is she suffering from?"

"How serious is it?"

"Is there anything we can do?"

"Is she going to be alright?"

Felim waited for the blizzard to abate, before reassuring them that Bamma was physically strong but that it might take some time for her to get over Mary's death. He told them to get the pharmacist to make up an emulsion of Parishes Food and cod-liver and to give it to her twice daily. They must talk to her as much as possible and feed her every bit of news and gossip they come across even if she seems to resent it at first.

The girls resolved to follow his instructions to the letter.

Chapter 5

Mooney's Field

Felim walked back to Springfield through the long grass of Mooney's Field in reflective mood. It was strange that he should have entered Cabra Cottage for the first time, not as a friend or neighbour but as a doctor on house call. They did not seem to mind that he was not quite a general practitioner yet.

All the Berfords and Kerrigans had been in Springfield as children. Philip Berford and his sisters along with poor Lilly Kerrigan and her brother Dunny were frequent callers to what they called 'The Big House', until they were young adults.

When he was old enough to ignore parental interdictions against entering cottages in and around the estate, the habit was well established and both the Berfords and the Kerrigans left him wait at the door when he called. Not that he had minded very much by then. He had become so dependent on the long talks with Philip during even longer walks through Sallcock's Wood, along the Royal Canal or just sitting in the sun in Mooney's Field, he had been prepared to overlook almost anything.

The same long grass of Mooney's Field was billowing all around him in the summer sun a decade or so earlier. Philip had picked up a long golden stem to chew. Felim used to think it a most endearing habit. He was always nibbling at something — a leaf from a bush, a blade of grass or a piece of straw — anything to aid his concentration as he teased out weighty matters. That day his mind moved with the wind between the questions of love and freedom. At one remove he agonised as to whether true love could endure carnal knowledge and at another wondered if the Irish class system would survive the coming Republic.

The stem of ripening hay collapsed across his bare chest as the two sixteen-year-olds sunbathed in that long, hot holiday just before Philip began training as a surveyor in the Midland Great Western Railway and Felim entered the College of Surgeons. It was only the end of June and Philip's body was already turning from olive to amber.

"If we band together as a nation, even the great power of England won't be able to break us," he said, his chewing becoming more zealous. "The Penal Laws all but eradicated learning and the famine devastated what was left of our culture. It will take the combined efforts of the entire race at home and abroad to rebuild this shattered nation. Individual effort mostly benefits the individual concerned."

And Felim, luxuriating in the camaraderie of that handsome youth, his best and longest friend, endured all that pedantry. He even deliberately weakened his own argument so as not to be confrontational while, at the same time, offering sufficient opposition to prolong the glorious interchange of inconclusive ideas. "Wouldn't we be better served looking to the successful models around us? Britain and Germany became great powers through individual effort — everyone looking after their own interests making the state powerful and its people prosperous. Look at how well America is doing. *Laissez faire* may be the best way forward for us also."

Felim's words caused a fresh bout of nibbling on the harvested stalk but then a shadow fell across the sun-warmed bodies.

"We had enough of your *laissez faire* in the great famine, right enoughsky," intruded the unmistakable voice of Dunny Kerrigan. "Individuals like your grandfather making a fortune selling Indian corn as people died in their thousands, mouths going green from eating grass. And in the meantime, the richest empire on earth excused itself from feeding their starving Irish subjects in case it would interfere with the market. Fair enoughsky Mr Mooney!"

Dunny, who could be so comical most times, always seemed to turn things nasty whenever the Irish Question arose. But it was Philip who delivered the *coup de grace* that day.

"True for you Dunny. Individualism has seen the greedy getting progressively richer while the rest of the nation struggles for survival," he said pointedly. His words landed like the smack of a wet fish. At that moment, Felim felt that he and the Mooney family were on one side of a line running through that unharvested field. Facing them were the Berfords, Kerrigans and perhaps the whole communion of the Gael.

Now as he reached the gates of Springfield, Felim looked back across Mooney's Field to Cabra Lodge at one end and Cabra Cottage on the other. He pondered awhile on his house call to the cottage and was amazed at his conclusion. The loss of poor Lilly would be a devastating blow to the Kerrigans. But they would get on with the business of life and the rearing of her little infant girl Essie by the soldier who never came back from the war. But who would have thought that anything could lay waste to the redoubtable Bamma. If she broke, the family might fall apart. Who then would rear Mary's baby?

The following evening Nelly entered Bamma's room with the tonic made up according to Felim's instructions by Jozé chemists of Dame Street. She stuck to her guns through a barrage of aspersion and censure until Bamma took two large spoonfuls of the creamy liquid. Then sitting on the edge of the bed, Nelly disgorged all the news and gossip of the day in a rush, barely pausing to take breath. When she got to the bit about Lena handing in her notice to look after Mary's baby, Bamma sat bolt upright.

"Did I hear you right? Lena giving up her good position in Pims. Has she taken leave of her senses?"

"Don't fret, she'll get plenty of private orders and somebody has to be here to look after the baby and you when you're so poorly."

"Fret is it? Me fret and sure what would I have to fret about will you tell me?" If Nelly could have shrunk deeper into herself she would have done so gladly. With her youngest daughter totally silenced, Bamma railed on. "And have you thrown up your good position as well?"

Nelly could only shake her head in answer.

"You lot can't be left to your own devices … none of you. I can't even die in peace."

Nelly ran down the stairs to Lena as soon as her mother began to rise from the bed. Bamma put on her black frock and wrapped her sleeveless bib with the tiny blue flowers around her, before tying it off in a bow at the back.

Down the steep stairs and into the kitchen, she went straight for the range, and began to clean out the grate with gusto, all the time scolding Nelly for letting it go out and Lena for not having the brains she was born with.

Behind her back, the faces of the two sisters lit up with pleasure for the first time in weeks as they hugged and giggled in complete silence. Bamma was indestructible after all. Things were getting back to normal.

Chapter 6

Molly Wilson

The special train from Kingsbridge Station was scheduled to leave at first light, stopping only at the Curragh main line platform and Kildare, for those two destinations were, according to the Great Southern and Western Railway posters, the best vantage points for viewing the Gordon Bennett motor race. Molly Wilson knew that the very best place was Ballyshannon Cross but that was seven miles from the nearest railway station and the GS&W Railway Company wasn't about to highlight that fact. She had been a keen automobilist since the moment her father came home at the wheel of his Renault, nine horsepower Aster Motor, costing an amazing fortune of £150.

Reading one of the posters plastered all over the city, she told Philip Berford that the Gordon Bennett Cup was going to be the biggest and fastest international motor car race in the world. And, since it was Britain's good fortune to host it, she for one had no intention of missing out on the opportunity of witnessing the spectacle. She left Philip in no doubt that if he didn't feel inclined to take her, she would jolly-well get someone who would.

Sitting in the train in Kingsbridge station before the first light of day, Molly had the whole compartment enthralled, talking about the details of the race. Philip, gazing adoringly at her as she spoke, was very pleased with himself. He was twenty-five, and spending a day's paid leave out in the country with his own sweet Molly, the best-looking girl in Dublin.

But what would happen if Bamma found out? Suddenly guilt seared him like a red-hot poker. He knew what she would say. She would remind him that his sister was only in the clay a few short months and that he was showing scant regard for her by gallivanting at a race meeting. In the dark of the Inchicore tunnel, he crossed himself and asked Mary for her forgiveness.

Philip imagined that many of the passengers sharing their compartment would comment later on how opposites attract. If his skin was sallow then Molly's was so fair it was almost translucent. And whereas his hair was a mass of black, unruly curls, hers was so blond, straight and fine it had the texture of finely brushed hemp. Despite his foreign looks, he had the hazel eyes of the Celt while Molly's were the pale blue of the Saxon. But they would clearly see that he was so much in love with her, he wouldn't have cared less were she Jew, Greek or Turk, yes, and even West British, judging by her accent.

He hadn't been keen on going to the race. He would have been content to spend the day walking along the Royal Canal out by Ballyboggan or even beyond Ashtown and maybe have a picnic by the tenth lock before strolling home in the twilight.

On the way home, they might go in somewhere quiet and out of the way for a good 'coort' ... like that time coming home from the Phoenix Bazaar when he had been amazed at how far she had let him go. How his caressing fingers had discovered she was wearing old-fashioned drawers instead of the bloomers he had been expecting. The confusion when his fingers slipped from one silky texture into another. The way he ran out of Mooney's barn and into the fields of the estate for fear he might lose control of himself. But Molly found him out there tracing his fingers along the pulleys of the steam-powered, combined harvester standing idle. She had soothed his turmoil, talking softly and running her fingers around his hair and ear in asymmetric motion. He knew then that he loved her ... and told her so ... and she said that she loved him too ... and she linked his arm back to the barn and they just stood there chatting.

Then slowly, almost casually, she undid her bodice until the sight of her naked breasts started his heart pounding again until he could hear it in his ears. But this time he did not run out into the fields but cupped her gently and kissed her softly over and over on the mouth and then on her silky nape where the wispy hairs tickled his nose until gradually their breathing kept pace with his racing heart there in the hay in Mooney's barn the day they became one.

Now, in the train, Philip became ever more silent in the presence of so many strangers, but still managed to keep Molly constantly in his vision by pretending to look out the window at the scenery passing in the pale light of dawn. It was as though he feared that if he lost sight of her, she might disappear forever.

Philip was glad he had insisted they go all the way to Kildare town to watch the race rather than the viewing stand at the Curragh where the military camp would be too close for comfort. He was quite happy to be the envy of every young man at the race but would not endure the rough British soldiery gawking at Molly and passing remarks. Besides, someone might recognise her and he did not like being reminded of her family's connections with the army.

She had frightened him with her talk of America that evening when they had *café au lait* in the City Arms Hotel in Prussia Street. Suddenly the laughter left her voice and she told him gently but firmly that he must make up his mind and soon. She was twenty-three and could not waste any more of her time if there were to be no prospects. She said that her cousin had written to her from Philadelphia offering to sponsor her out to America. There was plenty of work out there with good money for those with a bit of go in them, Molly said. Her cousin had gone out only four years earlier and was doing very well — married to a captain in the police force and with two lovely children.

She would wait for an eternity for him but she wasn't going to waste her youth waiting on the pleasure of Bamma Berford or her bold Fenian men. He felt a slight shiver remembering the edge in her voice when she told him: "I believe in the future … America is the future … the motor car is the future. The Fenians belong to the past, we should be looking to the future."

He had begged her to give him time, even just a short while until he got around Bamma to win her blessing. "Sure haven't we continued our courtship despite all?" he said, and then tried to get her to understand what it meant to his mother seeing her only son walking out with a girl from a Bluecoat family. It was to no avail. He would have to make his mind up soon.

As the locomotive approached Sallins for Bodenstown (and Wolfe Tone's grave), its progress was suddenly arrested by the over-enthusiastic application of the brakes. The train lurched, the wheels screeched, and Molly buried her face into his breast while holding onto him for dear life. At that moment, he wouldn't have cared if the pin had slipped from the wheel and ended his life, for he knew he would never be as happy again.

He would talk to Bamma tomorrow. He would make her see that there would be no life for him at all if it wasn't to be a life with Molly Wilson.

Chapter 7

Gypsy Berford

Gypsy Berford sailed down Prussia Street on her 'safety' bicycle dressed in her clerical-grey, tightly waisted skirt that reached all the way down to the heel of her high-buttoned, patent leather boots. She was married to Andy Kennedy and had taken his name, but to most of the people in the Stoneybatter area she was and always would be Gypsy Berford.

The herd of cattle flowing up the road against her divided into two streams as she glided through, reforming behind her into a single body of steaming nostrils and swishing tails moving towards the model abattoir on the North Circular Road.

Her attention was drawn to the men erecting scaffolding outside Mrs Trench's to carry out long overdue repairs to her roof damaged in the 'Big Wind'. The house next door had kept its roof but not its tenant. Gypsy was amused to see young Jimmy McNeill with his bride of less than twelve months on his arm, hopping the knocker off the door so soon after the TO LET sign went up in the window.

Gypsy kept her arm semaphored in the fully extended position from the time she entered the delta formed by the confluence of Prussia, Aughrim and Manor Streets. Sitting upright on the bicycle, she stuck her arm out at exactly ninety degrees from a back as straight as a stair-rod. It was her intention to cross to the other side of the road at Stoneybatter and she was leaving nobody in any doubt as to her purpose.

Parking her bike at the kerb, it became immediately apparent that matters in her brother-in-law's home were far from right. If she was shocked by the flies swarming out of the byre at the side of his dairy, she was appalled at the insistent, loud lowing of animals neglected of their first milking, and it nearly noon. She had been quietly observing the slide in standards in McNeill's Dairy since her sister Mary passed away and was now more convinced than ever that the time for quietude was over.

A bell tinkled over the door as she pushed it open and again when it shut firmly behind her. She made several noises to attract attention, including polite coughing and dropping copper coins onto the marble-topped counter, but no one came out of the back kitchen to serve her.

Even the aromatic pipe tobacco could not mask the sour smell about the place. When her sister was alive, God rest her immortal soul, you could have eaten your dinner off the dairy floor. Now she was not so sure she'd even buy a jerrycan of milk there no matter how generous the tilly. She called out 'shop' repeatedly while banging on the marble-topped counter with two copper pennies until, eventually, the kitchen door opened.

James McNeill's muscular frame filled the opening. He was stooped and showed every day of his forty-six years. He looked at her for the longest while, fascinated by an overlay of Mary's features that formed and reformed on the slightly harder outline of her sister's face. Gypsy's no-nonsense manner metamorphosed in the air into Mary's confident voice. Eventually, reality broke through and he heard her say that his son was thriving on the sweet milk from the young cow he had given Bamma ... heard her explaining the ingenuity of the feeding device his mother-in-law had contrived.

Gypsy spent ages bringing the conversation around to normal everyday things. James didn't know how she managed it, but somehow or other, as they talked about their respective children, the raging foot-and-mouth disease and the imminent royal visit, she had taken off her coat and hat, boiled up the big iron kettle on the gas stove and set about scouring every utensil and counter-top in the shop and every pot, pan and dish in the kitchen.

As she busied herself about the place, she told him that Dublin Corporation had voted to deny the king a 'Loyal Address' under pressure from Arthur Griffith's National Council. James, sitting with a cup of tea on his lap, said the Corporation was doing the right thing for once. Gypsy said that there was sure to be mass demonstrations against the visit and thought that it would do marvels for the cause.

"There's going to be a monster protest meeting in Dublin ... everyone says it's going to be the largest in years. Wait and you'll see ... something good will come out of this," she said.

He turned the conversation around to the Transvaal Committee and the great meetings of '99 where he met his lovely Mary and how high hopes had been then. He began to tell her about Mary's great plans for the dairy but his sister-in-law pulled him up short, grabbing her opportunity before it passed. She told him that he and his family would be far better served if he went back to the cattle dealing. He could then afford to hire a woman to look after the dairy and the children for they certainly needed a woman about the place.

With shop and kitchen spick and span, Gypsy, James and his three little children sat around the well-scrubbed kitchen table. The children tucked into fresh cuts of thickly buttered bread washed down with milk from gleaming mugs while Gypsy and James continued their conversation over steaming mugs of tea. After an age of drawing quietly on his pipe, James looked around his gleaming home and allowed that having a woman about the place was probably best for everyone.

Gypsy had the bit between her teeth and began writing out an 'ad' there and then, promising to place it in the *Freeman's Journal* before the day was out.

'Respectable Catholic father seeks housekeeper. Duties include three children and light shop work. Suit strong, healthy, RC woman, not afraid to roll up her sleeves. References essential.' Gypsy said there was no time like the present and that she would cycle into town that very afternoon and place the ad.

Emboldened by her success, Gypsy said it would do no harm at all if he were to drop by and see the beautiful son her sister Mary had borne for him, the next time he was passing Cabra Cottage.

With that, she swept on her coat and popped her hat onto her head. The bell over the shop door jangled for several seconds after she had shut it firmly behind her. She peddled down Stoneybatter and Blackhall Place in first gear, dropping into second for the drag along the quays, then freewheeled around the back of the GPO to Prince's Street and the offices of the *Freeman's Journal*.

Chapter 8

Life without Mary

James McNeill struggled as best he could to get on with life. His grief still scorched deeply but he was ever finding new ways of dealing with the pain. By staying busy he could better live with the sense of amputation that remained even after it surrendered some space to a growing acceptance that Mary was gone forever. Sometimes, when he was particularly lonely, he found himself engaged in conversations with her, and in times of trouble, invoking her name. Nevertheless, getting on with everyday matters was proving helpful. He would give Gypsy that.

The new housekeeper was a sensible woman from Carlow, called Bridie Byrne, who was easy to please and eager to please. She kept the house well, the dairy spotless and seemed to get along with the children. James knew that Peter, Kate and Queenie would need time to get to know yet another woman, but so far, things were looking good in that department at least.

He noted that the development had the approval of his eldest son Jimmy. It was a long time since anything he had done received that young gentleman's approbation. His subterranean anger could break through the surface at any time.

The arrival of the housekeeper left him bereft of excuses for not getting out and doing what he was good at — buying and selling cattle. True, he hadn't actually bought or sold any yet, but the farmer he'd been negotiating with would move and soon — his animals were as fat as they were going to get.

"We'll leave him to cool his heels for a week or so," James told Mary as though she were by his side.

Walking out in the chill of dawn and back in the warmth of the day, he felt the first creeping of a thaw drift along the edges of his soul. The arguing and bargaining over the price of such a fine herd of cattle had recharged his mind and he even began wondering whether he should become active in the campaign against the visit by the English king.

As the hedgerows came to an end where the Navan Road became the Old Cabra Road, James launched out in a deep baritone:

"And once more returning, within our veins burning
The fires that lit up that dark Tallaght Glen,
We raise the old cry anew, slogan of Conn and Hugh,
Out and make way for the bold Fenian men."

His da had died by the glenside near the Old Bawn River in Tallaght. If ever there was a nation beset by traitors, it was Ireland. "From the Norman invasion to the Fenian uprising, it's been spies, informers and placemen that did us down. No one knows that better than yourself Mary," he told his departed.

His absorption in things historical was intruded upon by the sound of steel on stone. Looking across the road, he could see a group of masons repairing the boundary wall of St Joseph's Deaf and Dumb. Realising he was at the edge of Mooney's Field, his eyes turned to the milch cow he had given Bamma and was delighted to see that it was bursting with health, grazing near the gable end of Cabra Cottage.

He rambled over and, as if by instinct, began an examination of the beast. He talked softly to her as he looked into her mouth and then, lifting a leg, he gently pressed on the soft pads of her two toes. Satisfied with the animal's state of health, his eyes wandered around the field until they settled on the wickerwork bassinet standing in the sunshine by the cottage door.

He felt drawn towards the reedy basket moving gently between its huge wheels. He drew its delicate lace curtains and was transfixed by what he saw. A gurgling, bubble blowing, milky-roundness looked straight back up at him. He could see Mary Berford's dark beauty in the tiny, laughing face and was delighted to see something of himself, too, in the emerging features of their son.

It was the great wonder of Dublin's North Union Ward. Little girls stopped skipping to watch and young boys let their jackstones drop in amazement. No one had ever seen the beat of it. A full-grown man with the build of a bull was pushing a child in a bassinet the length of the Old Cabra Road. In Prussia Street, Gypsy Berford was combing her hair in the sunlight coming through the front window when the sudden still in the street made her look out.

What she saw made her smile for the first time since her sister died. The son of the Fenian McNeill marching towards Stoneybatter, steering a high-wheeled bassinet and looking as awkward as a new nanny.

Chapter 9

The Gordon Bennett Race

Dr Felim Mooney had no difficulty picking out Philip Berford among the hundreds of people swarming out of Kildare railway station. The easily-tanned complexion that made him the envy of all the boys in Cabra during summers swimming in the Royal Canal continued to make him conspicuous as an adult. He also stood out from the rest by having on his arm the beautiful Miss Wilson who, Felim thought, looked as fine a lady as he had ever seen.

Philip attempted to duck back into the throng but Molly, recognising the young doctor behind the wheel of the new Wolseley 9, steered her young man towards the car. Sitting beside Felim on the high leather double seat was his father, Columbanus Mooney, who said cheerily: "Hop into the back young Berford, and we'll take you and your young lady to the very centre of the action."

Mr Mooney was not only the owner of Springfield House, landlord of most of Cabra, including, at one time, the land under Philip's home, but was also the esteemed chairman of the Dublin Tramway Company. He had used his influence to secure a good position for Philip with the Midland Great Western Railway on whose board he also sat.

Rattling along on the back roads between Kildare and Ballyshannon, Mr Mooney expounded on the virtue of staying abreast of modern developments. It was, he said, the foresight of the Dublin Tramway Company in changing over to electricity that had seen it survive and thrive while companies who stayed with horses declined and died. Turning to the Gordon Bennett Cup, he declared: "This race will demonstrate the high efficiency of the petrol motor — the transport of the future."

While maintaining a deep concentration on his driving, Felim attempted to engage his old friend in conversation. "Perhaps speed will leave the dominant impression. But consider the wonderment of machines that can endure terrific momentum, road shocks, sudden retardation, acceleration and still continue to perform their beautifully rhythmic functions."

Ballyshannon was alive with automobiles and Molly glowed with the delight of arriving at the very nerve-centre of the race in a swanky new motorcar.

Over fifty cars had been stationed in the club garage from as early as five o'clock that morning and, the facility being nearly full, Mr Mooney was advised by an official to park his with the overflow in the surrounding fields. As they dismounted, a sedan arrived carrying leading English members of the British and Irish Automobile Club: Mr Mark Mayhew, Mr Henry Norman, MP, the Hon. C. S. Rolls and Colonel Crompton, R E. A steward wearing a yellow halyard directed the sedan to park in the garage.

When the English group finally took up their positions on the stand Mr Mooney brought his entourage over to join them. Colonel Crompton drew everyone's attention to the pilot car.

"Would that be the one with the word PILOT, inscribed in large letters on front and back?" asked Philip Berford with barely concealed sarcasm.

Colonel Crompton then told his friends that the larger circuit was a triangle of just under fifty-nine miles and the smaller circuit was a triangle of just over forty-eight miles.

"A triangular circuit must be a geometric novelty in England," interjected Philip Berford helpfully. "In this country circuits tend to be circular to comply with the definition." Felim smiled, Molly glared. The English pointedly ignored the remark.

When it finally got underway the race lived up to expectations. From start to finish the issue was in doubt, and the interest unceasing – especially in the English drivers, Jarrott and Edge. The ladies on the grandstand gasped behind little lace handkerchiefs as each Mercedes, Napier and Panhard hurtled towards them, then rushed beneath their seats with a great growl of acceleration.

Never one to suppress her feelings, Molly Wilson let out a whoop of excitement when the first racers ploughed through at full-throttle. The gentlemen surrounding her merely noted the time, team and provenance of each driver and machine as it passed.

Philip Berford stood quietly, and at times, quietly mortified — trapped between his social betters and the English gentry they were so set upon impressing.

Molly started to tell them about the interview in *The Irish Times* with the famous French racer Monsieur Fournier in which he claimed to have driven at nearly eighty-six miles per hour. But the English gentlemen turned around to watch the starting post as the next driver got ready, leaving her only the Cabra group for an audience.

Colonel Crompton remarked on the ingenuity of Jarrott using a gauze bonnet on the Mooers, "thereby elevating the science of weight-cutting to a pitch that even the Germans have not attained."

"There's ingenuity for you," said Philip when the engine stalled because Jarrott had left his brake on.

"Steady on old man," said Felim in a low voice. "It's only a race, let's not restart the 'Nine Years War'."

Then the man dubbed 'De Caters, the eagle-eyed and debonair' went off like a rocket in his white Mercedes waving to the spot in the grandstand where stood the Baroness de Caters.

Edge came flying down the hill towards the stand, his arrival heralded by a shriek from the whistle of a traction engine stationed in an adjoining field. His pace was stupendous, sweeping past the enclosure, and hurtling under the grandstand,

Jarrott did not show on the next lap, much to the consternation of the English members. To the surprise of everyone, a car rushing down the hill pulled up at the starting line. It was Baron De Caters on his second lap stopping to reassure everyone that Jarrott was not badly hurt. His magnanimous act cost him minutes in a race where seconds were precious.

Back at the junction of the Marlborough and Ardscull roads, farm workers standing along the ditches had been bemused by the conversation between the French nobleman and the English ace.

"Can I do anything for you?" said Baron De Caters.

"What are you doing here?" asked the Englishman, disentangling himself from the fence he had just crashed through.

"Oh, I am racing," said De Caters.

"Well, go on, go on then and race!"

De Caters reported the accident at the next control, and a request for help was telephoned to Surgeon Ormsby at Ballyshannon. The President of the Royal College of Surgeons immediately dispatched Dr Felim Mooney to the accident scene.

"Will you come with me Philip for the adventure that's in it?"

"Thanks all the same Dr Mooney, but I would rather stay here with Molly."

Felim took off in a rush and reached Jarrott's side in less than an hour, driving the Wolseley 9 at great speed by a cross-country route. He was stunned by Philip's use of his formal title but was too preoccupied with the task in hand to dwell on it for long.

The gentry on the stand told each other that Baron de Caters was a very gallant gentleman indeed and they loudly cheered him every time he passed. Molly said she thought Felim even more gallant, the way he dashed off to administer medical assistance to an automobilist in trouble. Mr Mark Mayhew said, "Quite."

When Felim returned about three hours later Molly threw her arms around him, wanting to know every last detail of his adventure.

His return was barely noticed by the coterie of Englishmen who were busily discussing their country's chances in the light of Jarrott's retirement. The hopes of England were now confined to Edge alone. When he came by over half an hour late, with his engine firing on only three cylinders, the English members assumed an air of resignation. Molly asked Felim if he could amputate the grin off Philip's face.

With the competitors thinning down, Jenatzy, De Knyff and De Caters were making an astonishingly close fight of it. Round after round they roared past the grandstand, one close on the heels of the other.

The Chevalier De Knyff finished the race at half-past five amid great cheers. His car was in excellent condition and the tyres hardly showed a scratch. Jenatzy, for the Germans, finished about three minutes later than De Knyff for the French. The Hon. C. S. Rolls declared it a victory for the *entente cordiale*. Philip Berford cut his flow short saying, "As the German champion started number four, it is fairly safe to regard him as the winner unless De Caters makes quite extraordinary time in his last round."

Jenatzy was indeed the winner, with an average speed of 49.2 miles per hour. The fight for second place was very close but France's De Knyff just pipped it.

Soon after seven o'clock Mr Hutton set off to patrol the course to declare the race over. On the back and front of his car he had a large sign that read, RACE OVER. Despite the unambivalent nature of the message, Edge, England's great hope, came across the finishing line after everyone had gone home.

That was long after officials wearing yellow halyards had approached the group in the stand and announced that Lord and Lady Dudley requested the pleasure of the company of Mr Mark Mayhew, Mr Henry Norman, MP, the Hon. C. S. Rolls, Colonel Crompton, RE, Mr Columbanus Mooney, Chairman of the Dublin Tramway Company and Dr Felim Mooney for refreshments in the Vice-Regal marquee.

Molly just stood there dumbfounded as the Mooneys moved away from Philip and herself towards the Viceroy's tent with the rest of the British and Irish Automobile Club members. She was hoping Felim would give some sign, some indication as to what she should do, but the young doctor was devoting all his attention to his father who was busily talking at the Viceregal party.

Philip took her elbow and steering her towards the exit, babbled away cheerily about the fun they would have making it back to Kildare railway station. He would hire a pony and trap and they would have a fine time, bumping over the back roads on the jaunting car all the way to the station. To lift her spirits, he sang:

"Come, come, beautiful Molly
Come for a drive with me
Over the mountain
And down by the fountain
Over the valley
Now won't it be lovely?"

It was a great embarrassment to him, drawing attention to himself in public like that, but he felt well enough rewarded when she started to smile again.

The great cavalcade of motorcars was acclaimed with long and lusty cheers all the way back to Dublin by the vast crowds lining the roads to greet them.

"Truly this was a great day for Ireland," said Mr Lisle Jr.

"And an even better night for Irishmen, what?" said Mr Mooney.

In the mirror, Felim saw his father slap the well-padded thigh of his friend, and dreaded what was coming next.

"Young fellow! Take us to the Gloucester Diamond and don't spare the horses."

"You dreadful man," said Mr Lisle Jr., delivering a friendly punch to Mr Mooney's shoulder. Mr Mooney, deciding it was time to cement the relationship for the evening, handed him his silver hip flask filled with Power's Gold Label Irish whiskey. Mr Lisle unscrewed the top, took a deep draught and, returning it to his friend, said, "A great day for the Irish indeed." They both laughed uproariously at the pun, and when the laughter subsided Mr Mooney almost imperceptibly brought the conversation around to matters of business.

Felim loved his father dearly and held him in the highest respect but at times like this, when he was finessing a business deal, his feelings towards him came close to awe. His regard would probably survive another encounter in the Gloucester Diamond. One thing was certain, however, the stocks of the Dublin Tramway Company would be firmer for the night's work.

Philip and Molly trudged along the back roads to Kildare town. With no hackney cabs to be got at any price, they had little option but to 'shank's mare' it all the way to the railway station.

Philip recognised the horse before he did the driver. It was the dray belonging to his brother-in-law James McNeill, and sitting on the driving seat was his eldest son Jimmy and his new wife.

"Come in, Cabra, I know your knock," said the young McNeill.

While the automobilists were tooting their horns through the small villages between Ballyshannon and Dublin, the two young couples shared the McNeill's bread and cheese and passed around a canteen of milk. When they got to Kildare, instead of turning the horse left for the station, Jimmy reined him right for the Curragh and Dublin. In the back of the cart, Philip played every air he knew on his piccolo, while Jimmy McNeill carried the lyrics in a rich baritone voice.

Resting with Philip in the hay at the back of the cart, Molly Wilson's soprano was soon contributing contrapuntal harmony to the quartet's rendition of *After The Ball Was Over*. They played tune after tune, until they turned off the quays at Blackhall Place and headed up Stoneybatter for home.

Chapter 10

A sacred promise

A day out with a girl is like dining in style — it's the way it ends that's important, Philip thought as he whiled away his time in the parlour, waiting for Molly. This was turning out to be a great outing, one of the best. There had been moments of anxiety, he'd be the first to admit that, but here they were with Molly's house all to themselves and things were looking very bright indeed. It occurred to him that he was entering into an occasion of sin but quickly suppressed the thought by convincing himself that nothing need happen. He would be going to his Sodality confessions in Aughrim Street tomorrow in any event. That put aside for the moment, he began diverting his attention.

A lovely warm, bees-waxed feel about this room. Furniture handed down from generation to generation of Wilsons I'd say. Georgian, yes that's what it is, or maybe Queen Anne.

He took out his gold pocket watch and flipped open the lid, not because he wanted to know the time but because he loved the elegance of the timepiece and its double-Albert chain with the watch on one end and tiny matchbox on the other. Solid 18 carat gold every art and part of it ... Jesus! There we go again ... double-Albert ... even the bloody chain me watch hangs on is named after the consort of the famine queen ... is there no end to it?

He ran his hand around the curve of the table's smooth-polished edge. Inlaid. The table was made from solid walnut but the pattern around the edges was created by inserting little slivers of different timbers. Now, the whole thing is called after the decoration rather than the function — an inlaid table ... goes with the inlaid drinks cabinet.

Don't suppose Quartermaster Wilson lashes out the brandy very often. Retired now ... did very well out of the army, him. Not like the poor feckers hopping about Dublin on peg legs or arseing around in a bowl. He has his fine redbrick in Aughrim Street ... Marlborough Terrace, no less ... good education for Molly ... motor car. Make a fortune those fellows selling buckshee boots to the natives out in India and Egypt and God knows where else.

He turned the huge globe on its brass axis until he located Ireland. There's more of it, he thought. They name Ireland as one of the British Isles so that it seems perfectly natural that they should govern it. They just go off and call somebody else's country a British Isles without asking anyone's leave or pardon ... well nobody is ever going to hear Philip Berford refer to Ireland as a British Isle.

The days last forever in mid-summer. He flipped the red-gold lid of his fob watch to check the time. It was half-past ten and the sun was only then beginning to set, sending rays of yellow-gold dancing lightly over the white-gold of Molly's hair, that she had put up high with silver combs. He thought the loose strands on the shell of her nape had taken on the quality of gossamer in the light of the sun. He stood transfixed as she crossed its golden beams carrying a silver tea tray. He was lost in wonderment at the way she managed to do such commonplace things with an air.

"Molly, I love you more than anything in the whole, wide world," he said.

"Even more than Mother Ireland?" she asked with the soft lustre of a knowing smile as she laid the tray down on the polished walnut.

"Molly," he said almost pleadingly, "didn't you see the way those people treated us today? It makes little difference to them whether you are Bluecoat, Fenian or Home Ruler. We are all tarred with the one brush. They think of us in the same way as they do Indians and Arabs — a subject race — good soldiers so long as we have white officers."

Molly dropped her eyes for she felt the evening was taking a most unfortunate turn, and when she spoke her voice was so low he had to strain to hear it. "Philip, my parents, like myself, were born in this city and have as much right to be called Irish as you or anyone else. We are also British ... generations of Wilsons have played their part in building this Empire ... we're very proud of that. We are also very proud of the peace and prosperity the Empire has brought to the world ... including Ireland. So shall we leave it at that?"

Moving quickly to prevent a permanent chill descending upon the evening, Philip said: "And your father ... how is he these days?"

"Keeps himself busy. Always out organising something or other. On some sub-committee for the Royal visit to Dublin at present … down in Cork today advising on the decoration of their royal route. Won't see him again until tomorrow evening."

Philip hoped Molly hadn't noticed the flush-faced greeting that piece of news received. And though he was excited by the revelation, he worried that the royal visit had crept back into the conversation.

"Will you be out waving your little Union Flag for the occasion?"

"They are our King and Queen and I wouldn't miss seeing them for diamonds," she softly replied. "Daddy and I are grateful that we are getting the opportunity to show our loyalty. Daddy says that Dublin Metropolitan Police won't put up with any nonsense on this occasion." She reached out and caressed his hand. "Please don't get involved in any outrage that would put you in jail where I would not be able to see you."

"I won't for your sake my lovely Molly. Would you stay away from the celebrations for mine? We could go somewhere nice together and spend the day away from all the fuss and bother."

Seeing how much it meant to him, pleading with his big, little boy lost eyes, she could not but concede. "Alright Philip my sweetheart darling. I will, just to please you."

Then they held each other and made a solemn covenant not to take any hand, act or part, either for or against the royal visit. She thought he looked like a child longing for everyone not to fight so she squeezed his hand gently and kissed him softly on the lips and told him again that she would stay away because it would make him happy.

They stood by the French windows as the sun went down and watched the tulips, which had opened their petals wide to absorb the day-long light, purse to a close as the evening changed from gold to pewter.

Putting his arms around her, Philip said suddenly, "Molly, I want you." And she, tilting her head towards him replied, "Then promise you'll come away with me to America."

Putting a finger across her lips, Philip said "Hush!" and promised her faithfully that he would look into it.

The bedroom was a tribute to Quartermaster Wilson's odyssey through the more exotic parts of the empire. The rug was a rich, double-knot Persian and Philip could feel his feet sinking into its deep pile as he followed her towards the screen. She removed her rings and bracelets and placed them on the mahogany dressing table that was a richly carved cornucopia of fruit and berries draped around the glistening forms of naked Ceylonese girls.

Then she gently removed his jacket with one hand, deftly undoing the stud that released his starched collar with the other. Philip fumbled with the rest of the shirt until Molly was able to run her fingers lightly over his bare tanned chest and arms. Then kissing him sweetly on the lips, she slipped behind a screen, decorated with erotic paintings the likes of which he'd never imagined. Philip sat on the side of the four-poster bed, watching undergarments rise up in waves before coming to rest across the top of its delicately carved frame. Then Molly stepped out from behind and walked slowly towards him.

In the yellow light of the gas lamp, her breasts were little golden apples that she placed against his face to taste, to kiss, to take the upturned stems into his mouth and feel them grow more defined as she moved him from one to the other and then downwards to where her navel tasted smooth but salty and he dropped to his knees as she gently guided his face ever downwards.

And he, losing himself in her, became oblivious of the world outside.

She lay beside him on the deep pile and caressed his dark muscles lightly to slow his rushing heart. But his eyes were not wide enough nor his mind deep enough to store away the great treasures laid out before them. He tried to take in the line of her body, lying there with her head propped up on one elbow, her palm under a delicate jaw, her long fingers nesting a clearly defined cheekbone. Head inclined, her fair hair flowed down one side, revealing a long, slender neck. The line curved downwards from rounded shoulder to the narrow of her waist before rising again to form the most exquisite S-shape. Her breasts were so close, he thought he could smell an autumn orchard.

They made love once more, and more slowly — Molly allowing her fingers to linger over the matt texture of his sallow skin, kissing him warmly on the mouth, then withdrawing provocatively, running

46

her hands over his muscular back, then exploring his body with gently probing fingertips, lips sucking softly on his neck then biting more deeply on his shoulders.

Their dark and fair skins entwined like sisal and jute, they slept on the Persian carpet while the gas lamp flickered its warm yellow light.

Chapter 11

Of love and sin

All day long in the Broadstone railway offices, Philip's mind was in turmoil. Over and over, the same questions swirled around in his head — how could a being created by God to be as divine as Molly be an occasion of sin?

By the time the working day was finally done, Philip was glad to be heading for the open air to clear his mind. With Molly's father due back from Cork, he had little option but to return home to Cabra Cottage.

Taking the short-cut through the loco sheds, his ears were bombarded by the noise of shunting engines hitting the buffers, or were surprised by the silence of others changing direction on a turntable so finely balanced, their hundreds of tons swung *volte face,* almost effortlessly by one pair of hands. His nostrils were filled with the smells of hot metal, oil and steam, evoking the passion that had consumed him the previous night.

Exiting the railway property by the passage that led into the gap between Upper and Lower Grangegorman, he would have to pass by her house in Marlborough Terrace. His spirits lifted at the very prospect and he began to imagine her smile of surprise if she should happen to look out her front window and see him passing. It would light up her whole face and the very imagining gave him a delicious flowing sensation in the bottom of his stomach. Even if he didn't see her, being on the same street as his beloved was worth more than gazing at all the beautiful pictures in the National Gallery.

There was a secondary motive behind the circuitous route home. Bamma waited in the guilty recesses of his mind. Going around the bend in Lower Grangegorman, he was subconsciously pleased to be delaying the moment when she would face him in the flesh. But right then, the anticipation of Molly's bright face faded that spectre into the background shadows.

As the Women's Penitentiary loomed Philip decided to cross the road. He stopped suddenly at the kerb as the bell of an ambulance car clanging its way towards the Richmond Hospital brought him back to earth with a bump. It became crystal clear to him that, had he been hit by a shunting train going through the loco sheds in Broadstone, or run down by one of the many runaway horses that plagued the city, he would have gone straight to hell.

He was filled with the visions of it as revealed by the saints and told to him in classrooms of tiny boys by fierce Christian Brothers. If he were to die that very minute, all his senses would be tormented by ugliness and pain for all eternity. His sense of touch that he had abused so totally would be seared by everlasting flames; his sense of smell would inhale only the stench of corrupting corpses. How would he face his maker with the degradation he had fallen to with his tongue? He would be condemned to taste only brimstone forever. He would never hear anything again but the screams and curses of the damned. He would be left forever in the position in which he landed in that dark pit on which even the eternal flames would throw no light.

The right course of action became perfectly clear to him. His first duty was to God and his immortal soul. He would get six o'clock confessions in the Church of the Holy Family in Aughrim Street before the monthly sodality. He wouldn't wait for normal confessions on Saturday and if he was wrong about the timing of the confraternity confessions, he would call on Father O'Carroll in the presbytery and ask him to hear his sins straight away.

Walking briskly along Lower Grangegorman he decided to be on the safe side and began reciting 'The Act of Contrition'. "Oh my God I am heartily sorry for having offended thee and I detest my sins above every other evil ..." He was so lost in prayer he passed Kirwan Street without noticing. Realising he was no longer walking around the bend but was at the only piece of straight road in Grangegorman — the stretch that ran alongside the expanding lunatic asylum — he turned on his heel and headed back up the way he had come.

Walking alongside the Grange of Gurmund for the second time, he drew deeply of its sweet-smelling air and wondered if his sister Mary would think that the love he and Molly shared was a mortal sin. Mary was so full of life despite observing all the religious formalities ... all those books she had on comparative religions. They didn't all take such a damning view of the sins of the flesh as the Holy, Roman, Catholic and Apostolic Church … not as far as he could remember in any event.

His face flushed as he remembered the erotic scenes represented on the screen in Molly's bedroom. They were from a Hindu temple — religious art in a manner of speaking. Say if the Hindus were right and the Catholic priests wrong all the time — had anyone ever thought about that, he wondered.

On the other hand, of course, there were the Muslims who thought it a great sin if a woman exposed so much as her nose to anyone but her husband. For them, even the 'aul wans' leaving the Exposition of the Blessed Sacrament on a Sunday night would be nothing more than a gang of barefaced harlots.

He reached the North Circular Road and, with no sign of a tram coming, he continued walking until he came to the junction of the Old Cabra Road and Prussia Street. The spectre of Bamma confronting his overnight absence with Molly rose before him and he made a snap decision to visit his married sister, Gypsy, in Prussia Street.

Gypsy would help him concoct a story that would explain his being out all night to Bamma's satisfaction. She might even accompany him to Cabra Cottage as moral support.

So, instead of turning right for home at Hanlon's Corner, he went left and was soon knocking at the door of number 46 Prussia Street. In place of his sister's welcoming form, her husband stood in the doorway in braces and collarless shirt. Gypsy had been sent for. There was a bit of trouble up in Cabra Cottage.

Philip stammered that he had to go to his sodality in Aughrim Street and would follow her presently.

Making his way to the church, his nostrils recoiled against the summer air, fetid with the stench of animal blood and excreta.

The little hatch door would slide across. He would ask the priest to bless him for he had sinned, and a month had elapsed since his last confession. Father O'Carroll would question him about every detail of what he and Molly had done together and, as was the way with that particular gentleman, it would be through the medium of geography.

"Think of her body as the map of Ireland my son. Did you fondle her around the Sligo region? Did you touch the twin peaks of

Benbulben and Benbo? Did you take Belmullet into your mouth? Did you enter Ireland's one and only fjord at Killary Harbour?"

At the gates of the Church of the Holy Family, he could see 60 Marlborough Terrace just up the road on the opposite side. Though it was mid summer, the wall lamp had been left on to light the dark hallway, for he could see it illuminating the fanlight over the front door. Molly must be at home, probably in the drawing room playing the piano or perhaps in the bedroom dressing for dinner ... putting on something low-cut to show off that long, delicate neck of hers. Perhaps pinning that finely carved cameo brooch just above her breasts.

How could he even contemplate subjecting the beauty of their bodies interlaced in perfect, harmonious union to a voyeur's guided tour of Irish topography? No, he would not break faith with Molly whatever the cost. He would not heap embarrassment of himself upon betrayal of her, be it religious duty or no.

He walked on past the church relieved by his decision, but got no real respite for his heart was pounding with the prospect of passing her house. In the window of number 60 Marlborough Terrace he saw the cause of his joy and turmoil drawing the curtains of her bedroom window. Their eyes met and hers opened wide with surprise for a brief moment before lighting up with the delight of seeing him ... *him* ... the most beautiful girl he had ever seen in his life was expressing such obvious pleasure at seeing him and he had questioned the miracle!

This brief contact between them gave purpose to the whole day. It was the moment for which the day had begun and everything else that had happened or might happen fell away into insignificance. She gave him a light flutter of a wave with her fingers that played on his heart like grace notes and lifted his soul so high he thought he was floating up the street. It carried him right up to the North Circular Road on a stream of clean air and onwards to the Old Cabra Road to Cabra Cottage. With her delicate fingers playing gently on his heart he was resolved to face Bamma and whatever consequences might flow from his love for Molly Wilson.

Chapter 12

Maryanne Little's mighty establishment

Felim Mooney was coming to the conclusion that his father never wrestled with his conscience because he had two that he kept in strictly separate compartments. It seemed to Felim, whenever he thought of the matter, that he took out one for use in his public life and the other for very private use.

To the board and management of the Dublin Tramway Company their chairman was a paragon of virtue who drove a hard bargain but stuck to his side of it. To the groundsmen and servants of Springfield he was one of nature's gentlemen — a man who remembered everybody's name and took an avuncular interest in their lives and those of their children.

To the madams of Montgomery Street and the Gloucester Diamond he was an old rogue with a fancy for young girls, mostly two at a time.

The light that had turned the pasturelands around Naas into golden meadows changed the Grand Canal to a pale string of silver as the automobile rattled over the Third Lock Bridge in Inchicore. Along the Esplanade, Felim observed a lamplighter igniting the mantles along the quays that sent ribbons of yellow rippling across the Liffey while, inside the railing of Croppies' Acre, his predecessors lay, uneasily awaiting the day when Irishmen would no longer fear to speak of '98.

"I've a story for ye," Mr Mooney piped up quietly to his friend Mr Lisle in the back seat. "Did you ever hear about the old woman in Wexford who looked over the half-door and saw the landlord having his way with her daughter in the ploughed field? She screamed at the top of her voice, 'Arch your back Mary, and keep his lordship's balls out of the mud.'"

The two older men rolled around the back seat of the automobile slapping each other on the thighs and roaring with laughter.

"Well, that's a good one all right," said Mr Cecil Lisle Jnr. Then, taking out a silver flask of whiskey, he said, "We might as well polish off the last of mine, seeing as we killed yours off before Rathcoole."

"No," said Mr Mooney, "Kill comes after Rathcoole." This remark reactivated the laughter until their complexions were quite plum.

As the Wolseley 9 pulled into Gloucester Street, a Sedan arrived outside the door of Mrs Maryanne Little's establishment carrying leading English members of the British and Irish Automobile Club: Mr Mark Mayhew, Mr Henry Norman, MP, the Hon. C. S. Rolls and Colonel Crompton, RE.

"Away with you boy to Cabra and an early bed," said Mr Mooney to his son. "Mr Lisle and I are just popping inside to do a bit of business over a few drinks. We'll take a cab home when we're done."

"There, there, it'll all be over soon," was the softly whispered refrain Annie Deveraux heard through the breathless panting behind her. She had been leaning on the back of the sofa to relieve the strain, but had got so tired, made a cradle of her arms to rest her face. Squeezing her eyes tightly shut to stop the tears from flowing, she wished she were back on her parents' farm overlooking the sweet Slaney.

Her skirts were hitched halfway up her back and her bloomers were lying in folds around one of her ankles. She thought it would have made quite a comical picture if it weren't for all the pain — she bent over like someone playing leap-frog and the purple-faced old gentleman puffing away behind her, whispering, "Now, now, dear, it won't be long now."

Two doors down the hall, Cecil Lisle was enjoying the 'Sonnix Sandwich' that came highly recommended by his friend and crony. They were no more than seventeen or eighteen years old and he wondered where they got all that experience. Both had beautiful, well-rounded figures and very full breasts, but he could not help noticing the stretch marks terracing the little potbellies on the two romping lassies. Then it occurred to him.

"Fillies trained by Columbanus Mooney could jump through hoops by the time that rogue was finished with them," he chuckled to himself.

*****

The chaffing became so intense for Annie Deveraux she began to cry silently into her arms. She knew better than to allow a gentleman the likes of Mr Mooney see her shedding tears.

"Cry in front of a client and you'll be crying with hunger soon enough," the madam had told her when she first went on the game. Mrs Little was very good to her. Found her a place for herself and the child and regularly got her men that were big tippers.

"Laugh and smile a lot," she had advised. "There's nothing so easily parted as a man and his money when he thinks he's given a girl a good time." She knew it would soon be over by the way his breathing had quickened and by the severity with which he was digging his nails into her hips.

As Mr Mooney busied himself with buttons and studs, Annie quickly dried her eyes on the soiled, damask doily from the back of the sofa, pulled up her bloomers and smoothed down her long dress, then spoke to Mr Mooney with face beaming.

"Well, I hope you and your friends have a lovely time at the speed trials in the Phoenix Park tomorrow," she said with a wide smile that revealed all of her tiny, milky-white teeth.

"I'm sure we will, my dear, I'm sure we will, with God willing," said Mr Mooney closing her palm over a gold sovereign. "A little something for yourself for being such a good girl. I'll fix up with the lady of the house presently," he said, then left to rejoin his friends.

Mr Mooney was most surprised to find an empty anteroom. Sure I might as well have a drink while I wait, he said to himself as he poured a generous measure of Power's Gold Label into a large tumbler.

Annie Deveraux crept down the stairs and over to the corner shop to buy milk for the tea and the baby's bottle and some bread and margarine for her supper. Then she went to her tenement room in Empress Lane as fast as her discomfort would allow, to be with the infant she had left in the care of the big girl from upstairs. She thought she mightn't be missed for a while even on such a busy night.

Felim felt the need to rest his eyes and stretch his limbs after the long drive. He had an even greater need to make some sort of sense of the scene he had just witnessed and to place it into some kind of order. Removing his cap and goggles he began to stroll through the Monto, considering the possibility that, not only did his father have two consciences, but that this duality extended into his political beliefs as well.

Coming to terms with his father's ability to balance the roles of devoted, Catholic spouse with that of impregnator of domestic staff had taken years. He now had to reconcile his being a leading Home Ruler with his readiness to share the nation's women with the same English, ruling class that was denying Ireland its rights in the first place.

He remembered the first time he'd become aware of his father's proclivities – having his way with two of their maids. A hackneyed story perhaps – country lassies going into service and yielding to the blandishments and promises of men who were masters of the world they inhabited. If they fell pregnant, they lost their employment and the shame of having a child out of wedlock meant they could not return to their parents' home.

For many, the brothels of the Monto and Linenhall were their only means to feed and shelter themselves and the child. Felim's own frequent visits to such establishments as a medical student had taught him that. His experience as a junior hospital doctor had revealed it would only be a matter of time before they ended up in the Westmoreland Lock, disintegrating with the pox.

Yet his father's contribution to this train of misery and degradation did not diminish his love and respect for him. In a strange sort of way, it seemed to symbolise his virility and his heroic lusts for life. That he continued to maintain such appetites way into middle-years had to be admired, he told himself.

Felim had always envied Philip Berford his clarity of thought and wished that he could believe things were so simple.

"Ireland of all the strands is our nation," Philip had said with great conviction as they strolled one day through Sallcock's Wood. "No matter if you descend from Gael, Viking, Norman or English planter, you are now part of the Irish nation — a nation in its own right. Not one that is subject to England."

Felim was never that sure. He was confident enough about his Irishness and shared his father's desire for Home Rule, but not a total break with Britain. A separate assembly to protect Irish rights and develop native industry was one thing, but to be set adrift from the mightiest empire in the world was another. He knew he was Irish, but also felt British in the way that he supposed the Scots and Welsh did.

Keeping your cake and eating it, Philip called it. "We are not part of this empire. We are a subject race, there only to serve its interests and the needs of its ruling elite — to provide cannon fodder for its armies, servants for its stately homes and flour to dust the wigs of their hanging judges."

"And girls for its brothels," Felim thought as he strolled out of Montgomery Street.

He tried to date when it was that they had begun to drift apart. His going to the College of Surgeons had begun a rift that widened when Philip began training as a railway surveyor on the recommendation of his father. Awkwardness had crept gradually into their meetings until it became easier to avoid them altogether.

There had been no reserve when they met at Mary's funeral. The formality of the occasion made the meeting easier as did the formulaic expressions of condolence. 'Sorry for your troubles' sounding so limp an offering when people are lost to grief and yet it eased them once more to conversation. After the 'removal', they talked for hours about the great times they had had together as children. He wondered why the coolness had come back with such vengeance at the Gordon Bennett Race. He knew it was a difficult position for Philip to have been in and yet he still maintained that clarity. Felim realised he was also envying his old friend for returning from the race in the company of the beautiful Molly Wilson.

"Hey young fella, are yeh a master baker or wha? Your dough is rising!" The voice coming from a woman standing in the darkened doorway beside him stopped him in his tracks.

"A tanner a wank, one and six a ride," she said, taking him by the hand and leading him into the hallway. The smell of urine and cabbage-water wafted out of the hall, and by the light of its gas lamp he could see the rosy, red cheeks of a wasting consumptive and teeth rotting from the arsenic used to treat her venereal disease.

"Sorry ma'am, I'm just dropping off my father," he was surprised to hear himself saying as he broke away from her grip and made his way back into Montgomery Street. He could still hear her screeches of laughter as he turned into Gloucester Street and dodged down Empress Place. "He's just dropping off his Daddy, the pair of dirty whoremongers, did yis ever hear the like?"

Chapter 13

Bamma

For valuation purposes the rates office had it listed as an outhouse, but to the Berfords it was always the scullery. In all weathers Bamma could be seen through its wide-open door, sleeves rolled up beyond the elbows, peeling potatoes, washing vegetables, pummelling meat or gutting fish. Cooking was done on the kitchen range, but she would not have mess in the house so all preparation was carried out across the yard in the scullery.

Mondays were washdays and she spent the bulk of them out in the scullery, hands, arms and elbows reddened from washing soda, scrubbing the family's linen up and down the corrugated wooden washboard before running it through the great mangle in the yard. Then she would stand back in satisfaction, admiring the laden clothesline billowing in the wind.

Cabra Cottage, together with its outhouses and surrounding three-acre field, was bought on a 199 year lease from Mooney's Estate by Bamma Berford and her husband-to-be, just before they married thirty-seven years earlier in 1866.

Bamma had good reason to remember the date. It was exactly a year, a month and a day before she brought Mary, her firstborn, into the world. It was also the year before the Fenian uprising. Another glorious failure, her Seamus was lucky not to have ended his days in an Australian stockade or an English Jail. He survived '67 and all the repression that followed, to bring a little education and a sense of national pride to the slum children of North King Street. But he did not survive the cholera leaching out of the surrounding tenements. He left Bamma alone to rear four daughters and a son in the granite cottage with the solid scullery in Mooney's Field.

She stood by the earthenware trough, gutting herrings for a Friday dinner. Fish was food for the brain and kept the family observant on the day of abstinence. Like all Dubliners, she believed the silver harvest from Dublin Bay the best in the world.

The scullery suddenly darkened, making her cut her finger. "Get out of my light, bad cess to you whoever you are," she said. "Look what you've made me do."

"I'm dreadfully sorry Mrs Berford. I just called by to see how you are," said Felim Mooney making his way across the flagstones to examine the wound.

"Leave it alone for God's sake, it's only a scratch."

"Still and all you ought to cover it. You know what septic poison can do."

"There's no need to make a fuss. I'll put some carbolic soap and sugar on it when I'm done here."

She began scrubbing the muck off the mound of potatoes under the running tap and throwing each one into an iron bucket.

"Half the population of Dublin is living on bread and dripping. Your children don't know how lucky they are."

"You'd think so, wouldn't you?" she said pointedly. "Have you by any chance seen Philip in your travels?"

"Yes indeed I have. We had a fine time together at the motorcar race yesterday out in Ballyshannon. Bumped into them by lucky chance coming out of Kildare railway station with his lovely young lady."

If the dark glare had not told Felim the gravity of what he had done then the interrogation that followed certainly did.

"What was her name, this so-called lady?" Bamma asked in a voice tortured with restraint.

"Molly Wilson I believe."

"A blondie one full of airs?"

"She was fair surely and very pleasant indeed."

"I'm sure the men think so. If you took them to the race where are they now?"

"Made their own way home. Father and I were invited to meet the Viceroy…"

"Viceroy is it? Now if you would be so kind Dr Mooney, I have a family to feed."

Felim crossed Mooney's Field wondering why encounters with the Berfords left him feeling punctured by guilt.

He could still hear Bamma's voice reverberating around the bare stone walls. "Mary you were the finest by far … our prettiest and brightest star … a great joy to your father and mother. We were so proud when you followed in our footsteps — a Fenian teacher — passing on the torch."

Fresh tears flowed with the memory that it was Mary's childish sibilance that had given her the name she was known by. Christened Banba, after one of the Gaelic names for Ireland, it became conflated with 'mama' in the toddler's soft, watery mouth and came out as 'Bamma'. Both she and her husband so delighted in every utterance of their lovely daughter he took to calling her Bamma himself, as did everyone else in their turn, until she answered to nothing else.

Mary's death had shaken her belief in everything. The neglect of doctors might have caused the childbed fever, but only God could have brought down the Big Wind.

Looking after the baby brought some kind of purpose to the long days and nights and he had been taken away from her when the man of the house was not there to protect them.

If she weakened now, everything would fall apart. She had to stay strong, even if it made people think she was hard and unfeeling.

Chapter 14

Return of the Prodigal

Entering the kitchen, Philip felt as though he had walked into a wake. Lena, Gypsy and Nelly were sitting around the walls in stony silence. Not that there was anything surprising about silences in Cabra Cottage. When Bamma patrolled around her family's honour or good manners, quietness was often the best policy but Gypsy's silence was a bad omen. Though the quality of the stillness was not unique, Philip sensed prescience like a heavy summer's evening just before an electric storm.

He greeted them all with a cheery and, in the circumstances, badly misplaced humour: "God save all here, excluding the cat," he said. Gypsy was the only one to answer with the customary, "and may He and His holy Mother bless you." Lena and Nelly just looked at their hands. Bamma, busying herself cooking on the range, did not turn around or recognise his presence.

Philip hung his coat on the hallstand, removed the cuff-studs from his shirtsleeves and, rolling them up, began washing his hands for dinner. As he poured water from the bucket into the basin, he considered with great trepidation the cause of the heavy atmosphere. He knew that spending the day with Molly would be cause enough, but if Bamma got a sense that he had also spent the night with her, there would be hell to pay.

Taking his place at table he said, "I was one lucky man yesterday," and went silent to gauge the impact.

"Why so?" asked Gypsy.

"I got a chance to go to Kildare on Thursday ... my day off you know. And what do you think? Coming home, the last train was full with the crowd from the Gordon Bennett motorcar race and not a seat to be had. If it wasn't for young Jimmy McNeill I'd be there yet."

"What was he doing so far out?" asked Gypsy helpfully.

"Branching out into horses ... buying and selling on the 'QT' from his father I think. Very hush-hush about it all. Anyway, he only recognises me among the big crowd on the road to Dublin and gives me a lift all the way to Prussia Street. Slow enough mind you … it was so late when we got there, he insisted I spend the night. Bowl of porridge and all before I set off to work this morning."

"Wasn't that very Christian of him?" said Gypsy to the black back of her silent mother.

Philip made a mental note to square up the story up with Jimmy on the first chance he got.

The girls set out five places, each with the correct amount of crockery and cutlery. No one in the Berford home ever picked up the wrong eating utensil. Years of being struck on the knuckles with the back of the long bread-knife had ingrained table manners into every one of them.

When she saw that everyone had settled into their place, Bamma brought the pan of sizzling herrings to the table and smashed it over Philip's head, sending him sprawling across the wooden boards and the fish slithering all over the bees-waxed floor.

With the empty pan still swinging in one hand, she pulled his head back off the table with the other until their faces met. Her eyes stood out like organ stops protruding directly into her son's face, cutting off any escape.

"Where were you, you lying whoremonger, when your home was being invaded and your dead sister's child stolen away from us?" Without pausing for a reply, she continued. "You were out gallivanting with that camp-follower while your little nephew was being kidnapped … weren't you … weren't you? What would your father say, light of heaven to him, if he were alive and spared to us this day, ay?" No one dared move or speak until the tempest had blown itself out and everyone knew it had a while to run.

"Did I ever think I'd live to see the day that a son of mine would bring disgrace to the family name. To the longest day that anyone can remember, the Berfords were renowned for being fierce in the defence of their home and country … until you … you …"

She suddenly stopped talking and in the long silence that followed, the family held its breath. With a voice impelled by rising contempt she said, "And you, the last male Berford — the one we are depending upon to continue the family name — you bring shame on it by fornicating with that 'Bluecoat' whore. You're a poor dependence." Seeing him wince, she thrust deeper. "Ask yourself, what kind of a girl would let a man spend the night with her? Only a

64

British Army trollop would." Then lowering her voice till it was barely audible, she said, "You'll take up with her over my dead body, young man. I'll put the widow's curse on you first."

Nelly screamed in terror at what was being called down upon her lovely, gentle brother, but Lena held her face against her breast and stroked her hair until she calmed, then dabbed her own doleful eyes with a little lace handkerchief.

Gypsy's face was a mask. All her life she had seen her mother rail against superstition and yet she would call down curses when it suited her purpose. Bamma could be as violent as she liked to her son knowing that he was too manly to ever raise his hand against any woman, much less his own mother. She was contemptuous but Bamma could only guess at what she was thinking. It would never be expressed to her face or to anyone else. For behind it all, Gypsy too held her mother with awe and love.

"Lena and Nelly! Don't just hover around the place like a pair of drones. Clean up this mess." The two young women worked quickly, picking up the herrings and fried onions, then scrubbing and polishing. When everything was spotless, they laid the table for dinner once more. With the kitchen back in order, Bamma proceeded to serve the rest of the food.

Gypsy concentrated her efforts on cleaning up her brother and seeing to it that he was all right, at least physically. He would have a major bump on his head but that would heal a lot sooner than the wound inflicted on his heart. Bamma would keep that raw for as long as it took.

Gypsy knew how much her young brother loved Molly Wilson and instinctively felt that if their love were to be crossed, he would never marry another. Looking straight up into Bamma's tightly set face she said, "Wouldn't it be ironic if the Berford line, that survived centuries of rack, rope and prison, were to die out now because a man was not let choose the girl he loved."

Everyone froze in the audacious air.

"There will be no Bluecoats in this family and that's an end to it."

Being a practical woman, Gypsy moved to repair what damage she could. There was little she could do about the scurrilous attack on Molly Wilson or the gratuitous curse. She could, however, ease Philip's mind about his sister's baby. Philip loved and feared

Bamma, but Mary was the big sister who gave him all the mothering he craved but never received from Bamma. He had nearly burst with pride when she named her first child after him. Her death had hit him hard, but left him more attached than ever to her son.

As they continued the meal without enthusiasm, Gypsy placed her hand on Philip's and said: "There's no need to worry about Mary's baby. I saw him myself passing down Prussia Street in the care of his father and it looked only right and proper."

Bamma glared but Gypsy pretended she did not see. "You must visit your namesake. I'm sure that you and your friend would be welcome visitors in Stoneybatter."

When the meal was finished and the girls had carried the dishes out to the scullery to wash, Philip made his way to the stairs and the refuge of his bedroom.

"No Bluecoats in this family," Bamma said to his disappearing back.

Chapter 15

The Drummond Institute for Girls

Molly Wilson stood at the window of the Drummond Institute for Girls and gazed out at the Liffey Valley. Her eye followed the course of the river, lost in wonderment at its work of untold millennia, cutting a deep gorge through the Strawberry Beds on its way to the sea.

"Good morning Molly ... a penny for them."

She turned on her heel and placed a hand on her startled heart. "Dr Mooney! What ever are you doing here?"

"Annual medical I'm afraid. Don't look so concerned. I will only be examining the girls. The usual once over — tums, gums and bums."

Blushing at the forwardness of the remark, Molly replied: "The girls will be delighted with the change. Old McConchie was a terrible old grouch."

"Flattered I'm sure. But they won't be bothered by the old boy anymore. They called time on him last Easter."

"So sorry to hear it. And you're the replacement?"

"For my sins Molly ... so sorry for interrupting the day dream ... you seemed lost in thought just then."

"Oh, I was just thinking how marvellous it was the way the river cut its way to the sea no matter who ran the blooming country. Look at it, exposing layers of strata without a thought in the world for the royal visit or the pro and anti factions that are getting so excited about it."

"I see. Royal visit becoming a bone of contention then? I feared there might be a Bamma problem along the way."

"Aren't men a terrible contradiction all the same?"

"Nothing truer. They can be big and powerful as you like and still be helpless in the face of a strong woman."

He looked for as long as it was polite at her slender form, her skin translucent in the morning sunlight and wanted to say that any man would be a fool not to do what she commanded, that any man should be glad to be a fool for her sake. But she was Phil's girl so he said, "My word! We are very deep for this time of the morning. So who's winning the battle between the lovely Molly Wilson and the redoubtable Bamma?"

"You're very sharp … mind you don't cut yourself."

"You haven't answered my question."

"I might if only I knew."

"Molly, the main reason I popped in was to apologise for yesterday. I know it must have seemed terrible but I was so caught up with looking after my father, I forgot that you and Philip had no transport. I'm so sorry. How did you fare?"

"Don't bother your head about it. Everything worked out for the best."

"You're so kind. Must dash … meeting with the Lady Superintendent for instructions … speaking of strong women. Call me if you need anything Molly … anything at all."

Returning to her desk, Molly began preparing the morning's lesson on *The Iliad* and *The Odyssey*, smiling at the knowledge that her sixth formers referred to the two works as 'The Idiot and the Oddity'. But she couldn't concentrate for wondering who would win if it came to a choice between mother and lover. At one point she became convinced that Bamma was in for a jolt if she didn't change her tune. At another she would convince herself that Philip was so bound by love and fear, she would only keep him with his mother's blessing. She instinctively felt she had to make him more dependent on her than he was on his mother. She believed she had one big advantage. He was full of the mysteries of womanhood. She would show him plenty more … a bit at a time … enough to put a reel in his head for many a day to come.

She was just observing how the heat of summer, coming on top of a long wet winter, had caused grins to develop in every one of the six oak panels in the classroom door when it was flung wide open, bringing her train of thought to a sudden halt. Miss Rousselle, Lady Superintendent of the school, marched across the echoing floorboards, heavy footed in her high-buttoned boots and stood over her with a back as straight as a ramrod.

She addressed the young form mistress in her most peremptory manner. "Miss Wilson, you will note that Drummond has been requested to provide fifty of its best girls to form part of the guard of honour for their majesties, during the presenting of colours at the

Viceregal Lodge on July 24th. Miss Cappathwaita, Miss Kearney and your good self will help with our young ladies. I will be in command. The king is to inspect the Hibernian boys and the queen will do similarly with the Drummond girls."

Handing Molly a list of names, she continued, "See to it that your young ladies are on parade in the yard, dressed for inspection by 0830 hours tomorrow morning. A great honour Miss Wilson. We have been bestowed a great honour indeed. Rehearsals every morning until the big day. One other matter. A newspaper chap wants some background material. I've given him permission to talk with you. I'm far too busy to be entertaining that sort of person at a time like this. The interview may take place while your class is having its medical. That's all."

Executing a smart about-turn, Miss Rousselle exited the room as abruptly as she had entered, leaving Molly an absolute ball of excitement. She would be so close to their royal majesties, she could hardly breathe at the prospect. She couldn't wait to get home and tell her father. He would be so proud to see her standing there with her young ladies as the queen passed down the line. She began to imagine how she might react if her majesty stopped to pass a word with her and nearly died at the thought of it! In all her excitement she momentarily forgot her pact with Philip.

She smelled the fellow before she either saw his dishevelled form or heard his slurring words. Turning around, she beheld a fat, slobbering shambles of a man who pulled a dog-eared card from a shiny waistcoat pocket announcing 'Percival Sneade, *Freeman's Journal.*' The smell of stale beer and cigarettes was so overpowering she could barely take the handkerchief away from her face to answer his questions. Despite his state of inebriation so early in the morning, he painstakingly wrote down all the details he got from her on how many girls would be received by their majesties ... the names of the teachers who would be in charge including her own. He was very keen to get quotes on how she felt about meeting the Royal family.

"I suppose you might get a more accurate picture by attending the actual ceremony in the Park," she said impishly.

"As well to get the facts right from yourself miss ... for fear anything slips past me on the day, you understand."

"Slipping from a bottle by any chance?" she said with a smile.

"Now, now miss. It's nice to be nice. What did you say your own name was?"

"Wilson. Miss Molly Wilson."

The following days passed by to the rhythm of marching feet. Up and down the stone yard they went, the Lady Superintendent barking them to attention just to stand them at ease again, then to right wheel and left wheel in endless circles. Molly couldn't stop her mind from wandering and when it did it roved to Philip Berford — to his slim, muscular body and dark, Mediterranean features that could hide nothing for all their brooding. She began to ache for him, despite the incongruity of such feelings in a square full of drilling feet in the early morning. And she remembered too well the promise she had made to him.

What if she lost him? Molly allowed herself the indulgence of sweet anguish until a sense of loss started somewhere in the centre of her chest and flowed down to form a knot in the pit of her stomach.

She knew that Bamma would wield her role in the big pageant like a weapon if she got to hear about it and, in Dublin, that would only be a question of time. Why couldn't a royal visit be like the Gordon Bennett Race she wondered— a spectacle everyone could feel part of and enjoy?

But she knew she had no option. She would ask Dr Mooney for a note diagnosing some complaint that would satisfy the Lady Superintendent about her absence at the Viceregal Lodge. She was now certain. She would not break faith with her Philip, even for a chance to meet her king and queen.

Chapter 16

An Unhappy Correspondence

76 Prussia Street
Dublin
4 July 1903

Mrs B. Berford
Cabra Cottage
Dublin

Please
Mrs Berford i want to Let you know I have Been to the convent,
as you advised in your last note. i went with Mrs trench and Mrs
Dooley. i was telling them about the child and how it was that it was
still in the house and no one to mind it saving my Father and how it
was clear to all that a man on his own cannot look after a new born
infant. i was asking them the best thing my Father could do with it
and the two Nuns told me that its Grandmother should take it and
She was the best entitled to it. They said that it is such in the case of
death. i was telling them the way things was during the week with the
child not feeding and my Father at his wits end not knowing where
to turn. They bid me send this letter up to yous. its for pity sake im
doing this and respect for its Mother that is in the clay. i gave him
dogs abuse for taking it from its own. i told him how it was that the
child was feeding well and happy enough when it was with yous up
in Cabra Cottage. He is in such grief for his wife your dear departed
daughter who is in heaven and now he is in fear for his infant son. it
is pitiful to see such a strong man bent by so terrible a burden of
cares. the Nuns said that there is no time for wasting if the child is to
survive this week. so as a Friend let me know what you say about
this note till I tell Mrs trench and Mrs Dooley and the Nuns. so you
must only do something for it and not let it die an unnatural death.
so let us know tonight. send word back with my little brother Peter.
Yours Sincerely
Young Jimmy McNeill

*****

Cabra Cottage Dublin
4 July 1903

Mr J. McNeill Jnr.
76 Prussia Street
Dublin

Dear Mr McNeill

Your note has given rise to a great deal of alarm for the safety of my grandson. The child's condition would seem to have deteriorated considerably since we last communicated.

Let me state at the outset that your father was most precipitous in the way he removed my daughter's child from the care of her kin where, as you correctly acknowledge, he was safe and thriving. I cannot tolerate my household being again turned upside-down at the whim of your father who, in the past, has shown scant regard for the feelings of others. The most charitable construction I can place on his behaviour thus far, is to conclude that he is a man who acts without thought for the consequences of his actions. Please communicate this to him.

I must also ask you to tell him about the heavy burden already borne by my family and myself in trying to do our best by our dear departed Mary and her child. I am not a young woman any more and caring for a newborn infant on top of the rest of my duties caused a considerable extra strain. In addition, my daughter Lena was obliged to give up her good position in business to be a second mother to her sister's baby. While she was prepared to pay this high price to mind the child, it became an unacceptably high tariff when there was no child to mind as a result of his impetuous action in kidnapping the baby from outside our home on 23 June.

You must tell Mr McNeill Senior that his was an intolerable deed and one that could not be countenanced a second time. He must realise that my household cannot be pulled thither and yon at the behest of his sudden impulses. Therefore, I will not consider taking the child back into the care of my family, unless I get copper-fastened guarantees that my grandson will be reared in my home to the age of majority, without let or hindrance.

72

You must advise your father to go to a solicitor and get him to devise a legally binding agreement to give effect to my decision in this matter. I'm quite sure Messrs Gavin Lowe, or some other of the cattle auctioneers with whom he deals, will be able to recommend a suitable law firm for the purpose.

Get him to tell his solicitor, when he has acquired one, that the child must be made my ward or, if that is problematical, then a ward of my son Philip Berford. Your father must sign over all rights to the child and agree to never interfering in his upbringing again. Indeed, he must agree to not approaching the child ever again under any circumstances, even to crossing over the far side of the road should the danger arise of a chance meeting on the street. Please convey my conditions to him. They are final, unalterable and not amenable to either negotiation or amendment.

Time is of the essence. You must move immediately to get this matter resolved without further delay. When your solicitors have the papers drawn up, you may have them sent to me for my approval before we proceed to a final settlement in this matter.

Yours Sincerely
Banba Berford (Mrs)

*****

Chidley & Gannon
Solicitors
Commissioners for Oaths
23 to 26 Arran Quay
Dublin
5 July 1903

Mrs B. Berford
Cabra Cottage
Dublin

Dear Mrs Berford,
I have been asked to act on behalf of my client, Mr James McNeill of 23 Stoneybatter in regards to the matter of the care of the infant, Philip McNeill. In pursuance of this affair, I have drawn up an agreement (encl.) that is acceptable to my client on the proviso

that you move quickly to take care of his infant son. You will see from the attached documents that my client agrees to all the conditions as set out by your good self. He undertakes to hand the child over to your care and agrees that it becomes the ward of your son Philip Berford.

I have sought a hearing with a judge in chambers this very afternoon so as to expedite the matter. I fear that your gender and eminent age might give his Lordship pause. Seeking to make your son Philip Berford the Guardian would be most helpful, given the time constraints we are under.

My client further undertakes not to interfere with the rearing of the said Philip McNeill, and, in furtherance of this provision, will seek to avoid all further contact with him from the date he returns to your care.

In cases such as this, where the urgent well-being of a child is concerned, and where there is no conflict involving religion or social station, and where the parties are in agreement, the courts are often disposed to speedily facilitate the outcome desired by the families concerned. Therefore, may I request that you signify your acceptance or otherwise with the attached proposal by return. Further, if the proposal meets with your approval, could you please arrange to be present at the Four Courts this afternoon, together with your son, Philip Berford, to facilitate the smooth transition in the matter of the care of your grandson, should the court deem it right and proper.

Yours Sincerely
Berchmans Gannon Solicitor

*****

46 Prussia Street
Dublin
6 July 1903

Mr J. McNeill Jnr.
76 Prussia Street
Dublin

Dear Jimmy

Please convey to your father my profound sense of sorrow and guilt at the terrible travail he has had to undergo, and for which I feel at least partly responsible. I thought my heart would sunder in the Four Courts yesterday to see that strong, proud and honourable man cry uncontrollably as he handed over his son, perhaps forever. Tell him that the sympathy of all we Berford girls was with him, just as surely as was that of his beloved Mary, Light of Heaven shine upon her. I know that she is interceding for him with the Blessed Virgin that she might get her Son, Our Saviour, to lighten the dreadful loss he must endure in the days, months and years to come.

Tell him that I came to him in pure friendship and for the love of my sister in the grave and the child she left behind. I believed then, as I do now, that the interests of the child, and everyone else concerned, were best served by his being reared by his own father. I have no reason to doubt my judgement that he was, and is, more than equal to the task. Tell him that it was fortuitous that the child would only feed for Bamma and no fault of his. So he must not blame himself that the baby began to fail under his care, but rather put the fault on me for having instituted the situation in the first place.

It is generally believed, and the court yesterday accepted, that men possess neither the nature nor the skill to rear an infant. None of them have seen, as I have seen, your father nurse his dying wife with a tenderness beyond the capability of most mothers. He has a gentleness when about children, women and even animals that stands in great contrast to his powerful mien.

Ask him not to fault my mother too much. She acts in what she considers the child's best interests, though the manner of its execution might seem harsh. She had a hard life, being widowed young with children not much more than babes. She had to rear and educate us all without support, other than her own hard work and strength of will.

I hope your father finds consolation in the knowledge that his son will be well cared for in Cabra Cottage. My sister Lena will not allow a wind to blow upon him and my sister Nelly will dance attendance on him night, noon and morning. As his new Guardian, my brother Philip will ensure that he grows into a fine, educated Irishman of whom your father will have just cause to be proud.

Reassure him that, when the dust has settled, I will call into the dairy in Stoneybatter, from time-to-time, to give regular reports on his son's progress. He can rest assured that I, too, will be keeping an eye on the child and will be happy to step into the breach should the need arise at any time in the future.

We must all trust in God and bend ourselves to His Holy Will. His ways are not our ways and, who knows, but it may all be for the best, in the best of all possible worlds.

Please read this letter to your father ASAP. I hope it gives him some consolation. I'm sure he will get comfort from the rest of his children: yourself, your brother Peter, along with your sisters Katie and Queenie. Remember me to them all.

I remain
Yours Faithfully
Gypsy

*****

23 Stoneybatter
Dublin
20 July 1903

Mrs H. Kennedy
46 Prussia Street
Dublin

Dear Gypsy

Our good friend Harry Head was so good as to write these words down verbatim. As you know, I cannot read or write.

May I first thank you for your letter to me by way of young Jimmy. The kind words of comfort you offered came at a time when I thought my soul and body were passing through the cold, dark flames of hell. Some awful sin must have been committed in the past by myself or some long-forgotten generation of McNeills. The court hearing was a most bitter episode, coming so soon after the death of my sorely missed Mary. When she passed away on Good Friday, I thought I had dropped into the deepest pit of pain, but there was more yet to travel. Giving away our son on the steps of the Four Courts convinced me that suffering and loneliness is a bottomless thing.

Please do not reproach yourself in any way for the great misfortune that has befallen me. Your advice was sound and I have never regretted acting upon it, not even for a minute. It was only right and proper that I should have attempted to rear the son that bore my name and the beautiful aspect of his departed mother.

Had we been more fortunate in the matter of the housekeeper, things might have come to a different pass. God only knows, we took great care in the woman we selected to mind him and my other children. The lady chosen was ideal in every respect of age, temperament and education. Who could have foreseen that the unfortunate creature would suffer the loss of her own mother so soon after taking up her position, necessitating a return to Carlow to look after her elderly father?

Perhaps it was all foreshadowed, but for my sins, I got no inkling of the crisis that was brewing. I have never seen a child, nor yet a calf or cub, so determined against taking nourishment. He seemed to be pining away. Perhaps it was the loss of the mother whom he hardly saw, or maybe he missed the society of her people in Cabra Cottage. Whatever the cause, he would not feed for his father, nor for the 'Lucky Woman', not even when the same good woman brought along her cousin, the wet nurse.

You must please understand that it was because I knew he had been feeding for Bamma and thriving so well under her care in Cabra Cottage, that I so readily agreed to her conditions. I did it all so that my son might survive and grow up to be a fine Irishman like you say in your letter, and a credit to his mother who sacrificed herself.

Not being part of his life is just another cross for me to bear. I will try to bear it with fortitude and seek consolation and fulfilment in the rearing of my three small children. Heavens knows, they have been through enough, losing two mothers in such a short space of time. Peter is still only nine and his sister Katie, seven. Queenie is just turned four and a bit dawny still. They all deserve greater attention from their father if they are not to go the way of their baby brother, or join his mother in the clay. I will try to be a better father to them and to protect them from further hurt.

I thank you from the bottom of my heart for offering to keep me in touch with Philip's progress. Can I ask you to do one more favour for me? It occurs to me that his new guardian, having the same Christian name, might cause confusion. I do not know why it should be such a bother to me, but I worry that he will become known by some unflattering diminutive: little Philip, Pip or worse. I think it would be best if my son were called Phil to distinguish him from his Uncle Philip. Don't tell anyone that it was my suggestion, just gradually introduce it by calling him Phil yourself and, perhaps later, encourage Lena and Nelly to do likewise. It will soon catch on.

I was going to close the dairy to concentrate on my cattle dealing. However, in the light of the current situation, it occurs to me that keeping it open will prove conducive to my receiving reports on my son. Who knows, perhaps he will drop in himself one day when he is old enough to act on his own behalf. We must live in hope!

I remain
Yours Faithfully
James McNeill
X (his mark)

Chapter 17

The Royal Canal

Philip Berford thought that neither the Ponte Vecchio in Florence nor Venice's Rialto could surpass the tenth lock bridge in Ashtown at that moment. It was better than he ever imagined those renaissance cities in all those days dreaming in the National Gallery. He was strolling by the swan-glided waters of the Royal Canal with Molly at his side, pushing his ward in a spanking new bassinet as though they were a brand-new family. Everything was magical.

There had been so much anguish in his life of late, with Bamma's icy silence cracking the air in Cabra Cottage. Then there was all the to-ing and fro-ing with Mary's baby ending up with him having to take on the onerous duties of guardian.

His distress began to fade as soon as he and Molly left the metalled road for the grassy towpath at Phibsboro. His mind became freer still when the great walls of Mountjoy Jail had disappeared into the distance and the world of back yards gave way to views across open ground. The surveyor in him delighted at the engineering harmony of two railway lines — Midland Great Western and Loop — running parallel with each other and the Royal Canal.

Looking across the well-kept fields of St Vincent's Orphanage for boys, the child began to cry. Molly picked him up and held him close to her breasts, gently caressing his back until he burped and returned to sleep. Philip watched enraptured. Away from the clamour of the city, peace descended slowly on him and with it a confidence that things would sort themselves out in time, just as they always did.

"Little Phil is beginning to thrive again."

"Yes, God bless him. Isn't he beautiful?"

"Touch and go for a while but he's grand now. And Lena seems to have got a new lease of life looking after the little fellow … hat business doing well too though I keep telling her she'll ruin her eyesight if she keeps sewing up hats by candlelight."

"So Lena is enjoying playing the mum then?"

"Yes, thank God."

Strolling towards Violet Hill he could make out the figures of men, backs bent into the work of harvesting hay with scythe and pitchfork all around Faussagh Lodge and Bloody Acre. He took to wondering about the previous day and how Molly might have filled in her time while the king was reviewing his troops in the Phoenix Park. He knew it couldn't have been easy for her so he was being especially attentive. It had been less difficult for him to keep up his end of the bargain. All he had to do was go to his work as though it were any normal day. He hadn't even enquired as to where the protests, promised by the National Council, were to take place. Still, he thought it better not to raise the matter with Molly, just in case it provoked some unpleasantness that might spoil their day out together. She was a bit quieter than usual and he suspected her mood was in some way connected to her being denied a chance to be part of the pageantry. In such circumstances, he considered that diversionary tactics were the best policy.

He drew her attention to the Loop Line that had swerved back again and seemed to be re-joining the parallel of mainline and canal only to cut underneath them both, heading off on its subterranean journey under the Phoenix Park. He said it was built by the British so that they could move troops from the Curragh camp to the centre of Dublin in the event of an outbreak of disorder without having to hazard the city streets on the way.

But Molly, heedless of the engineering wonder, was lost to things that might have been. *The Irish Times*, reporting on the big day in the Park, said that Queen Alexandra, inspecting the girls of the Drummond Institute, had stopped to chat to one of the teachers. It might have been her if it hadn't been for her promise to Philip. She even felt a tiny bead of sweat developing on her upper lip at the thought. Her father would have asked her to repeat every syllable that transpired between them over and over again.

"Let us pass together under 'Inspiration Bridge'," said Philip as they walked under a low masonry arch. Pointing at the dressed, grey limestone, he went on, "It was on those very stones that Sir William Rowan Hamilton scratched out the equation that formed one of the foundations of Algebra. A great flash of genius by a great Irish mathematician and physicist."

"I squared equals J squared equals K squared equals IJK equals minus 1 and whatever your having yourself sir," said Molly rattling off the still visible formula. "With a name like Rowan Hamilton, I suspect he was more likely to be one of our lot rather than one of yours."

"Will you wipe that smug grin off your face," said Philip daring to squeeze her around the waist, sheltered by the arch from prying eyes.

Emerging back into the bright, she pointed out the green dome of Dunsink on the lea of a hill above Finglas village. "And that was his observatory," she said.

"Look! Look!" said Philip, pointing excitedly at a family of mallard ducks, walking in a single-line formation down the field that sloped away from the canal towards the Tolka River. "Aren't they only gorgeous waddling along behind their mother?"

The waters of the canal were wide and river-like by Ashtown but they lay without a ripple on that July evening with the smell of new-mown hay resting on the still air. They took their ease by the Tenth Lock, with the only disturbance to the smooth surface of the waters being caused by the swans gliding around in pairs. Molly was sitting on one of the huge arms of the lock gate, gently rocking the baby in his bassinet, eyes shut, face tilted to receive the warm rays of the sun. She seemed transported to some distant place not accessible to him and it made him feel drawn to her and shut out simultaneously. He lay on the grass chewing on a ripened stalk, lost in wonderment of her.

He said in a rush, so sudden, it made him feel like he was a spectator at an unfolding drama he was unable to stop, "Molly, please be my wife and I will treasure you all the days of my life." He thought it amazing that he had plucked up the courage to ask her and was astonished at the million things that coursed through his brain while he waited through an eternity of cascading emotions for her to answer. He wondered if it would be a yes, no or maybe. He noticed that the stray lock above her ear was being left unattended for longer than usual and was surprised that he was sitting bolt upright. He wondered how Bamma would take the news and an icicle formed in his heart.

Molly turned to him. "Would you want to spend your whole life with a royalist?"

"Molly, I would be so honoured. I cannot bear to think of what life might be like without you … royalist or republican … what does it matter? Our love is strong enough to overcome all of that."

"Bamma will never let you marry into a Bluecoat family."

"Molly, please say you will … we will have such a fine life together. I may not be rich but all I have is yours for the taking. Don't trouble your head about Bamma. I'll take care of that," he said, not knowing if he could and hoping Molly would not pick up on it.

His sadly slanting eyebrows made him look a little like the brown and white cocker spaniels on the mantelpiece in Cabra Cottage. It gave her an irresistible urge to run her hand across his olive cheeks, to stroke his blue-black hair, to take him into her arms and shade him from all harm. She called him to her side and held his head to her breasts. Then calming his racing heart by running her fingers asymmetrically through his hair as she had done that first time they made love in Mooney's barn, she said, "I will. I will be your bride and share a life together whatever might befall."

A rippling motion told her he was crying silently into her breasts. Down, deep in that warm, safe arbour, Philip knew that he would never again feel such happiness and wished, not for the first time, that life would end there and then if it could not go on in that way forever.

But the sun continued to lower in the evening sky and hunger woke the sleeping infant. They walked in almost total silence — both lovers afraid that anything said might spoil the magic of what had passed.

Chapter 18

Things fall apart

Philip was surprised to find everyone had gone to bed except his mother and the evening with still some little time to run. His mug was on the table and Bamma was warming the milk for his cocoa on the range. He noticed that she had also laid out that morning's edition of the *Freeman's Journal* beside his placing. A hot bedtime drink and the papers! Was this the thaw or a treacherous shift in the ice?

He began telling her his good news, babbling on about how she would be gaining another daughter after losing one so tragically ... "The Lord giveth and the Lord taketh away ... doing it the other way round ... as is so often the case." He became so over-enthused, he didn't notice that the more he ran on about Molly making an ideal wife, her being an educated woman and a teacher, the more ominous the silence became.

"Save your breath to cool your cocoa," she said coldly, then more coldly still, "and read your paper."

He was not at all surprised at the saturation coverage of the royal visit — the highlighting of the welcome the king had received in Dublin and not a mention of the protest he was sure must have taken place. He was glad he had not taken any hand, act or part in demonstrations, especially as Molly had consented to be his wife. He was more convinced than ever of the wisdom of the pact they had agreed upon.

REVIEW IN THE PARK
A MAGNIFICENT SPECTACLE
Roared the headline over a report of the happenings in the Phoenix Park the previous day.

A smaller article by a Percival Sneade under the heading of **PRESENTATION OF COLOURS** was ringed in purple.

"Yesterday at the Viceregal Lodge, his majesty received a large contingent of the boys from the Royal Hibernian Military School to whom he presented a new and very handsome set of colours in commemoration of ... and to mark the esteem, etc., etc. At 10.30

boys arrived … numbering around 400 … under the command of Colonel Wynard, commandant, and Major Smyth, Adjutant … drawn up in lines … staff disposed in the following order … boys presented their usual smart appearance, bright military uniforms … attractive touch … colours presented by the king to replace those presented by him in 1852 as Prince of Wales.

"On the left rear of the line, the girls of the Drummond Institute, Chapelizod, which corresponds for them to the Hibernian School for the boys, were stationed to the number of about fifty in charge of the educational staff."

The pace at which Philip read the article quickened.

"At 11 o'clock his Majesty the King, accompanied by her Majesty … Princess Victoria … Countess of Dudley, Duchess of …"

He sped through the verbiage faster and faster.

"New colours emblems of discipline, obedience and good conduct … three cheers for the King — hip hip hooray with a right good will before the boys marched off to the strains of their lively and inspiring school-marching air, *British Grenadiers*."

Philip's reading became as laboured as his breathing on the next passage, heavily underlined with indelible pencil.

"Immediately afterwards, her Majesty the Queen inspected the girls of the Drummond School, who were in charge of Miss Rouselle, Lady Superintendent, assisted by Miss Cappathwaita, Miss Kearney and Miss Wilson. The later young lady from Aughrim Street will not long forget the words of encouragement she received when her majesty spoke to her personally…"

Philip could not go on – there was only one Miss Wilson on the teaching staff of the Drummond Institute and that same Miss Wilson had just promised to be his wife. The value of that promise exploded in his head like an artillery shell.

"Do you see now what you are getting yourself into. Your Bluecoat tart up in the Park toadying up to that dirty, English adulterer. What do you think of her now? Make her your wife would you? I'd put the 'Widow's Curse' on you first. Your right hand will wither … your children, should you be so misfortunate to have any, will be born with the gimp. The 'Widow's Curse' I tell you, to carry to your grave."

Philip's head was spinning so much he nearly fell over as he made for the door. Even the air blowing across Mooney's Field from·

the Great Midland Plain wasn't sufficient to cool the fever in his brain. In minutes he was on the Old Cabra Road and running for Marlborough Terrace.

He would have it out with her right then. He would know why she could be so duplicitous. He would find out which solemn promises meant anything to her and which didn't. He would ask if her two-faced attitude extended to everything or just the things she wanted badly enough.

At Hanlon's Corner he stopped briefly before going in and ordering the first whiskey of his life. The bar foreman, looking at his pioneer pin, asked if he was sure in advance of handing him the glass. Philip removed the pin from his lapel and threw it into an ashtray. A drunk he hadn't noticed sitting beside him at the counter picked up the pin and proceeded to lance a large boil on the back of his neck with it using the bar mirror as a guide. He was so concentrated on removing the boil's purple core, he drooled continuously down his droopy lower lip into his drink.

Picking up his glass, Philip lowered the fiery liquid in one go and gagged. The foreman handed him a glass of water that he swallowed as fast as his rasping windpipe would allow, then stormed out of the pub and onto the street.

On the North Circular Road the scattering of young couples still coming from the Phoenix Park in the fading daylight of mid-summer were gathering into a circle to watch a man bullwhip the flesh from a fox terrier. At the corner of Aughrim Street, a big country lad with a mouth full of rotten teeth grabbed him roughly by the lapels and shouted into his face, "Give me a fucken tanner for a night's kip." Breaking free, he could hear the stitching tear in his good jacket.

As he drew nearer to Marlborough Terrace lights were coming on in the houses as blinds were drawn. Even from behind he could clearly recognise them — Molly and Felim walking arm-in arm down Aughrim Street towards her house.

Nothing surprised Maryanne Little about the strange and unusual needs of men. But when the dark, young gentleman returned to the anteroom and asked for a pen and paper, she couldn't help asking if the girl had been so good that he needed to take notes.

Philip took the writing material to a table and sat on his own. It had been a big day. He had been promised and betrayed, betrothed

85

and jilted, had his first drink and his first prostitute all in less than twenty-four hours. He felt he must rearrange his life into something he could manage. He would deal with her now. Felim could wait until later.

He picked the pen up and began, "Dear Molly …"

"What have you done?" Felim asked, picking himself off the drive leading to Springfield. Dusting himself down while Philip squared up to him again he tried to piece together the incoherent shouting his friend had engaged in prior to landing a punch to his face.

"I've done what I should have done years ago. Given you the smack in the chops you long deserved, you shoneen bastard. Stand up here and I'll give you the rest."

"Don't be a bloody fool all your life. I meant what have you done about Molly?"

"Given her her marching orders. You're welcome to her. She's more one of your kind than ours. The perfidy of it — becoming engaged to me one minute and then going out with you as soon as my back was turned. Step up here now and I'll beat you good-looking."

"Out with me? What are you talking about?"

"The other night … linking her down Aughrim Street. Did you think I wouldn't see you?"

"What kind of a horse's arse are you at all? It was late at night for God's sake. I was escorting her home from my surgery like any civilised man would do. It's only a half dozen doors up the road from her house."

"Your surgery? I didn't know you had a surgery …"

"Well I do and she was there as a patient."

"What was the matter with her? Was she pregnant?"

"She just wanted a doctor's note excusing her for being absent from work … didn't want to be at all the ballyhoo up at the Viceregal Lodge with her school. I could get struck off just for telling you that."

"A likely story!" he said turning his back on his old friend to run across Mooney's Field and home.

"I hope you're satisfied!" he shouted at Bamma as soon as he came in the door. "She's gone forever … you've ruined my life … I'll never wed another … there'll be no more Berfords after me I

86

promise you that. Where's my coat and wallet? I'm going down to Hanlon's. Don't wait up for me."

Chapter 19

Flight

It will be just wonderful being in a country where the seasons can be told without measuring the length of the days, thought Molly Wilson as the dark bulk of the transatlantic ship emerged from the enveloping drizzle. She could scarcely make out the shapes of the women wrapped in shawls and the men in sodden cloth caps passing her window in a continuous stream. But the big, four-master rose above the Queenstown quay to impress its presence despite the enfolding mist.

The weather was so much kinder and predictable in Philadelphia. Everyone told her that. She would be far better off in America being treated like an equal instead of living as an oddity in her own country. All her lady friends had said so.

Philip wouldn't listen ... wouldn't move ... held fast in the twists of widow weeds and Irish history till he drowned. They might have had a wonderful life together, if only he had listened.

She looked down at the two letters resting in her lap to read again and for the hundredth time. The one from her cousin told of the endless number of teaching positions in the city of brotherly love. She would be snapped up by one of the private schools in Philadelphia in no time and earn decent money for a change.

The unseasonable cold that had been seeping into her stomach the whole journey formed into a black knot that kept her fastened to the spot when the train stopped. As all the passengers began bustling over their baggage, all she could do was to clasp her purse close to her breast and look out the window.

Her father had been so brave standing on the platform at Kingsbridge — back straight, eyes to front, his walrus moustache waxed more stiffly than ever. He talked crisply to her at the open carriage window about the details of the journey; the ticketing, the transfers; who and what to look out for. He was doing so well until the train began its slow, staccato throb out of the station. Then his eyes took on the pitch and slope of his drooping white moustache and she knew he was crying even though he made no telltale movement to wipe away the tears.

She had spent ages that morning looking out her bedroom window, admiring the orderly sweep of Marlborough Terrace until it met the chaos and excitement of the cattle-market. Beyond its sprawling lairage lay the Old Cabra Road. She quickly averted her eyes to follow the street in the opposite direction as it moved towards Stoneybatter and the river. She would miss little Phil … miss taking him for walks along the Royal Canal.

The houses were smaller, more dingy from the Church onwards. She could not quite see Stanhope Street Convent but could almost hear the catcalls of the children in its schoolyard:

"Proddy waddy on the wall, a half of loaf will do you all."

She looked back into the room seeking comfort in the detail of its richly carved dressing table, four-poster bed and delicately painted silk screen.

"When the devil rings the bell, all the Proddies go to hell."

"Queenstown … Queenstown … all passengers must alight," the big, red-faced man with the peaked cap was shouting in his seesaw voice as he moved along the corridor. Seeing no sign of motion in the fair-haired girl with the huge, blue eyes, he bent towards her and said softly, as to a child, "I'm sorry mam but the train terminates at Queenstown. You'll have to get off here. Can I get you a porter to help with the luggage?"

She gave him a sixpenny bit and found enough voice to say, "Thank you … yes … would you fetch a porter please?"

Her father would miss her terribly and she him. She had not noticed him getting old for he went briskly about his days. But he looked so stooped and worn, standing alone on the platform as the train pulled away.

Miss Rousselle was more of a war-horse than a headmistress but she had reason to be upset at her absence during the presentation to the Queen. "Deserting your post," was her term.

Yet Philip could believe she had broken her promise. Prepared to take the word of a lazy beggar from the *Freeman's Journal* basing his story on interviews in the school the day before the royal presentation. "Like the rest of you people, too busy getting drunk to honour your duty," she had written to him in a fury when he had so dishonoured her.

It wasn't the loss of her salary that was forcing her to go, useful though it was. Her father would see to it that she would want for nothing. There was no question about that. She would not be able to stand the long days with nothing productive to do. Then there would be those chance meetings so common in Dublin. It would be too much for her to bear.

She wiped a circle on the clouded window with her gloved finger and through it saw a short porter pushing a long, flat handcart down the platform towards her carriage. She glanced at the other letter resting on her lap. She would force herself to read it again. It would steel her for what lay ahead … help her bear the wrench and the tear of it all.

Dear Molly
I am truly grateful to you for revealing your real nature before it was too late, though it would have been better were it not done so publicly. That you should make so little of our solemn vow was bad enough but that I should learn about it, not from your own lips, but from the pages of a penny newspaper beggars belief. I will never be so naive again.

I spent last night with a prostitute in Montgomery Street and found more truth and honesty for a half crown than I could ever find with you.

As you found it impossible to be true to one man, I will never devote myself to one woman again and for that I thank you.
Yours faithfully,
Philip Berford

"Excuse me your ladyship. Your luggage is all on the cart whenever your ladyship is ready. You might follow me when it suits you, your ladyship. There's a bad fog this evening and the dock can be very slippy indeed. Take your time now your ladyship and I'll bring you all the way to the gangplank. I'll make sure no harm comes your ladyship's way."

She was ready now and was delighted to follow him to the ship. She told him as much as she placed a shilling into his waiting palm. Then she folded the two letters neatly and placed them in her purse. It was going to be a long journey. She would need them both before it was done.

91

PART 2

Chapter 20

Tailor-made hero

Phil McNeill hated being a tailor's dummy for his two aunts though he loved them both dearly. He was seven and it wasn't fair that he should still be asked to stand up on a stool on the kitchen table wearing a ball-gown while Aunt Nelly pinned up the hem. He could hardly wait for September. Number one — he would be leaving the junior infants on the Navan Road; number two — he would be moving in with Aunt Gypsy and Da Kennedy in Prussia Street and number three — he would be joining the Countess Markievicz's Fianna Boys. Best of all, he would be going to school with the big lads in Brunswick Street. His aunts would have to get a real dummy like the ones in the shop windows in town to hang their gowns and hats on.

'Brunner' was a tough school but he would soon be drilling with Fianna Eireann and would be well able to look after himself. He would miss Aunty Lena, especially the way she played cowboys in her knickers, and he'd miss Aunt Nelly who could talk and breath with her mouth full of straight pins without ever swallowing one … not even once. But he wouldn't miss standing up on the rickety old stool every evening while Aunt Nelly pinned up the mantle gowns that fell from his shoulders to the tabletop. Nor would he miss balancing Aunty Lena's model hats on his head just so that she could see how they matched the gowns from the distance of the far kitchen wall.

He couldn't refuse Aunty Lena anything. She was soft and warm and full of fun even if she did squeeze him too tight sometimes, filling his nostrils with the sweet scent of lavender. She was always first to pick him up when he was hurt and to make him laugh when he was frightened.

Easter was coming and he was up on the table balancing a big hat full of fruit and satin roses on his head with Nelly's gown dragging out of his shoulders. What would happen if Sonny Kerrigan were to walk in? They were going to lay down their lives for Ireland (when they got their green tunics and slouch hats). Bamma would miss him then. She wouldn't be too keen to crack him across the knuckles with the blunt part of the kitchen knife and he there bleeding his last for his native land.

He couldn't wait for September when he and Sonny would join the Countess. They'd be marching down Prussia Street and the whole length of Stoneybatter on their way to the Slua hall in Blackhall Place. Uncle Philip would come down from Cabra Cottage to see him off. He'd be bursting with pride at his 'Aul Segotia' all dickied-out in his new uniform and bandoleer, marching to the strains of 'On for Freedom Fianna Eireann'. Ah! It's in your breed like the 'Auld Fenian Gun', he'd say.

Bamma would be proud too, he thought, and then got a fit of the shivers at the prospect of her inspecting the back of his ears and neck and checking his underwear in front of everyone. She'd even do it out on the street, like she often did at the school gate. He had got such a jeering off his school pals he had to give two of them fine bloody noses to put a stop to it.

"Too many flowers and not enough fruit," said Lena as she took the hat off her nephew's head. "We can't take a chance like that with Mrs Mooney's bonnet for the annual hunt ball, can we?" Unable to resist the temptation she stroked his olive cheeks and tapped his full lower lip with her index finger.

He was everything to her. He gave her cause for getting up in the morning, provided reason for her endless sewing the whole day long and was her greatest source of pride whenever they went out to take the morning air together. She loved looking at his dark handsome face — so like his mother. Now that he was getting so big, she could see the extraordinary heavy-boned frame of his father begin to emerge.

She would miss him desperately when he moved in with her sister Gypsy but would not protest. It was she who made the suggestion in the first place. Brunswick Street Primary was too far from Cabra Cottage for a seven-year-old to walk and unnecessary too with Gypsy's house only up the road. That had been her argument. Lena was determined to do all she could to secure his future before her own condition became too obvious.

"I was just saying to Phil that he'll be well used to Stoneybatter when he goes to the Christian Brothers in Brunswick Street," she remarked as her mother passed the table on her way to the door. Her subtly in trying to open the subject of his father and the fact that Phil would soon be passing his door several times a day was wasted on Bamma.

"Don't worry yourself unduly. All that was taken care of years ago. Keep an eye to your hats ... it'll suit you better," she retorted closing the door firmly behind her.

"What's wrong with Stoneybatter?" he asked.

"Nothing whatsoever," she replied twiddling the lobe of his ear between finger and thumb.

"Will you miss your Aunty Lena when you go to Prussia Street?" she asked, looking into his wide hazel eyes.

"Aunt Gypsy says she will bring me up to Cabra Cottage as regular as clockwork. Sure I'll have to be seeing Sonny Kerrigan all the time and I'll see you then won't I?"

"Sonny will be moving to Prussia Street too. His father has taken over the sawmills beside Aunt Gypsy and they are all moving into the cottage that goes with it. Isn't that grand?"

"Aunt Nelly and Uncle Dunny as well?"

"Of course. He'll hardly go without his ma and da now will he?"

"We're best pals. Sonny and I are joining the Fianna together in September. That's soon, isn't it, Aunty Lena?"

"Yes, my little Irish hero, but Con Colbert will have to bide his time until this little Fenian moves to Prussia Street. Blackhall Place is too far for my little soldier."

"Bamma said I ruined your chances."

"When did she say such a thing?"

"The day she put me out in Mooney's barn for sticking me fingers into the sugar and licking them."

"When was that?"

"When you were in hospital. It was the time Uncle Philip came home and found me out there without me trousers – she took them so I wouldn't run away – and went into one of his rages ... and told her if she ever did it again he would lock her out in the barn to see how she liked it ... and Bamma told him he was full of drink ... and he said it was little wonder when she had ruined his chance in life ... and he went out to Hanlon's again after his tea ... and Bamma cracked my arse and said I was nothing but trouble … and she said I killed me mother … and ruined your chance in life … and I was bad luck … always coming between a widowed mother and her only son."

"You're not to be using rude words like that. And don't pay attention to everything Bamma says. Sure it wasn't much of a chance anyway. Fachna had buckteeth, a cast in his eye and 'heh ushed to salk wid a moutd full of mashed shpuds'," she said, doing her burlesque imitation until Phil couldn't stand upright for the laughing.

"It's well you can laugh now," said Nelly as she made to follow her mother out to the yard. "How long is it since he darkened your doorstop?"

"Seven years. Spends all of his time now organising Arthur Griffith's Hungarians. Sinn Fein they call themselves."

"At least they had the decency to give the party a Gaelic name. That's what Bamma says anyhow."

But the questions had got her to thinking again about the chances that might have been. There was relief that the longing for a child of her own had left her completely. Phil McNeill had filled that gap. He had become all the child she would ever want and now he too was leaving. She could feel the bottom drop out of her soul as the ebbing of her life took away the things she loved in its undertow.

But Lena was not the sort of woman to indulge in self-pity. She had seen enough of that to last several lifetimes. Picking herself up again she said, "Won't it be grand growing up with Aunt Gypsy's family … more natural for you to be with other children. Móna and Dido will be like sisters to you and Gypsy thinks the sun shines out of your little bum," she said giving him a pinch on the bottom. "Let you be warned though. There's a fair rub of the teacher about her as well. Nothing as severe as Bamma, mind," she said lowering her voice. "And your Uncle Andy is real dote."

"I do call him Da Kennedy. He lets me."

"Don't I know. Sure we've all seen you stuck to him like a poultice, watching every little job he does about the place. You should call Aunt Gypsy Mother Kennedy. I'm sure she would be delighted with that. Then they'll be like a real father and mother to you."

"What happened to my father … after my mother died?"

"His heart broke *alanna*. What would you do if I were to give you a penny for yourself?"

"Get a bag of dolly mixtures and a big lump of twang."

Bamma and Nelly waited in the stone yard, shielded from the cottage windows by the scullery's granite gable. They knew it was Felim as soon as he entered Mooney's field dressed in his doctor's suit of charcoal grey. Even Bamma twisted her fingers as they watched his progress across the meadow. They did not greet him or offer him a cup of tea.

Their fixed stares asked only one question of him and he answered it directly. "Malignant tumour", he said as gently as he could manage.

Nelly put her hand to her mouth and began to cry.

"How long has she got?" Bamma asked without changing her expression.

"She might live two or even three years with proper nursing. And it will take a lot of nursing." He knew that Nelly would do her best but would not have the stamina. That was Nelly's weakness. Bamma could see anything through. That was hers.

"Who'll tell her?" he asked.

"She knows. We were the ones in ignorance," Bamma replied.

"I'll like to see her nevertheless. Can we have a few moments together?"

"Nelly, use your apron to dry your eyes. There's a trough full of sheets waiting for me in the scullery and it's about time you went home and got the dinner ready before your husband comes home from work. There'll be plenty time for tears before we're very much older."

But Nelly couldn't face the walk home across the open field and her with only her son for company. The dark was never so threatening as the open light, especially so on a day when her tenuous hold on life was being so clearly demonstrated. She would not go until the wide threatening world was shut out by darkness.

"I'll give you a hand. Dunny won't be home for ages yet."

"Suit yourself but first get Phil out of the house and send him over to the lodge to play with his cousin. Go on doctor, do what you have to do."

97

*****

As the two women pummelled and wrung out bed linen in the scullery, in the cottage kitchen, Felim set about his most delicate job as a family doctor. He was so skilled and gentle, Lena felt like a queen privileged by being awarded a French swordsman as an executioner instead of an axe man.

When the amount of time left to her became clear, she became more resigned than ever. She told him that the last seven years minding little Phil had been the best time of her life. She beseeched Felim to ensure that he did not see her in her last agony. "I'll spare him that and offer it all up to God that He might fill his life with health and happiness and find a way to unite him with his father. The poor lamb has had enough loss and separation in his little life. I want to leave him with only happy memories of his silly Aunt Lena."

He never looked smarter standing in front of her, the jacket of his new suit crested by the whitest Eton collar, holding his little cardboard suitcase in his hand.

"Sure you'll have fine times in Prussia Street," she said, holding the lad close to her breast.

There was warmth and fragrance there, like the humid air rising off the flower gardens in summer only the more comfortable for Lena's soft voice droning. "The Christian Brothers will give you a fine education. Study hard and sure you'll be a Minister of the Republic when that great day dawns."

In her mind's eye, Lena follows the lad, dressed in his school best, walking down Prussia Street with his satchel on his back. On he goes, his legs getting longer and stronger as his bag gets fuller and fuller, past the junction of Aughrim Street and Stoneybatter, sauntering towards the turn off for Brunswick Street. A man of stout build is standing in the doorway of a shop, his strong bull-like body hobbled, unable to reach out to the passing boy. With all her strength she wills him to enfold the lad in his strong arms and protect him.

"You're hurting me Aunty Lena," came the little voice trapped within her breasts. "I can't breathe with yeh", he said.

"Out with you now. Your Aunt Gypsy is waiting for you in the yard," she told him as she released her grip.

She clasped both hands to her chest with the joy of seeing him tear out through the door shouting, "Sonny, Sonny, I'm going to live in Prussia Street today! You can come down and play in the cattle stalls in the back yard. You won't mind, sure you won't Mother Kennedy?"

Chapter 21

Number 46 Prussia Street

Phil McNeill felt that he was getting luckier and luckier. Although he was only eight-and-a-half years old, this was his third and best home. He was determined to stay in Number 46 until it was time for him to die for Ireland.

He loved nearly everything about his new home, even his two cousins who were girls and so were always squealing. It was full of mysterious, secret places. The yard was a maze of disused wooden cattle pens that were the best places in the whole world for playing hide-and-go-seek, cowboys or even house with his two cousins.

The cottage had a back room that was hardly ever opened, filled with huge sideboards where he could hide and no one would ever find him. Then there was the bedroom upstairs behind the chimney with the stairs that were so straight Mother Kennedy had to come down backwards. Although he called them Mother and Da Kennedy he knew they were really Aunt Gypsy and Uncle Andy.

Mother Kennedy also had a scullery across the yard from the house, just like Bamma's, where she did all the washing on Mondays and prepared the meals every day of the week. It had the biggest mangle he had ever seen in his whole life. He and Sonny were going to put a farthing through it to see if it would be made big and flat like when the big fellas placed them on the tracks for the tram to run over.

They hadn't done it yet though they had the farthing on a few occasions. The lure of a twist of twang from Whacker Reilly's and the ages and ages of sweet chewing it brought always won out. But they were going to do it one day. The mangle could drag you in by your arm and make it all squashed and flat, oozing blood and mess. That's what his cousin Móna told him when she was ringing out his Fianna Tunic before hanging it up to dry. The mangle dragged in the bull's wool uniform and flattened every last drop of water out of it even though she was turning the handle with just one hand.

The cattle pens were the stagecoach, the livery stable, the saloon, the jail and sometimes even the cattle pens of some dusty town of a very wild west. Phil was always Jesse James and Sonny sometimes his brother Frank. On such occasions, they would walk up the yard, arms around each other's shoulders before jumping over one of the wooden gates to take on the posse in a corral shoot-out. On dry, sunny days, the gunfights became all the more real for the smell of old timber and dust coming from the decaying balks of wood.

Móna squealed as much as any girl but she knew lots of things that he didn't and he was beginning to think that that was the way it was with girls. It was not the only way they were different as he had noticed with embarrassment when Mother Kennedy was bathing them all in front of the range on Saturday nights.

And that was another thing that was nice about living in Number 46. He used to hate bath night in Cabra Cottage with Bamma pulling and poking at his ears and scrubbing the skin off him with the long-handled brush. Now he looked forward to bath night. Mother Kennedy always turned it into a sort of game — allowing them to splash each other and wash each other's backs with the flannel. He particularly loved sitting in front of the fire drying themselves with the air full of the fruity smell of jelly dissolving in boiling water, mixing with the more earthy one of steeping peas. And the three cousins taking turns with the long-handled fork to toast bread in front of the roaring range.

He even liked going to mass in Aughrim Street Church with Da Kennedy and the girls — all of them done up in their Sunday best. Mother Kennedy always went to an earlier mass so that she could be getting the Sunday dinner ready while the rest were out but she would inspect them all before they were let out the door — even Da. He loved the way she would slick down his unruly hair and fuss about his Eton collar then tell him he was a right little toff.

The excitement about going to the big school in Brunswick Street was wearing thin. The brothers there were always cross and leathering the boys for not being able to do the big sums and hard spellings. Sometimes they beat them for what they did and at other times for things that they didn't do. Doing something that you shouldn't do was a sin of commission and was punished with a good leathering. Forgetting to do something that you should have done was a sin of omission and was punished with an even bigger belting.

Walking into school at half past nine each morning, he knew that he would be beaten before it was time to come home for lunch at half-past twelve. Then going back in the afternoon for two o'clock, he knew he would be beaten again before being let out at four. He could never be sure what he was going to be leathered for. Móna had once spent a whole night teaching him how to spell Dublin and he got biffed for not saying capital D-ublin.

The brother's leather was the biggest problem but it was not the only one. There was the strange man who sometimes stood in the doorway of the dairy in Stoneybatter, his eyes always following like in the pictures in the art gallery. He had very sad eyes for a big strong man. Phil had been warned not to talk to strange men and he figured that this must be the strange man they were warning him about. When he told Mother Kennedy, she just ran her fingers through his hair until he felt calm and droopy, then told him it was nothing to worry about but never to mention it to Bamma.

One good thing about the school was the fights. He had been a bit frightened at the start though he would never have admitted it to anyone. But now that he was able to bash every one in all three forms of second class — A, B and C — he wasn't frightened about fighting anymore. He was still careful not to cross any of the lads from the higher classes. They were called the 'Big Kids' and they mostly didn't bother with the 'Little Kids'.

He went up to Cabra Cottage once a week with Mother Kennedy and the girls. As soon as he got in the door, Bamma would examine their knees for dirt, behind the ears and neck for 'high-water marks' and even their underwear to make sure they were bleached white and clean. On one occasion, she saw the 'rust' marks on the tail of his shirt and made a holy show of him in front off everyone.

The great thing about going up to Cabra Cottage was seeing Uncle Philip and Aunty Lena. Uncle Philip always let him play with his good pocket watch and gave him a brass thru'penny bit before going off to Hanlon's. If they were still there when he came back from the pub, he was likely to get a 'tanner'.

As the year wore on, Aunty Lena got quieter and quieter until she would just sit there smiling at him, not even asking him to model her hats or mess with his hair. Later still, she seemed to be always upstairs taking a nap.

Thursdays were *slua* night and he loved being dressed up in his green uniform even if the bull's wool tunic and trousers itched his skin. He felt like a Boer in his slouch hat and imagined himself out on the veldt giving the Tommies a right good hammering. He would love to have worn it playing war with Sonny out in the cattle pens but Mother Kennedy said it would get ruined.

He was getting great at parading to orders barked in Gaelic. On the *'parád áire'* command he would snap smartly to attention in unison with the rest of the boys and at *'seassaig arais'* he would stand with feet apart and hands clasped firmly behind his back, eyes fixed on the neck of the boy in front. When he grew up he was going to be like Con Colbert. Adjutant General Colbert inspected his *slua* on several occasions and once told Phil that he would make a great squad leader. It made him determined to learn his map reading, knots and short arms so he would be good enough to become squadron leader one day and maybe an officer with a leather Sam Browne belt when he was really big.

Maps were hard but the mountains were great for drilling and camping and preparing for the next great rebellion. The Countess told them, when they were at the Curragh camp, that for seven hundred years every generation of Irishmen and women had rebelled against English rule. It was a long time since the last rebellion so he knew that there was one due any day. He only hoped it waited until he was big enough to take part.

They had great times singing around the campfire at night. He had to laugh, though he didn't want to, when they were singing the 'Battle Hymn' (written by the Countess herself), "Armed for the battle Lord kneel we before Thee, bless Thou our banners God of the free ..." and Sonny sang, "Armed with a bottle Lord ..." and the Countess always going on about the evils of drink. He was ashamed for laughing because he would have loved the Countess to know that he would follow her into any battle. Sometimes he thought the Goddess Erin must have looked like her ... his mother too. He usually had to fight back the tears when they all sang:

"Ireland is rising, shout we exultant,
Ireland is rising hand grasp the sword
Charge for the old home
Down with the old foe
Living and dying

Ireland to free."

That song was powerful stuff and Phil felt that anyone who heard it would surely want to join in the struggle for Irish freedom.

He loved swimming in the mountain streams after damming them up with big stones even though the water was so cold it made his willie shrink to almost nothing and made him pee crooked. He didn't like OC Costello, who was a hairy man with bad teeth, getting into the water with all the boys. He particularly hated the way he liked to wrestle in the grass before any of them had had the chance to put their uniforms back on. Phil always got out of the water and dressed as soon as he saw the OC coming.

Even when he was home in Number 46, he liked to smell the wood-smoke off his tunic. It was a smell redolent of woods, damp earth, the warmth of the campfire and strength too — all of them bound together by their green uniforms and pledge to the Fianna Code of Honour. The smell would last until Mother Kennedy washed it in the big wooden trough out in the scullery across the yard and Móna rung it out in the great mangle.

"Is Queenie McNeill my sister?" he asked Bamma when he was visiting Cabra Cottage with Mother Kennedy and his two cousins.

"What made you ask that?"

"Ever since I moved into Third Class, a big girl has been giving me twang and lozenges through the school railings." His curiosity to find out about the girl was suddenly overcome by a fear that confessing to taking the sweets might get him into trouble, so he added, "I only took them off her because she wasn't a strange man … only a girl. But last week when one of the big boys out of Sixth Class was at me for the sweets, she came into the school yard and boxed his ears."

"What did she look like?"

"Red hair and freckles."

"And what did you do young man?"

"I soon told her that I didn't want any girl fighting my battles," Phil said, sure that Bamma would approve. "But do you know what she said Bamma?"

"No, but I'm very curious."

"She said she wasn't just a girl, that she was Queenie McNeill and that she was my big sister."

Bamma looked at him for such a long time, he wondered if she was going to put him out in the barn without his trousers. He took to wondering whether Mother Kennedy would allow her to do that now that he was hers and a Fianna boy, and when it might be, if ever, grown-ups stopped obeying their mothers. When she did finally speak, he was amazed at her voice — so calm. What she said was even more surprising.

"Yes, she is your sister, in a manner of speaking, but you are to have nothing to do with her or hers ever again. Do you understand what I'm saying to you?"

"Yes I do Bamma."

"And do you promise to me on your mother's grave that you will do as I say?"

"Yes I will Bamma."

"Then give your Bamma a kiss and go out into Mooney's Field to play. I want to talk to your Aunt Gypsy."

Phil was never so glad to kiss his grandmother and didn't even mind the way the whiskers on her chin prickled his cheek. He tore out the door and into Mooney's Field as though he had just escaped the gallows, wondering what kind of trouble he had made for Mother Kennedy.

"Is he having contact with his father?"

"He passes his dairy every day morning, noon and evening."

"That's not what I asked, Gypsy. Does he have contact with him?"

"I can't stop him from seeing the child pass his window."

"Has there been any contact that breaks the court order? Can I say it any plainer?"

"There has been no approach that I know of, if that's what you mean."

"Make sure it stays that way."

"Bamma, surely after all this time … it's so unnatural …"

"That's enough … there'll be no broken treaties while I'm around. Do I make myself clear?"

"Yes Bamma. Perfectly clear."

Chapter 22

The Irish Volunteer

The Number 10 tram pulled away from the park gates at the top of Infirmary Road, rattled along the tree-lined North Circular, picking up passengers from its tall red-bricked houses with the well-kept gardens. Then it moved on past the teeming cattle markets and onwards to the prosperous village of Phibsboro, where it passed Philip Berford walking purposefully into town to attend the inauguration of the Irish Volunteers.

Walking proudly beside him, punctuating each step of the journey with one question after another, was his ward and nephew Phil McNeill. "Why are they going to be called volunteers? Why won't they be paid? Will they be in a union? What's an Orangeman? Why don't the British leave Ireland? Why do the Orangemen want them to stay? Can I be a volunteer when I'm old enough?" Each one was asked more for the warmth of the response than for the quality of the information.

They heard the double-decker before they saw it and Phil knew that a part of his uncle longed for the comfort of its upstairs seats where he might puff his pipe and enjoy a bird's-eye view of his dear, defiled Dublin all lit up by gaslight. His Uncle Philip loved his native city despite the dirt and the squalor. Indeed, there were times when little Phil felt his guardian was in danger of loving Dublin even more than Ireland herself.

"Can we take a tram Uncle Philip? Me legs are worn out."

"Not during a strike son. Never let it be said that the Berfords reared a scab. Big Jim Larkin says he'll see grass grow between the tramlines. It'll happen yet with the help of God."

It was said with more hope than expectation. The strike, begun in August, had become a lockout and was still dragging on and it nearing the end of a bleak November. Trade unionists and their families were everywhere begging or queuing at soup kitchens and Christmas would soon be on top of them.

"Which is the worst, a scab, an informer or a man that hits a woman?"

"Well, only a coward hits a woman … worst form of cowardice that … even worse than deserting under fire. A scab is a very low form of humanity altogether. He's the sort of fella that takes bread from the mouths of starving families. Never let it be said of you that you were a scab or a woman beater. But there is nothing lower on the face of the earth than an informer. They are the buggers that kept this nation subject to the British Crown this past seven hundred years. Sell their best friends, their own family … the entire bloody nation given half the chance and all for what? For a few lousy coins of blood-money, that's what."

As a railway draughtsman, Philip was not himself a member of Mr Larkin's union and so remained unaffected by the strikes and lockouts that followed one on the other all that year. Nevertheless, it was easy to see that he was full of admiration for the workers' leader who was so fearless of the Dublin Metropolitan Police despite all the baton charges and the 'Black Marias'.

Their conversation was interrupted by the screeching of iron wheels on steel tracks caused by the tram turning the bend at Doyle's Corner. As it drew abreast of them, Philip recognised the conductor standing on the platform. "Be gob, it's 'Revolver Murphy' from Inchicore. Do you see the leather moneybag Phil? The fecker has a gun in that bloody bag and he's let everybody in the Spa Road Tramsheds know that he'll shoot the first person who tries to take over his tram. He'd get away with it too most likely. Probably get promoted to inspector when this is all over."

"Up Jem Larkin and pay no one!" a snotty-nosed urchin no older than Phil himself shouted at the surprised conductor before wiping his nose in a sleeve that had more holes than cuff.

"Is yer mother a big woman, Murphy, yeh big, fat, fucken scab?" shouted a dishevelled looking man, shivering without an overcoat in the cold, damp, November air.

"Hey choke the chicken!" shouted a shawlie who appealed to the gathering crowd to "Send hunger's mother to his fucken relations in the castle."

Murphy drew a military pistol from his leather money pouch with one hand and gave the brass bell-plunger an urgent double thump with the other. The tram lurched forward, gathering speed by the second before disappearing down Berkeley Road and out of sight of the hostile crowd.

Phil held his uncle's hand tightly in front of his chest, moulding his body into his side from hip to ankle.

Philip lit up his pipe using only his left hand so as not to disturb the boy. He took several long puffs, releasing each with a gasp of contentment. As the crowd dispersed, they too began to move, picking up the pace once more as they followed the tram into Berkeley Road and down Berkeley Street. Reaching North Frederick Street, they adjusted their stride to flow with the stream of people heading towards the semi-circular Rotunda in full view at the beginning of Parnell Square.

Ragged men clamped their arms around the railings of the crumbling side streets and watched the growing throng with the passive eyes of lairaged cattle.

"Here we are son. We'll soon see if Carson and his Ulster Volunteer Force can get away with cocking a snook at the rest of us — parading their guns for all the world to see. They're right about one thing — the British only understand force. Well two can play that game. Right?"

"Right enough Uncle Philip."

The Rotunda was packed to the rafters. Phil had never seen a building so crowded not even the church for late mass on Sundays. They entered the auditorium just in time to see a man mounting the stage looking for all the world like a headmaster.

"That's Eoin MacNeill," said his uncle in his church voice.

The crowded room hung on the schoolmaster's every word. Phil could almost feel their blood rise like the boys in his class when the 'Brothers' told them how the British massacred men, women and children in their thousands on Vinegar Hill in 1798. But Phil found it increasingly hard to follow MacNeill as he slowly explained what was happening in the country and what everyone should do about it. He couldn't even risk asking Uncle Philip anymore. He'd just close his eyes and put a finger to his pursed lips as though he was interrupting during the 'Consecration of the Eucharist'.

He did his best to concentrate. He was out at night and all the lads in Brunner would be raging. He could see his Uncle Dunny at the far side of the hall and Sonny wasn't with him. That made him feel special and if he could tell the 'Brother' what was said at the meeting this night, he mightn't get biffed at all on Monday.

"The Tory Party policy in Ulster has been deliberately adopted to make the display of force and the menace of armed violence the determining factor in future relations between this country and Great Britain." He could almost taste the anger of the crowd.

"Drive them out," a shout from somewhere in the back rippled on top of a myriad calls: "Burn everything English except their coal."

"Perfidious Albion."

Then a deafening chorus of voices all around shouting, "Up the Republic … Up the Republic … Up the Republic …"

The man on the stage held up his hand and there was silence. "If Irishmen acquiesced to such a policy, they would be surrendering their rights as men and citizens."

The crowd was on fire.

But the voice on the stage droned on and on and Phil, way past supper and bedtime, placed his head on his uncle's lap just to rest for a minute.

"If we fail to take measures to defeat this policy," the voice on the platform warned, "we will become the most degraded population in Europe and no longer worthy of the name of Nation."

Phil could barely keep his eyes open as MacNeill spurred them up with a final appeal. "They have rights who dare to maintain them, but rights can only be maintained by arms. It is time to form a body of Irish Volunteers to secure our rights and liberties."

By that stage Phil was fast asleep on his uncle's lap. The last thing he heard was, "Begob that's done the trick."

He did not see nor did he hear the tumultuous response the speaker received when he called on them to enrol in the new force. He didn't even feel his guardian taking off his overcoat or slipping it under his head so he could continue to sleep stretched out on the chairs when the time for action came. Nor did he witness him joining the great surge to sign up. They did not write their names in their own blood like his uncle said the Ulster Volunteer Force did in the North but they wrote them down with a determination that surely signalled the inevitable beginning of the inevitable end of yet another great empire.

By the time he got to the front, Philip had become so ecstatic he released the flood of thoughts coursing through his fevered brain on the nearest person to him — a thick-set man handing out papers from behind a wooden table.

"This is the turning point, this is the turning point," he repeated excitedly before realising that he was addressing his brother-in-law, James McNeill. The recognition caused only a momentary pause. "James this is it," he said, "I do believe that this is finally it. This is the moment we have all been waiting for all these generations. It's a great day for Ireland ... a great day indeed."

James waited until the torrent of words had quietened before interrupting to ask, "And how is your ward these days?"

"A fine young fellow, James, lovely lad ... only ten years old and already following in the family footsteps ... a Fianna boy ... lives with his Aunt Gypsy down in Prussia Street now, you know."

"I know. I've watched him passing the dairy every day for more than three years."

"Up in Cabra Cottage today," Philip lied in an attempt to change the dangerous turn the conversation was taking. "My sister Lena's been very poorly ... not looking too good, I'm afraid ... Dr Mooney says it could be any day now ... herself and Phil are very attached ... it will break his poor little heart."

"I'm sorry to hear about Lena ... lovely woman ... heart's blood of good nature. And how's your mother?"

"Taking it very bad. Nursed Lena herself through it all ... looked after her like a baby ... did everything for her!"

"Great woman in a crisis. It's in the aftermath that she needs watching."

"Bamma is not the woman she once was," Philip said defensively. "Times move on James. Age has softened her and Lena's long illness has drained the strength out of her."

"But she would be still strong enough to enforce a court order, would you say?"

"James, I hardly think this the proper time or the right place for such talk."

"Right then," said James proffering a wad of enlistment forms. "You're an educated fellow, it will be no trouble to you to fill one of these out. You could help the cause greatly by assisting others less endowed than yourself to do likewise." Then, almost as an afterthought, he said, "You're right about one thing. This is the moment … the best chance we've had since the men of '98 took up the pike … better than bloody '67 and that's for sure."

Philip took the papers from his brother-in-law and joined the men milling around the enlistment tables. But the meeting with James and his opening up the old question unsettled him terribly. His discomfiture grew with the building fervour all around as men grabbed forms from his hand, sought further information, demanded pencils and the spelling of the streets they had lived in all their lives. His head pounded and expanded until he felt that it would burst wide open if he didn't get out of the crowded rink quickly.

He found in the air and spaciousness of O'Connell Street's broad boulevard what his brain and lungs longed for. Holding the window ledge of Mooney's Licensed Victuallers, he swallowed the cold, damp November air as though it was water at an oasis.

"The pint tonight is only like mother's milk," a drunk said to him, wiping the froth off his moustache with his cuff. His exit released the warm vapours of Guinness porter and tobacco into the night air. Before he knew it, he was at the huge mahogany and brass counter ordering a pint of stout and a large Gold Label to sip while he waited for the pint to settle. He grimaced as the whiskey rattled its way down his throat like a shovel of hot slag. Peace came gradually as the warmth spread upward from his stomach to all parts of his body, eventually reaching his head to soothe away the spasms in his brain. If the fiery whiskey soothed, the creamy stout cooled his throat, completing the feeling of wellbeing.

"Same again," he said to the barman in the big white apron endlessly polishing the glass in his hand.

"Certainly sir. Powers and the stout is it?" he said, already pumping the black liquid into a pint tumbler. "Great meeting beyond, I believe," he said handing Philip the second glass of whiskey.

"Yes very good."

This time the whiskey began to burn the sharp edges off his great loneliness so that it didn't cut at every turn. He swallowed the rest of the glass with one gulp and set about the second pint as soon as it was placed before him.

"Will we see Home Rule in our time, do you think?"

"We will with the help of God and better too."

"Better?"

"The Republic man. That's where we're heading — an Irish republic."

"Ah, Jaysus now sir, that'll hardly happen in our children's time, never mind ours. Sir … your change. You're forgetting your change."

But Philip was already out the door and heading back across the street to the Rotunda. When he got to his place in the emptying hall he found James sitting beside the sleeping boy, running his fingers through the unruly mop of black curls. Without uttering a single word, Philip wrapped his ward in his great coat and carried him out of the building hugging him close with both arms.

"Prussia Street," he said to the cabby, then slipped onto the comfort of the quilted leather upholstery, boy and man welded together as if they were a single entity.

Chapter 23

Half a soul

Phil waited by the window for his turn. He ran his fingers over the surface of a leathery aspidistra wilting behind the shut sash. He traced each broad leaf's firm green centre to where they faded into khaki towards the wilting edges, always avoiding the frayed holes at the tips.

Behind him, Mother and Da Kennedy sat stoically together, Uncle Dunny did his best to calm Aunt Nelly and Uncle Philip questioned Uncle Felim in earnest whispers.

"You may go up and see her now," Bamma said softly, so softly it took him a minute or two to realise what was meant.

He moved up the familiar stairs and down the long corridor that seemed shorter somehow and the number of doors had shrunk to three. He stood before the second door fixed by fear of premonition until a slender finger lifted the latch. "It's only Aunty Lena. Go on in and talk to her," said Essie Kerrigan with her softest chapel voice. "I'll wait for you outside."

"Thanks Essie but you'd better wait in the yard with Sonny. You know what Bamma's like."

He turned and followed the slowly swinging door into a room of total darkness. Standing there in the still black, he wished Essie had stayed with him.

"Aunty Lena … Aunty Lena … Aunty Lena …" He whispered around the room.

"Go over to the window," said the faint yet familiar voice from under the lower end of the hipped ceiling. He slinged across the room until the heavy drapes revealed their floral pattern.

"Open the curtains just a little chink, and let me have a look at you," she said. Voice warm and thin as skimmed milk. He had intended asking her why he never saw her anymore. Why she was never around when he visited Cabra Cottage. Why she never came down to Number 46. Nourished by her presence, he did as he was bid. He had always found it impossible not to do as she asked, though she seldom asked for anything.

He could locate exactly where her voice was coming from but could not see her face with the sidelight blinding from the slanting sun.

"Tell me all about yourself and what you've been up to this while?" Voice getting rounder. Butter coming back.

Phil told her about 46 Prussia Street: the secret room and hiding places, the Fianna Code of Honour and his recent promotion to squad leader.

All the while, Lena was transfixed by his beautifully carved face, framed by curls of the blackest hair. He was firming up well. The puppy fat was becoming taut muscle around a sturdy frame.

"You're the image of your mother. Did you know that? You have her clear, olive skin and long eyelashes … and her lovely hair. Girls would give anything to have what you've got."

"I could model a hat for you if you liked. No one would see me up here in the dark."

"Aren't you very good. But there's no need darling. I won't be making hats anymore."

"There's great cattle stalls in Mother Kennedy's yard. Did you know that?"

"I know them well … are you being a good boy for her? Good sons make good husbands. Remember that and you'll get a wonderful, healthy girl for a wife one day."

"I never knew my real mother."

"No! But weren't you the best boy in the house for your Aunty Lena?"

"I suppose."

"And didn't I love you as much as any mother could?"

He stumbled towards the voice, following the slope of the ceiling with his hand until he found her bed, fumbled for the tender cusp between her neck and shoulder, softly snuggled his face till he found the proper place and then her arms enfolded him as he knew they would.

Tears flowed silent down her sunken cheeks to his wild, unruly hair and she was grateful. Grateful for that moment, grateful to Dr Mooney for the laudanum that kept the gripping pain at bay. She could slip away now knowing that everything had been looked after.

"And what are you going to be when you're a man?"

"I'm going to be a blacksmith like Harry Head and make things from iron." Then to please her he said, "Or maybe a teacher and teach children things without strapping them at every hand's turn or making little of them in front of everybody."

"That sounds wonderful. You'll make a great teacher … It's in the family, you know. Bamma and your grandfather, Lord have mercy on him, were teachers … so was your mother, light of heaven to her, and Mother Kennedy before she married."

"Tell me about my mother again."

"She was tall and very beautiful … dark like you … bright as a pin and full of life … doted on you … for the short little while she had you."

"What happened to my father?"

"Your father loved you too. Loved you so much, he kidnapped you once so that he could bring you up himself," she said as the pain returned to stab her through the centre of her gut. "Will you go down to the scullery and rob some of Bamma's apples for me and we'll have a little party of our own?"

"Sure thing Aunty Lena," he said, rising delighted. She was coming back to her old self again. Taking Bamma's stored apples was a dangerous operation but he had done it often in the past for the apple parties Lena and he held on the blind side of the bed under the eaves.

He stole quietly down the stairs and slipped out the front door for fear he might be noticed and asked to do some message or chore.

Crossing the yard to the scullery, Essie Kerrigan called out: "Hey Phil! Let's make peashooters. There's some real straight stalks over by our house."

"And I got a box of hard peas," said Sonny.

"Can't today … on a message for Aunty Lena. See you later on."

Lena regretted nothing. She had got her way in the thing that mattered most to her — Phil's rearing. As the pain gathered strength, she clung to the image of his dark features framed by long, curly locks so black they gave off a bluish hue.

*****

"I can't take the pain, I can't take the pain anymore."

The scream from the house froze him in mid-count by the apple box in the scullery. As the howls continued, he coiled himself beneath the trough, clamping his head between wrists and elbows.

"Sweet merciful Jesus, why didn't you take me in the beginning instead of my daughters one by one?" Bamma shouted at the heavens. "I asked Him to take me when Mary died. But He didn't think I had suffered enough. I asked Him to take me instead of Lena, but He denied me that too." Her declamations became entreaty as she petitioned, "Lamb of God, take me now for I can't bear any more pain."

Uncle Philip was at the foot of the stairs as Phil sneaked in to the front door, his gansey half full of apples despite all apprehension. His guardian placed an arm around the boy's shoulder telling him his Aunt Lena was already with his mother in heaven. "They're having great fun up there, eating all the fruit they could want and toasting bread on long, golden forks," he told the boy.

Phil was taken aback by how quickly they lowered the coffin into the big, mucky hole in the ground. He quite liked the priest reciting the *de profundis*, it sounded magical and rhymed like a poem, but he hated the rosary and found himself counting backwards from ten on his fingers until it was over.

As the mourners began to move away from the grave, his Uncle Philip placed his big hand on the boy's shoulder. "Say a little prayer for your mother. She's buried there, just behind where you're standing."

The headstone had fresh lilies growing out of a stone goblet on its plinth and carved words that told a story of which he only knew a part.

'Mary McNeill (nee Berford)
Died Good Friday 1903 aged 36
Deeply mourned by her loving husband James and son Phil
May she rest in peace'

"Is that me there?" he said fingering the last name chiselled on the weathered Wicklow granite.

"Yes, that's you alright. You're the only son she had."

"And that's my father then. His name was James wasn't it? Is he down there too?"

"No. Just your mother. Let's say a prayer for her soul," he said, crossing himself. "In the name of the Father and of the Son and of the Holy Ghost …"

Chapter 24

Friends again

Maryanne Little ran a comfortable, secure and affable establishment. The heavy, red velvet drapes and deep-pile carpet contributed a sense of enduring opulence while the golden cowled gaslighting flattered all that looked into the many gilded mirrors. Her fragrant girls had no pains, moods or demands reclining in their many coloured mantles. At the end of a shift they walked away from all attachments, starting afresh with each new batch of clients at the beginning of each new sunset.

The ambience so suited Philip and Felim; it became inevitable that they would run into each other in her house of comforts at some time or another. When they did, no reference was made to their presence in a brothel. And once it had happened, they continued to meet there periodically after closing time when the choice lay between home and the warm conviviality of Mrs Little's anteroom.

For her part, Maryanne Little regarded the two gentlemen from Cabra as 'bread and butter' clients. They were not big spenders, but neither were they any trouble and they were regular. They drank a lot but never got messy or complained about the whiskey being watered so long as it kept coming.

The Cabra regulars were liked by all of the girls, though none could remember when they were last asked for anything other than company. They mostly arrived before midnight to drink and talk until they surrendered to sweet oblivion. On waking, they would walk home before dawn's grey light showed up the moth-holes in the dust-laden curtains and the gilding wearing thin on the golden mirror frames.

The talk would go on all through the night. Politics mostly: Sinn Fein versus the National Party; Home Rule versus the Republic; constitutionalism against direct action. Even as the clouds of war gathered over the great powers, even as the ruling cousins of Europe squared up to each other with massive armies, the Cabra pair dug trenches either side of Irish nationalism's opening divide. It suited them both. Ireland was all that was left of Philip's passions while Felim never really had any to speak of.

"Today was one of the proudest days of my life," Philip Berford confided to his childhood pal, now greying from fair to distinguished along the temples of a lived-in face. "I saw the Volunteers unload any number of rifles and ammunition out in Howth and who was there playing his part in the full Fianna uniform but my very own ward, Phil McNeill."

"And who was there to defend the innocent citizens of Dublin on Bachelor's Walk?"

"You're asking the wrong bloody question as usual. What right did the Scottish Borderers have to fire on the people of Dublin?"

"The point is this. If you go about putting guns into the hands of ordinary citizens you must do so in the certain knowledge that people are going to get hurt. Where was Clarke and the rest of his Fenian cronies when the shooting started along the quays today?"

"They weren't armed men that were gunned down on Bachelor's Walk, just citizens going about their daily business. And in anyway, what would your man, Redmond, have done?"

"The Nationalist Party has to be seen to be in control if we are to be trusted with self-government. We can't have private armies run by a crowd of Fenians and felons."

Philip loved this. The raw edges of his nerves soothed by whiskey and his old friend in great argumentative form. It was promising to be one of the better nights.

Felim was even happier. He had been bewildered for years by the tensions that had built up between them. When they first bumped into each other by chance in Maryanne Little's, there was no discussion on what had parted them, just two sad men glad to pick up from where they had left off when boys became men.

Philip held his glass above his head in both hands like a priest at the consecration and admired the light glinting through the golden liquid from the gas lamp for a few moments. "You have an interesting view of who has the best interests of the country at heart and no mistake."

Felim was silent for a few moments, chewing the inside of his cheek as he always did when concentrating. "We'll never get Home Rule if the very men who'll govern the country are not seen to control the thousands marching and drilling all over the place. You can see how right Redmond was about that. The Home Rule Act is now on the statute book."

"But put on ice until this business with the Kaiser is settled," Phil shot back before continuing in a more measured way, "Isn't it interesting that Pearse and Clarke had the pragmatism to back down? If they had taken the same attitude as your man, the split in Irish ranks would have been fatal."

"What do you think Britain would do to an Irish Volunteer force that stepped out of line while Crown Forces were dying on the Continent?"

Philip lay back on the couch and twirled the whiskey around in his glass, smiling. "Crown Forces dying on the Continent … Begob that sounds very hopeful altogether."

Chapter 25

Opportunities of war

By September, the Great War had got underway, and war produced enormous opportunity. As one of the best cattlejobbers in the town, James McNeill could earn a tidy profit working only on market days in Prussia Street. The dairy did good business, boosted by its share of 'shawlie' separation money. Queenie kept the shop spotless, was good with customers and careful with money. James called her his little manager.

For the first time in his life he had money and the time to do what he willed. As the British Army extended trenches across the mud of Continental Europe, he devoted himself almost full-time to the Volunteers of Stoneybatter.

Buying and selling livestock took great skill and he had that in abundance. Successful cattlejobbers could calculate figures quicker than a ready reckoner, give an acting performance worthy of the stage and have the capacity for delaying completion that would put a chevalier to shame. James found the pipe a great prop — drawing on it ponderously, filling it carefully, lighting and re-lighting and sometimes engaging in the complete cleaning ritual while an anxious vendor reddened with impatience.

It was returning from one such journey with full pockets and an empty pouch that led to a very private meeting, with the old Fenian, Tom Clarke. The cattle were all crammed aboard the boat for Liverpool when, on a whim, he changed his routine to search the city centre for the dark aromatic shag that had become scarce as hens' teeth since the outbreak of hostilities. Strolling up Parnell Street, he dropped into a tobacconist shop in Number 75A and came face-to-face with the leader of the Republican Brotherhood.

A young woman was serving him with great courtesy when the unmistakable face of Clarke appeared behind her. His hair was white and wispy and his moustache drooped sadly on his yellow face but his eyes still sparkled as they did during those hushed meetings at his father's house in the long ago. The same indominitable presence that inspired men to devote themselves to 'the cause' at numerous meetings he had attended in the more recent past still shone through in the brown and murky atmosphere of the little shop. Clarke's soft whispers sent the girl to serve another. Then turning to James said, "Well if it isn't the 'Great McNeill'. You'd be the eldest of them wouldn't you?"

"Yes Mr Clarke. I'm James."

"I've often remarked that you were the spit of your father … a great man, God rest his soul."

"He was to be sure. Light of heaven shine upon him."

"Not a lot of good tobacco about since the war started … terrible scarcity altogether. I keep a little in reserve in the backroom. Come with me and we'll see if there's anything that takes your fancy."

He led James from the shop into a Fingal's cave pungent with golden-brown abundance. Glass jars crammed the dusty hardwood shelves that terraced every wall. One by one, the old man decanted shag for him to smell, to twirl between finger and thumb, and even to roll with the ball of his hand and fill into his pipe until his head swam with all the sweet intoxication.

He puffed and sniffed beneath an overlay of gentle incantation. He was of course his father's son. Everyone said it. And Ireland needed men of the Fenian breed now that her hour was fast approaching. He had been watched since joining the Volunteers and everybody liked what they saw. They wanted men to stiffen the resolve of the rump that stayed true despite the blandishments of Asquith and the Redmondites. It was true for Clarke when he said that the McNeills had always answered their country's call and so would he.

"Con Colbert tells me you've a lad in the Fianna down in Blackhall Place … you needn't tell me … I know the whole story … your fortitude is remarkable. I thought you'd be pleased to know that the Fianna boys will all come into your bailiwick along with the Volunteers of the Stoneybatter area."

"Our hour is coming surely. I'd be happy to play my part in whatever role I'm given."

"Good … good … it's settled so. Now if you'll just kneel down by the chair, I'll administer the oath."

James left the little shop in Parnell Street with a pouch filled with the best of shag and his father's place in the Irish Republican Brotherhood. Mary would have been so proud, though the IRB being a secret oath-bound society, she would not have had the pleasure of telling anyone. Pity. Dropping the word would have been enough to shut Bamma up whenever she spouted on about the green blood flowing in the veins of her swarthy children.

He stood on the dairy doorstep taking in the fresh air and the passing world, as was his habit when tea was done.

The faint sounds of marching feet intruded on the rhythm of this Stoneybatter evening. As the beat grew louder, his eye was drawn to a column of boys dressed in green coming into Manor Street, each youth swinging his arm as high as the shoulder of the lad in front. At the command, they sang out, keeping time with their marching feet.

"On for freedom Fianna Eireann
Set we our faces to the rising sun
And the day in our own land when strength and daring
Shall end for evermore the Saxon crown."

He thought his heart would burst as he watched his youngest son, green tunic crossed by a leather Sam Browne belt, barking out commands in Gaelic. Handsome and intense, just like his mother. James felt that rush of pride mixed with apprehension he assumed had been the lot of rebel fathers since the English first invaded.

The way was clear at last. Henceforth he would stay by his son's shoulder like a Guardian Angel. There would be another blow soon. He would look out for him as they went together into the gap of danger even if Bamma and the law forbade it. Bamma had been outflanked. He could meet his son as often as he liked in the subversive world of the Irish revolutionary movement. She could hardly report that to the authorities. That would make her an informer. The Berfords and the McNeills were at one in their belief that informers were the lowest form in creation.

"Sure what do Fenians care for the English law?" he said to a surprised Queenie as he went back into the dairy wiping a hand across his eyes.

Chapter 26

Skinny Lizzie

Lizzie Nolan was a tall, wiry girl of 13 who could get through any amount of washing on Mondays, wheel six or seven of her younger siblings down to Thomas Street to save tu'ppence on the groceries on Saturday and still find time to visit her grandparents in Back Lane. Indeed, her usefulness in a house full of kids was often too much of a temptation for her mother who kept her home from school every time things got on top of her. Not that her frequent absences seemed to matter to anyone in authority.

"You'll be educated but you won't be furthered," her mother would say to relieve a troubled conscience.

"I hope to God I can get a job in Jacob's when I'm fourteen, or sooner if I can borrow a birth certificate," she said to her best friend Maggie Smith as they both set off on a bright Easter Monday to visit their respective grandmothers.

"Well you can't borrow me big sister's, I've done that. Try and get the loan of someone else's. The biscuit factory is great ... you'll love it."

Lizzie also loved their new house. McCaffrey's Estate was so different to the rooms in Watling Street where there was always a soldier getting sick on the lobby and they had to share a dirty lav with eight other families. She couldn't believe her luck when Maggie Smith's family got the place next door to theirs in Dublin Corporation's first housing project.

Her father believed that everyone made their own luck but Lizzie was of the opinion that his being one of Councillor Alfie Byrne's cronies had a lot to do in their getting the key.

"I love Easter, don't you?" she said to her friend between the pealing bells of Christ Church Cathedral.

"I think it's better than Christmas ... our aul fellas getting scuttered for the week. I got a whole egg for me breakfast again this morning."

"I hate Christmas for that ... all the drinking and messing, but I love the rest of it; all the shopping and the excitement on the kids' faces in the morning. I love going to see me granny in Back Lane before the Christmas dinner. We always get the best presents … and they have a silver tongs for holding the sugar lumps and real china teacups that have matching saucers. It's a great mystery to me how every piece of crockery on the table is always of a set with not so much as an odd jug or cruet."

"Sugar lumps! She's a real lady, isn't she? And your grandfather is lovely and gentle … reminds me of Saint Joseph."

"Do you know what?" Lizzie interjected with a sudden burst of inspiration.

"No. What?

"I think I'll ask my Uncle Peadar if he would do me an obligement … if I could only find the words to ask him."

"Ask him today. Sure doesn't he live with your Granny in Back Lane?"

"If he's there, I'll pluck up the courage. He's something very important in the Citizen Army, you know … always out drilling with them and that other crowd. I don't suppose any of them would be out doing their manoeuvres over the Easter."

"I think that's a great idea. Your Uncle Peadar has a lovely hand. Sure the mothers of the Liberties have a path beaten to the door, asking him to write job application letters for all their youngsters. He'd have no trouble doctoring the date on the cert for you."

"I might just sneak the subject into the conversation while we're having tea … he might volunteer to do me the favour."

Lizzie couldn't wait to be swanning down the hill from McCaffrey's Estate in the early mornings with all the big girls chatting and gossiping as they made their way to the biscuit factory.

"We do be singing the whole day long in the press shop, sometimes sneaking the names of the bosses into the songs for the laugh," Maggie said. "It's great gas. Then we walk home, all linking in our shop coats after the hooter goes at six o'clock. You'll love it."

"I'd love to be bringing home wages to my mother. She'd be delighted with the extra few bob. Do you know what she'd do?"

"Throw a party?"

"Exactly. She'd send one of the younger ones down to the shops to buy lemonade and broken biscuits and we'd put on a little concert for her, like we used to on pay-day before my father got into the brewery."

Going down to the brewery gate on Fridays to collect her mother's money before it was all spent had become another one of Lizzie's chores, the only one she really hated. It was such a relief when he gave her one little gold coin because her mother would be all smiles. A big handful of silver and copper meant the housekeeping money had been cut. There would be tears on those days and no treats for the kids. When she got her job in Jacob's, she would make sure her mother would smile every Friday. She wouldn't wait until she turned fourteen to bring laughter back into the Nolan home.

The two friends parted at Cornmarket, each to spend the rest of the day with their particular grannies. Lizzie was her grandparents' first and favourite grandchild and they spoiled her rotten. But there was no tea, dainty cakes or chocolate eggs waiting for her this Easter. Instead, there was anxiety and fluster. She was met at the door with a request from her grandmother to go immediately to the College of Surgeons with her Uncle Peadar's lunch. She gave Lizzie a billycan of hot tea, a wrap of ham sandwiches and hurried instructions to go as fast as she could down the back of the Iveagh Buildings and on by the biscuit factory in Bishop's Street. There was trouble in the town and she beseeched her granddaughter to be very, very careful, to use only the back alleys and avoid the main streets. Above all else, she implored her not to talk to anyone, especially soldiers.

Chapter 27

The rising periphery

"Come back here with my lovely piano," shouted Anna Maddix, at the Fianna boys struggling down the stairs with her baby grand, hopping it off every wall as they passed.

The normally sedate pianoforte teacher of Arran Quay and North Circular Road was beside herself with anger and disappointment. At least two of them were past pupils and yet they could still show such disrespect for the well-tuned instrument. It was, she thought, typical of the times. Youth had such scant regard for other people's property. But this was not just her most beautiful piece of furniture, it had also been the focal point of their labours too (labouring being the operative word as far young Kerrigan was concerned).

"Where are you going with my property?" she demanded.

"We are commandeering it in the name of the Republic," replied Phil McNeill, his voice a curious mixture of regard and determination.

"I'll go straight to Mrs Berford and tell her all about your blackguardism if you put so much as a mark on it."

"Mark me bollix," said Sonny Kerrigan, barely under his breath, causing Phil to nearly drop his end of the piano with the laughter.

"It's many a mark she put on the back of my legs with her wooden ruler … her and her bloody lines and spaces. Bad luck to her aul face, the frosty-nosed aul …"

The rustle of taffeta and swish of silk followed them down the garden path. The familiar sound pursued them over the road and on to the railway bridge as the redoubtable, if ageing, Miss Maddix hurried and harried as much as manners and her long, figured and bustled dress would allow. By the time she gained the bridge over the Midland Great Western Railway, Phil and Sonny were already dragging her highly polished treasure onto the barricade they had been erecting on its west side.

"I'll have a word with your Uncle Philip on this matter. He'll give you something to remember this day by."

"Then you'd better climb down the embankment, miss, he's trying to aim that engine down there at the troop train steaming here from Athlone," Sonny answered.

Looking over the wall, Miss Maddix thought the world had gone mad. She was just in time to see Philip Berford, son of two respectable teachers, and him with a good job in the railway, jumping clear of a moving locomotive, his double-Albert watch chain swinging wildly from the waistcoat of his best suit. She never saw such a moronic grin as he had on his face, gazing admiringly after the runaway engine he had just sent steaming up the line.

Then, just when she thought things couldn't get worse, a group of Volunteers took up firing positions against the ramparts of the bridge. Turning their caps back to front to prevent the peaks obscuring their aim, they opened fire on the nearby railway station. Miss Maddix had had enough for one day. She hoisted the ends of her dress up off her high-buttoned boots and scurried back to the safety of her three-storeyed red-bricked house, the swish of her black silk audible between the volleys of rifle fire.

"Isn't this a great day for Ireland?" said Phil, standing on the top of the barricade. "The runner from the Four Courts says that the whole centre of the city has fallen to the Republic. The Tommies are being scattered without hope of reinforcement. Begob, Sonny, the Broadstone will be in our hands before the day is out."

"There'll be few reinforcements coming down that line today. Bejapers! Them Tommies are going to get a quare land when they meet that engine flying at them on the up line. We should thank God for your Uncle Philip and for being alive to see this day."

They might have had more to thank God about had they managed to get Philip out of Hanlon's Licensed Victuallers a little earlier. With all the excitement and inebriation he had completely forgotten to tell the Volunteers to switch the points at Liffey Junction. Word soon came down the line that the runaway locomotive had harmlessly derailed itself at Blanchardstown.

When it became clear that the approaching troop train was not going to be destroyed by that particular ploy, Commandant McNeill summoned Phil and gave him his first job as a runner — it was to become his main duty for the rest of the day. He was sent up the line to Blanchardstown with a request to the officer commanding the Volunteers there to blow up the permanent way to stop troops arriving in the city from Athlone. Adjusting his stride so that he landed on every second sleeper, Phil made his way westward.

Phil felt that rebellion was a whole lot better than working as a grocer's curate in Findlater's. Patting butter between two wet paddles all day long ... and all the aul wans with their quarterly accounts demanding deference and 'just a little sliver' extra for nothing ... fur coats and no bloomers.

Not that he would ever see the inside of Findlater's again ... ascendancy bugger sticking his half pound of butter under his nose ... accusing him of short-changing on the weight. It would have been enough to make a saint's blood boil. He wasn't so high-and-mighty when he took the loose butter out of his hand and squashed it into his stupid face. It was worth being sacked just to see Findlater's best creamery melting off his big snooty nose. Two and six a week as a first-year apprentice with seven more to go ... just to learn how to serve the 'quality' with rashers and butter!

When the English were beaten out of the country, he'd join the new army of the Republic and defend his country against all comers. That would be the way to spend your life. He might even become an officer with all the experience he was getting. It would beat the hell out of Findlater's anyhow.

He arrived in Blanchardstown in just over half an hour and was immediately sent back to Cabra to relay an order that had come up from Commandant Daly in the Four Courts. They were to blow up the bridges at both the North Circular and Cabra Roads to simultaneously block the railway line and render the roads impassable. Phil made it back to Cabra even quicker than he had gone out, taking the sleepers two at a time with greater confidence.

He was standing at the barricade talking to Sonny when the air around them concussed once, twice, three times under the blows of failed attempts to demolish the bridges onto the line. Then the screech of an artillery shell was followed by a louder bang that demolished the barricade they had so patiently built and strengthened with interlocking wire. Miss Maddix's piano was sent in smithereens all over the North Circular with the rest of the furniture, hand-carts and tar barrels that had been commandeered from the surrounding area.

The two boys were covered in the debris but were otherwise unhurt. As they ran for cover, they passed a Volunteer officer who had had the side of his head ripped away by flying shrapnel. He hung awkwardly down from the remains of the barricade by his ankles, his Mauser lying on the roadway beside him, still in its wooden holster.

Gaining the safety of Miss Maddix's music room, Phil and Sonny could see where the troops advancing from the Phoenix Park had placed their field gun in position. It had all their strongholds within its range. They could also see the Dublin Fusiliers snaking along the private pathway to reinforce The Broadstone station.

"Here, have a go," Sonny said, handing Phil the Mauser he had stuck inside his tunic as they passed the dying Volunteer. Phil attached the machine pistol to its wooden holster to form a stock, turning the weapon into a short rifle. Remembering nights of short-arms drill in Blackhall Place, he tucked the stock snugly into his shoulder. Then, looking through the bridge of the backsights, he tilted the weapon until he saw the bead of the foresight standing up neatly in its centre. Aiming just over one of the hedges along the pathway, he waited for a kitbag to appear. He squeezed his finger … *he squeezed his finger with the big signet ring on it when his Uncle Philip brought him to his office in Broadstone along the private lane for railway servants. His guardian was full of all the wonders they would see in the loco sheds and on the magical turntable, letting him stop on the way to pick blackberries from the bushes growing all along the sides. Uncle Philip's hand felt so big and warm and protective …* he squeezed his finger tighter. The stock kicked into his shoulder as the kitbag lurched sideways, away from the bushes and out of his sights.

"You got him … bejapers you got him sure enough," said Sonny babbling with excitement.

As Phil fought off the urge to vomit, the field gun discharged a shell that took the roof away, starting a fire that quickly spread along the attics of the terraced houses. At the same moment, the Dublin Fusiliers returned fire, directing a withering hail from rifle and machine-gun from both the laneway and the nearby railway station. Plaster and glass flew through the smoke as the two boys flattened their bodies against the floor for air and safety.

Suddenly the order to abandon positions was shouted up the stairs. Stumbling blindly downwards, Phil tripped over Anna Maddix's still body lying askew on the first landing. This time he did get sick but was caught under the arm by a Volunteer officer, built like a bull with the strength to match. James McNeill effortlessly held the two boys up as he ushered them out of the blazing house and into the relative safety of the street.

In the clear light of the day, Phil realised that revolution was a strange thing indeed with cattle-jobbers becoming field commanders and railway surveyors sending their precious locomotives to destruction for the cause.

The company was rallying for a frontal assault on the station but the commandant told him curtly that he would not be involved in the action. He had a special job for him. He was to use his knowledge of the area to find a safe route to the Four Courts and deliver an urgent dispatch to Commandant Daly.

Dashing down Rathdown Road and through the grounds of the lunatic asylum, he thought that poor Anna Maddix with her metronome and wooden ruler wasn't the worst of them. She certainly didn't deserve to go up in flames like a Viking warrior, or to see her lovely piano go before her.

He slid comfortably through the hospital grounds until he reached Brunswick Street where he began to hear the thud of shellfire and the crack of rifles coming from the direction of O'Connell Street. The narrow Red Cow Lane took him into North King Street and he decided to slip into the Four Courts by way of Smithfield and May Lane to avoid the Bridewell. There's no need to make things handy for them by walking into their arms, he thought.

"Halt, who goes there — friend or foe?" shouted a young man with an accent as salty and yellow as country butter. He was pointing the muzzle of a Lee Enfield 303 at Phil's face, so the scout came to a sudden stop.

"Friend," Phil replied at a snap.

"Advance friend to be recognised."

Phil took the mandatory three short steps towards the sentry, stood sharply to attention and shouted, "Phil McNeill, adjutant, Wolfe Tone Slua, Fianna Eireann with an urgent dispatch for Commandant Daly."

The sentry brought him into the central concourse of Gandon's masterpiece where Commandant Daly dressed in full Volunteer officer's uniform was supervising the erection of loop sandbagging around the windows of its huge, high dome.

The man with responsibility for the insurrection north of the Liffey read the note telling of failed attempts to hold or blow bridges or to block the MGW railway by any other means. The line from Athlone was still passable despite casualties of forty dead and wounded and a hundred taken prisoner.

Turning to his second in command he said, "Take a detachment to North King Street. Our outer defence cordon is going to be much nearer than anticipated." Then, scribbling his comments on the note, he asked Phil to deliver it to HQ in the General Post Office.

He was off again, darting down Mary's Lane and Mary's Street with the sounds of war getting louder and louder as he got closer to the Henry Street entrance of the GPO. This time he was challenged by a member of the Citizen Army at a very solid-looking barricade and was brought straight into the presence of their leader, James Connolly.

"Glad to see we're not the only ones blessed by the presence of military genius," the legendary union leader said, on reading the note. "Son, I want you to change into civvies and take an important message to Countess Markievicz. Tell her to get Mallon and his men out of their slit trenches in the Green where they are sitting ducks and back into defensible positions in the College of Surgeons and surrounding buildings. Can you remember all that?"

"Yes sir," Phil shouted back over the din and then repeated verbatim the message just given him.

"Good man, good man. Down with you now to the quartermaster and get something respectable that fits. I don't want you drawing attention to yourself with the place crawling with enemy forces."

Minutes later, Phil, dressed in a tweed jacket, jodhpurs and brown brogue shoes, set out on the dangerous journey across the river to the southside of Dublin, a place as foreign to him as it was to the invading English Army.

Unsure who controlled all the main bridges, he shot back down Henry Street and turned sharp left into Liffey Street. Crossing the river by the Ha'penny Bridge he entered the tiny back streets of Temple Bar at Merchant's Arch. He became lost so often among the small thoroughfares behind Dame Street it was a great relief to him when he finally got sight of his destination on entering York Street from where, he didn't know.

He was full of excitement at the prospect of meeting the Countess, the great lady who had founded the Fianna Eireann and had written their Battle Hymn. As he got closer to the College of Surgeons, he realised with great disappointment that his journey had been completely unnecessary. The Countess was already leading her men out of the Green under fire from a machine-gun nest on top of the Shelbourne Hotel. Bullets were taking chunks out of the walls at the top of the street.

At the corner of Cuffe Street he noticed a tall, wiry girl of about his own age, carrying a steaming billycan in one hand and a brown paper bag in the other. She seemed only mildly concerned by all the commotion. The city was well used to armed men spending their weekends drilling and making mock attacks on buildings. The shooting was just something else to be putting up with.

She was approaching the corner oblivious to the soldiers guarding the junction and heedless of machine-guns stuttering from the Shelbourne. Just then a pattern of automatic fire made its diagonal way down the buildings towards her. One of the Tommies dashed from his post on the corner, threw himself across her body, pinning her to the pavement.

Lizzie Nolan wasn't sure what to be most alarmed by — the soldier lying on top of her or the fact that he had spilled her uncle's tea. She couldn't make out what he was mumbling at her with his English accent muffled by the fistfuls of her Uncle Peadar's ham sandwiches he was stuffing into his gob. There was further cause for apprehension. A dark, foreign-looking, young man, dressed in an expensive tweed jacket and jodhpurs had a pistol at the soldier's head.

"Jesus, Mary and Holy Saint Joseph, we'll all be dead before this day is out," she shouted.

"Remove yourself from this young lady or you'll never see your pagan country again."

Young lady! He was talking about Lizzie Nolan from McCaffrey's Estate, who hadn't even got a job and he was referring to her as a lady. The darkest, handsomest boy she had ever seen in her whole life and he was ready to take on the British Army to protect her.

Slinging the soldier's rifle down the far end of the street, Phil warned him to lie flat on his face until he had counted to one hundred. Grabbing Lizzie by the hand, he dragged her down Mercer's Street and out of sight. He would have taken her into the first turning at Cuffe Lane only Lizzie pulled him away, telling him it was a blind alley.

"Do you know your way around this part of the city? 'Cause if you do I'll escort you home and you can direct me to the shortest way back across the Liffey to Prussia Street."

"Where's that?"

"Way up above Blackhall Place on the other side of Queen Street Bridge."

"What has you out wandering so far from home?"

"I'm a Fianna officer on very important business with Countess Markievicz. What are you doing rambling around in the middle of an insurrection?"

"I was bringing my Uncle Peadar his lunch," she said. Then added, "He's something big in the Citizen Army, you know ... What's an insurrection?"

She took him down streets he had never even heard the names of before — Golden Lane, Bull Alley, Carman's Hall, Crane Street — but he knew full well he was in his native city.

As they walked, she talked non-stop about her granny in Back Lane, their lovely new house in McCaffrey's Estate and her best friend, Maggie Smith. He told her things he had never told anyone before about his mother dying on Good Friday, the games he had played with his funny Aunty Lena, the reign of terror that was Bamma, Mother Kennedy, Uncle Philip and his best pal, Sonny Kerrigan. She noticed that he said very little about a father and so she said nothing about hers or about her granny in Faulkner Place.

"I'm going to get a job in Jacob's when I'm fourteen." The words were no sooner out of her mouth when she became afraid it would not impress the handsome boy from the other side of the city. So she quickly added, "It will give me something to do until I'm eighteen and can start training as a nurse." She had never thought of it before, but now that it was said, it sounded so good she decided to make it her plan.

He told her about getting a job in Findlater's without a birth certificate by telling them he was born in Scotland and that she could do the same in the biscuit factory if she wanted to. He did not tell her about being sacked.

*****

At Watling Street Lizzie directed him towards the bridge at the end of the hill that would take him close to Blackhall Place. He assured her he could find his own way from there. Then, looking straight into her eyes, he thanked her for being his guide and for her company that, he said, had greatly shortened the journey. Lizzie's knees turned to jelly as he spoke his farewell and she thought she might fall down with the delicious feeling flowing to the pit of her stomach when he took her hand to shake it goodbye.

The strength didn't return to her legs for a while after he disappeared at Ellis Quay on the other side of the water.

Phil threw the Mauser over the Liffey wall and walked home as though he were returning form the Fairyhouse Races.

PART 3

Chapter 28

Carrying the torch

Children, skipping alongside the grim lines of marching men, sang at the top of their voices.

"Vote, vote, vote for De Valera, leave aul Dillon at the door-i-o
If they don't let him in
Then we'll push the do-er in
And yis won't see yer mammies anymore-i-o."

The juggernaut of massed ranks marching six abreast moved on inexorably. A thousand burning bulrushes modelling light and shade turned each row into a line of serried faces.

"Begob, your National Party is on the ropes now for certain," Philip Berford gloated to his boozing butty as the juggernaut wheeled into College Green. The two men were standing on the plinth of King William's statue at the Dame Street end where they had a great view of the proceedings.

"They backed the wrong horse in the Rising and no mistake. They've lost every by-election since the boys came home from Frongoch and they're going to get a right pasting in the general election too, I'm telling you." Then, looking in wonderment at the thousands thronging the large diamond space outside the Old Irish House of Parliament, he said, "Dublin hasn't seen anything like this since Parnell's funeral."

Felim didn't reply because he was left with nothing to say. Like most moderate nationalists, he was appalled at how the British Government could always be relied upon to pull Republican fat out of the fire. They had turned the defeat of Easter week into a separatist victory by executing too many over too long a period. And ever since had been Sinn Fein's best election agent with conscription laws, arrests, forced feeding and all manner of counterproductive coercion.

It was a long time since he had seen Philip's face glow as it did in the light of the flaming kerosene. He seemed transported, calling out the names of the leaders as they climbed onto the platform and tossing his bowler up in the air. "Up De Valera, up Cathal Brugha, up Michael Collins ... Look, look, there's my nephew Phil, marching in the thick of it. Go on, yeh boy yeh! It's in your blood."

But concern soon overcame his sense of triumph. "Felim, did you notice anything about young Phil? He's over there on the left of the colour party."

"He's getting to be a real man, must be sixteen by now?"

"Yes, yes, but he's not wearing his Fianna uniform."

"Well he's in some kind of uniform. He's wearing a trench coat and cloth cap like the rest of them."

"Let's go somewhere for a drink," Philip said abruptly.

"Maryanne Little's or the Scotch House?"

"Jurys' is nearer and quieter. Come on, it's only up the road."

Sitting comfortably around the circular mahogany bar, Felim ordered two glasses of Jameson's ten-year-old whiskey and two large bottles of Guinness to chase them.

In the brighter light of the gas lamps, he could see the glow in Philip's face for what it really was. It wasn't just nationalist fervour and torchlight. Nor was it a symptom of robust health. It was something more disturbing. Observing him closely in the bar mirror, he could see that Philip was beginning to present the toxic bloat usually found under the skin of advanced alcoholics.

"I'm thinking of getting married," Felim said.

"That's rather sudden ... does the girl know?"

"No, as a matter of fact she doesn't. I haven't asked her yet but I probably will and soon."

"Anyone I know?"

"I doubt it. My mother has been doing rather a lot of matchmaking lately, so I thought I'd better do some choosing myself before someone is chosen for me. Her father is on the board of the GMW with pa ... she's been to Springfield on several occasions ... nice girl ... I think you'd like her."

"Has your father said anything about the other matter?"

"I'm afraid it's not looking good."

"What are they saying?"

"Well, they know it was you who sent their locomotive to destruction in Easter week ... can't prove it of course. Those that witnessed the event are either in agreement with the action, dead, or

144

afraid they soon will be if they inform the authorities. However, they have been watching you like hawks ever since."

"Who are you telling?"

"They say that of late your work has fallen off ... Philip, I'm quite uncomfortable about this."

"Go on, I need to know what the bastards are planning."

"Well, they are saying that your drawings are frequently unreliable, that your absenteeism is a cause for concern and that several managers have detected a smell of strong drink off you during duty hours. They feel they have grounds for dismissal."

"I'll fight them every inch of the way..."

"If you fight you'll lose, it's as simple as that and you know it."

"What alternative have I? I'm not going to allow them besmirch my professional reputation. I have always been one of the best railway draughtsmen in the country and I never drink on the job ... the bloody cheek of them."

"The alternative is not very attractive but it is a sight better than dismissal. If you are sacked from the railway, you'll find it very difficult to get another job in Dublin. And who will keep you and Bamma? She's too old to go back teaching and you have needs to maintain ... some of them quite expensive, I needn't remind you."

"What is it then?"

"My father recommends that you accept disciplinary action. It will involve demotion and loss of service. He says that that will keep you in the system and put you in a position to rise up in the company again at some time in the future. Perhaps when your Republic is up and running, it will reward the heroes of 1916's attempted putsch."

"Demotion to what?"

"Gate-keeper at a level crossing. There's a position coming up at Cardiff's Bridge."

"That's humiliation. Do they seriously expect me to take such a dramatic loss of status and salary lying down? And Cardiff's Bridge — they want everyone in Cabra to see my reduced circumstances. Well, I won't take it."

"It's the best my father can do for you."

Then in a desperate attempt to change the subject, he said, "Any chance that you'll be following me down the aisle? I mean if a confirmed bachelor like myself can take the plunge, there's hope for everyone."

"Bamma has the feet kissed off the statue of Saint Jude down in Merchant's Quay imploring him to find me a wife. I suppose it's appropriate that she seeks the intercession of the patron saint of hopeless cases. She's living in fear of the Berford name dying out. I'm the last male in the country to bear the name, you know."

"Then, get out there and do your bit. Get yourself a fine, big country lass that's good breeding material. Look out for one with strong haunches and a full bosom — have a bit of home comfort and oblige Bamma and Saint Jude!"

Philip knocked back the remaining contents of his whiskey glass, chasing it quickly with the stout and stared at the ceiling in silence.

Beckoning the curate with a slight flick of his head, he ordered, "Innkeeper … two large Jemmies and two bottles of your best stout. Come on Felim, let's drop it. We'll polish off these few and head for Maryanne Little's."

By the time they reached Trinity College, the rally had come to a close. The two men stood at the railings watching the Volunteers march back to their own areas for dispersal, shouldering blackened torches.

B Company from Cabra went past with Phil McNeill in the leading colour party. It was clear to Philip that his ward was now part of an army. Sinn Fein was a certainty in the coming general election. They would then make a grab for the Republic with the Volunteers their instrument of war. People were already calling it the IRA, though the lads preferred the full title — Irish Republican Army — loving the sound of it.

The officer commanding B Company wore full, formal uniform — green jacket, riding breeches, Sam Browne belt stretched across his barrel chest, his bull-like body straining every seam and fibre.

"*Clé, clé, clé, deas, clé,*" he called out as he went up and down the ranks. He kept a particular eye on the colour party marching at the head of the column, carrying the green, white and orange tricolour of the Republic.

A lower-ranking officer took up the rear, barking his own brand of discipline. "Lift those arms, yea shower of mother's pets. Yer not in the 'High-go Shites'. Yer in the army of the Republic now and that should be good enoughsky. Swing those arms yea shower of hoors, left right, left right."

Passing the gates of Trinity he tipped a wink in their direction. Felim and Philip knew for certain that it was Dunny Kerrigan and burst out laughing.

Crossing the Liffey, the column made its way up O'Connell Street past the gutted shell of the General Post Office, sticking out like a black, broken tooth in the middle of the main thoroughfare of the 'fair city'.

"*dFheiceadh fó clé*," shouted the commanding officer and all heads turned sharply to the left to face their scarred monument. They gazed upon it with eyes that blazed for the men who had sacrificed themselves there for the cause. It was two years since the Rising but the work of restoration had still not begun. The skeletal remains of the GPO and many more burnt-out shells of the once-fine buildings lining Dublin's broad boulevard were a constant reminder to a severely chastised city.

Falling steadily behind, Felim and Philip sauntered up the capital's main thoroughfare, turning right at the GPO, heading for Earl Street and the delights of the Monto.

Chapter 29

The Thread of Life

Sitting on the edge of her iron bed in the nurses' quarters of the Richmond Lunatic Asylum, it struck Lizzie Nolan that everything in the world was connected to everything else in ways that were most surprising. Who would have thought that the actions of the King of Bulgaria would end up costing her a permanent job in Jacob's biscuit factory, force her away from her lovely brothers and sisters and turn her into a madwoman's nurse two years before her time?

People hardly noticed when Tsar Ferdinand pulled out of the war but they sat up when the German Kaiser followed suit and called for an armistice as well. That put an end to War Office telegrams falling like dead leaves in a gale and everybody welcomed that.

Nobody was so pleased about what came next though. With no war to fight, all the men were packed off home without a job to go to and a sudden stop put to the 'separation money' for the women. Lizzie had even less to sing about. With no soldiers at the front, Jacob's lost its big order for mess tins and all the girls in McCaffrey's Estate were thrown out of work, including herself and her 'job for life'. Nobody she knew had thought about any of that when the King of Bulgaria threw in the towel.

A head peeped around the door and a beaming face beneath a mop of frizzy red hair said, "I'm your next-door neighbour, can I come in? I'm Essie Kerrigan. What's your name?"

"Lizzie Nolan from Mount Brown. Where are you from?"

"Cabra ... just the other side of the North Circular. I'd say by the look of you that Mount Brown must be like Valparaiso. Come on, I'll give you a hand to put your things away. Matron will be doing her tour of inspection any minute."

As they neatly folded her undergarments into the bedside locker and hung her few dresses and good coat on hangers, Lizzie told her new friend about Jacob's letting her go, despite her having a job for life. "Mr Swan and Mr Pew were quick enough with the forms for me to sign and I still pouring blood after the tip of that finger got cut off in the folding-press," she said pointing her truncated digit at Essie's face.

"How was it that you didn't faint?"

"How could I and they getting me to sign with my left hand while my right one was still caught in the machine? 'Just waive your right to damages and you'll have a job for life,' said Mr Pew all nice and sweet so that I could hardly believe it was him that was doing the talking."

Essie went into a fit of laughing as Lizzie put on her burlesque version of the event with all the airs and graces that went with the plumy accent she affected. "I might as well have wiped me bum with the same piece of paper for all the good it did when Jacob's lost the army order. You'd want to hear the songs we sang in the press-shop after the girls got their notice."

"You're a howl!" Essie said. "Were you long idle?"

"I was six months unemployed before getting into this place."

"Me too. Didn't you hate every minute of it — traipsing the city with an army of men and women looking for something to do?"

"God! I hope I never have to go through that again."

"Perhaps it was all for the best. After all, you wouldn't like the war to continue just so as you could stay in the biscuit factory, would you?"

"Oh no! There are too many young men hopping around McCaffrey's Estate on peg legs to want that."

"There are plenty of mothers in Cabra who'd be delighted to see their sons coming home in any shape so long as they came home at all. Didn't they all look like fine things marching off in their brown uniforms all the same?"

"Didn't they just. And do you know what? You'd get brained by my father for just looking at a soldier."

"My father was a soldier … didn't come back from the war."

"Oh! I'm very sorry for your trouble Essie. I had no idea and me carrying on. Was it Flanders?"

"No. Mafeking … or so they tell me … lost in the Boer War … before I was born. My mother was only carrying me at the time Lord have mercy on her too … she was killed on the night of the Big Wind."

"Oh, you poor thing."

"Not a bit of it. What you've never had, you can't miss. Me granny is great and Uncle Dunny is more like a big brother to me."

With the packing done the two girls sat beside each other on the bed and took turns to unfold their lives to one another. Lizzie told how the unexpected loss of her job had brought forward all her great plans but not in the way she envisaged. She had really wanted to be a nurse in Saint Kevin's in Mount Brown when she was eighteen. Ever since she came up with the plan that day walking home with the gorgeous, dark fella from the other side of the river, she always saw herself nursing in Kevin's. It was just down the hill from her house and everyone would see her walking to and from work in her crisp, white nurse's uniform.

"I used to dream about Phil McNeill, I never forgot his name, coming into 'casualty' after being wounded in another rising. I'd be gently tending his injuries, wiping his forehead and cleaning the blood from his jet-black curls. He'd have to be suffering from brain fever or become a complete idiot for me to be nursing him in this place."

She began to giggle at the audacity of her own remark but Essie didn't join her. Instead, she stood up from the bed. "Phil McNeill you say ... real foreign looking ... powerful build?"

"Yes. Do you know him?"

"You could sing it if you had the air. Aren't there plenty of young men on your own side of the river or did they all leave their minds behind in the trenches? You'll have to excuse me, I'd better get my own room sorted out before matron arrives."

Must have hit a tender spot, Lizzie thought as her new friend breezed out of the room. Essie definitely knew something about Phil McNeill. It was her first sniff of him since the Easter Rising and she felt certain that she was on the way to meeting him again. It would just be a question of time.

Lizzie eventually came to love the work and the *esprit de corps* that developed between all the nurses in her year. Essie Kerrigan was great fun and they became best pals but she never mentioned Phil McNeill again and Lizzie thought it better not to ask.

Time flew without a minute's pause. She passed all her exams that autumn and shed her trainee's stripes for the full white of the probation nurse. She had been looking forward to that since the first day she walked up the granite steps of the hospital.

What she didn't expect was the notice she was getting from the big six-foot policemen of the DMP. Some were fine young men but they were all 'country-mugs' with ruddy faces and hands like shovels. She knew that she would get a terrible ragging from Maggie Smith and the rest of them if she were seen walking out with their likes. The Shinners might take a dim view of it too. A girl could end up getting shot for having a walk around the Green and a ha'p'orth of dates with a rozzer.

"I saw him again yesterday," she told Maggie Smith during a half-day's leave in Mount Brown.

"Who?

"The dark fella."

"Where?"

"With the Big Fella and the Long Fella … carrying the rebel flag in College Green."

"Well you won't be seeing him doing guard of honour in that company for a long while. They've arrested the Long Fella and they say that the Big Fella has gone on the run. There'll be trouble in this country yet, the way they're all carrying on. What was he like?"

"He was only gorgeous, standing as straight as a die with the flag on a big, thick pole sticking out in front of him."

"Did he have anything else sticking out in front of him?"

"Maggie Smith, you're terrible altogether, you don't care what you say."

Chapter 30

War of Independence

Phil McNeill buried his right hand deep into his trench coat pocket for the familiar feel of his Webley 45. Once more, he ran his fingers over the milled-handle for its brailed message of reassurance, almost of comfort, as he walked through Mooney's Field. B Company, Dublin Brigade met across the road at the Deaf and Dumb in an outhouse provided by the Christian Brothers. Hidden behind the high walls of an institution where the inmates couldn't talk, and their keepers wouldn't, made it perfect for an underground army operating in a city crawling with soldiers, 'G' men and police.

Visiting Bamma and Uncle Philip was excellent cover for being in the vicinity at the same time on the same day week-in-week-out. And though he was happy to be seeing them, he was always relieved when it was time to leave again for the fresh air and lush grass of Mooney's Field.

"And how's my Bamma today?" he said coming in through the half-door with all the confidence of an armed man in a graveyard.

"Growing down like a cow's tail."

"Not a bit of it Bamma. I met Mrs Trench and Mrs Dooley coming out of mass in Aughrim Street only last Sunday and they were both saying what a big, straight woman you are and how you had more energy than a woman half your years."

"Hmm! Big standing like a dog sitting! Did you get a new position yet?"

"I did Bamma. Uncle Dunny gave me a job in the sawmills."

"I suppose you'll be 'under-dog', ruining your good lungs with all the dust of the world falling on top of you?"

"Divil a fear Bamma. Sawyers don't have 'under-dogs' anymore or 'top-dogs' for that matter. They went out with the Mohicans. They have modern, power-saws these days ... belt-driven by steam engines ... no need for anyone to slave down in a pit at all ... and it's only a few doors down the road from number 46. There'll be no travelling either."

Bamma had softened over the years but Phil still tiptoed around her capricious temperament. As ever, Uncle Philip was interested and interesting, exchanging views about the evolving military and political situation though he was developing a tendency to repeat himself. "How are things with Ireland, and how does she stand? as Napper Tandy once said," Uncle Philip asked, as he asked every Thursday, anxious to get the news from the horse's mouth.

Relieved at the interruption, Phil took off at a canter. "Since they suppressed the Dail in September, most of the leadership is on the run. But Dev's policy of social ostracism has RIC men leaving in droves and no one joining up to replace them."

"And what's the latest?"

"Did you not hear the rumpus up at Ashtown yesterday?"

"There was any amount of Tommies and rozzers to-ing and fro-ing and I coming in from work. I believe they nearly 'did in' the Lord Lieutenant."

"Ambushed him going in through the park gates … nearly got the bastard and all …"

"Wash your mouth Phil McNeill," Bamma said brandishing her old bread knife. "We'll have none of that kind of language in my kitchen … even if you are talking about that God's curse of a flunky. Sit up to the table now and tell us all about it and none of your vulgarity."

"The details are still a bit sketchy, Bamma," Phil said to cover his own peripheral involvement in the action. "Just that it was a near thing for the Viceroy … they got a few of his entourage though … tells you a lot when the king's representative in Ireland has to travel around Dublin in an armoured car. We'll force them into governing Ireland from bunkers yet."

As always, Bamma had put out a beautiful spread of ham sandwiches, boiled eggs, scones and soda-bread, jugs of fresh milk and pots of tea. The table was set with her best willow-patterned china, linen napkins and silver cutlery.

Knowing that Bamma and his guardian lived for the diversion his weekly visits provided, he greased the wheels of conversation with large dollops of information on the developing Anglo-Irish War. He told them the inside story about the first shots of the rapidly growing conflict, fired in a raid on an explosives wagon in Tipperary earlier in the year. "Soon, England will have to decide between launching a full-scale war on what they consider one of the 'Home Nations' or come to terms with an independent Ireland. And that's the truth of it."

"Hobson's choice. If they lose Ireland, the rest of the empire will not be far behind," said Bamma slicing large cuts off a steaming loaf of soda-bread

He did not tell them that Sean Treacy, the daring hero of the Tipperary raid, had become the model for every young Volunteer in the country. He was walking openly around Dublin with a revolver strapped to each hip in leather holsters. He'd seen them himself as they approached Ashtown gate and him covering them only by a loose-buttoned dustcoat: "To be quick on the draw," he had answered to the unasked question.

"And what makes this uprising different from all the others?" Uncle Philip asked and sat well back in his chair awaiting the wrong answer.

"What do you mean by different, Uncle Philip?"

"What is making it more successful than all the uprisings, insurrections and rebellions against English rule since Dermot McMurrogh Kavanagh brought the hoors over in the first place, all of 750 years ago?"

"The support of the people."

"Very important, indeed. But the Wexford Republic of 1798 had the support of the majority as did the Confederation of Kilkenny a hundred and fifty years earlier and all they gave us was a few more centuries of 'Croppy Lie Down'. The same was true for Eoin Roe O'Neill and all the other O'Neills … all the way back to the last High King."

"The three things necessary to win freedom from England is guns, guns and more guns," Phil said, parroting a recent pep talk given to B Company by Dunny Kerrigan.

"All very important in their own way, I suppose. Hard to see anyone having much of an uprising theses days without guns but Patrick Sarsfield captured a whole ammunition train at Ballyneety and still couldn't prevent Limerick from falling."

"The cities. This time it's not just out in the countryside. Dublin is a hot-bed of sedition so is Cork, Galway and the rest."

"What about the Invincibles, the Fenians and Robert Emmet — all set in the city and all noble, bloody failures?"

"OK. I give up, Uncle Philip. What's making the difference this time around?"

"In a word — intelligence. In the past, our side was always so riddled with spies and informers, the English knew more about what was going on than we did ourselves. This time it's the other way around. That's why they were able to mount an ambush on the Lord Lieutenant himself, like you were just saying. The IRA knew when he would be entering the park for the Viceregal Lodge and by what gate. Dublin Castle, on the other hand, probably didn't have a clue that an attack was in the air or who might mount such a thing."

It was little wonder, Phil thought to himself. Most of the Dublin Brigade didn't know either, but he did. He would have loved to be able to tell them that the same Tipperary boys who were at Soloheadbeg — Dan Breen, Sean Treacy and the rest — carried out the attack. They would have been so proud that he had been detailed to use his knowledge as a local to do some of the reconnoitring.

Commandant McNeill had asked for him especially … had him summoned to the dairy in Stoneybatter and gave him his orders over a cup of tea. He said he needed someone with a sound head on his shoulders to guide the country lads to the ambush site and show them the best route back to the city when it was all over. He had also given him the strictest orders to stay out of the fight. His job was only to scout out the area and to get them there and back in safety. The Commandant was able to tell him exactly by which gate Lord French was to enter the park and at what time. Gave him a quart can of milk for Mother Kennedy when he was leaving.

The living quarters above the dairy gave him the strangest feeling — *déjà vu* they called it — seen before but not remembered. It was like the time Aunty Lena had taken him on the pilgrimage to Drogheda to see the severed head of Blessed Oliver Plunkett and he felt he had known the town all his life.

There was something very unreal about the whole assassination escapade. They were all young lads, not much older than he. They looked as though they were preparing to go to a dance rather than an ambush — slicking their hair back with brilliantine, brushing down their clothes … competing with each other as to who had the best chance with a girl with a funny name in Bansha called Sheila Sean Mhór Ryan. Young Martin Savage was the quietest of them all and they mounting their bikes outside Fleming's in Drumcondra. He never returned.

From his position across the road in the Halfway House, he could see them lying in wait by Ashtown Gate, so still and quiet the everyday traffic passed by without noticing their presence. As the motorcade approached— state car escorted by an armoured car at front and back — he could just about see the muzzles of their guns slide forward through the grass at the top of the ditches. They let the first armoured car pass untouched. When the state car drew abreast of their positions they blasted it with everything they had. They weren't to know that the Viceroy was in the first car that sped off at the sound of shooting, taking no further part in the action.

They found regular soldiers a different kettle of fish to country peelers. Withering fire from the Lewis machine gun on the second armoured car was even cutting young trees in half as it raked the ditches all around. The Tipperary lads fought on bravely for a while but were eventually forced to withdraw, leaving the mortally wounded Martin Savage behind. Intelligence was the difference all right. The only problem was, there wasn't enough of it.

He hated not being able to tell them. As it was, Bamma was looking at him like a mother hearing the first mass of a newly ordained son. He longed to see their eyes lighting up with pride in his involvement. Uncle Philip would have got a great kick out of getting the inside story from his own ward. Were he to tell them, the information would never go any farther than Cabra Cottage, but it was against army orders. It was a dangerous rule to break.

Nevertheless, being in the know increased his stature at the table enormously. He almost luxuriated in his change of status at Cabra Cottage since he took up the gun for the Republic. Bamma now spoke to him as though he were the embodiment of all the Berfords and O'Tooles since the Battle of Sallcock's Wood. At times she leaned heavily on him to consider changing his name by deed poll from McNeill to Berford.

"You have the brains, looks and temperament of your mother, not to mention her colouring. She was a true Berford. You were reared as a Berford ... the only thing you ever got from the McNeills was their name and God knows there are McNeills enough in the world as it is. Your Uncle Philip is the only one left to carry the family name forward," she said rather pointedly. "Wouldn't it be a terrible thing for your mother that's in the clay if the Berford name were to fade forever?"

He wanted to tell her that his name was the only thing that was his as of right … that he had never known what it was like to have a real mother or father, only relations that played the part. His father had given it to him and become just another of the many subjects that couldn't be mentioned in Cabra Cottage. As a child, he had fantasies about descent from any number of Irish heroes with the MacNeill or O'Neill surname.

He still held Bamma in such awe and respect, he replied, "You must have made that soda-bread yourself Bamma. There isn't a bakery in Dublin that can make soda-bread as good as that. Aunt Gypsy is always saying that anyone can make a rich cake but the real test of a baker is her ability to bake good, plain soda-bread."

"It's true for her. You can hide bad baking behind all the rich, sweet things that goes into a fruitcake but there is no deceit with soda-bread. It is plain and simple. It stands or falls by the skill of the cook."

And so the visits went, as Ireland sank deeper and deeper into war with its powerful neighbour. By the spring of the following year Cabra Cottage was greeting his news of mass resignations from the RIC with glee. Their delight turned to foreboding when he told them soon afterwards that the falling numbers were to be made up by a new breed released from the jails of England. He told them that the Black and Tans were coming and that an even stranger amalgam of ex-army officers called the Auxiliaries would be joining them.

He heard the unmistakable sound of the engine while crossing Mooney's Field and pulled up the collar of his jacket despite the warmth of the summer evening. He had just stepped onto the pavement on the other side of the Navan Road when the Crossley tender swerved from the Old into the New Cabra Road. The screech of tyres made him jump, as by instinct, behind the shrubbery in front of the Deaf and Dumb and draw his pistol.

When the lorry lurched to a stop, Black and Tans immediately began jumping off the back onto the pavement right beside him. Phil held his revolver tight to his chest, pulled back the hammer and placed his finger on the trigger, staying as crouched and still as a mountain hare under a hovering falcon.

From his hide between the bushes and the Deaf and Dumb's high wall, he observed the unfolding atrocity at close quarters. The Tans pulled a lad of about sixteen down from the back of the truck and stood him against the stone gatepost of the institution. In silence, the officer in charge took a Jacob's biscuit tin from the cab, walked over to the boy and placed it over his head. Without further orders, the Tans lined-up with their backs to the truck, raised their rifles and fired a volley into the biscuit tin. Then, shouldering their weapons by the sling remounted their vehicle and drove off at speed down the New Cabra Road.

When they were out of sight, Phil ran to where the boy had fallen. His head, riveted to the biscuit tin by a half-dozen or more projectiles, had doubled down between his knees. Phil knelt down beside him and recited the Act of Contrition into where he thought his ear might be. Somewhere inside him, he knew death was probably instantaneous but perhaps the soul hadn't left the body yet. In any event, prayer was never wasted.

He was interrupted by the screech of tyres as the Crossley tender did a U-turn and came racing back up the road to see what game their bloodied bait had drawn. Phil hurriedly finished the prayer before dashing down the Old Cabra Road, consoling himself with the certainty that there would be reprisals for this latest outrage — two-to-one was the rule. He would talk to Dunny Kerrigan at the sawmills in the morning.

Rushing past Cabra Lodge he could hear the sound of the lorry approaching the junction. It would only be a matter of seconds before it turned the bend and he would be in full view. He must either make a dash for the high grass in Mooney's Field or brazen it out.

Then something strange and wonderful happened. Two girls in nurses' uniforms emerged from the gate of Cabra Lodge, took him by the arms, one on either side, and linked him back up the garden path towards the cottage door. The tall, dark one took the revolver out of his pocket, lifted up her skirts and stuck it into the waistband of her knickers. They were laughing and talking to him as though they were all off on a summer outing as the British military sped past.

He quickly identified the redhead on the left. It was his neighbour and childhood friend Essie Kerrigan. It took him a few seconds to recognise the other one. It was Lizzie Nolan, the lively young girl who had guided him through the labyrinthine streets of the Liberties during the Rising more than four years earlier.

"Mrs Kerrigan saw a neighbour's child in danger from her bedroom window and sent the two of us out to rescue the laddie in distress," Lizzie said in her cheeky 'Liberty Belle' manner.

"Granny saw the whole thing from upstairs. Jesus, Mary and Joseph, Phil … the poor lad … aren't they terrible animals altogether?"

Phil was a particular favourite of Mrs Kerrigan who had great hopes for him and her granddaughter. They seemed like a perfect match even though Essie was older by a few months. "Sit yourself down now Phil and we'll make you a nice cup of tea," Mrs Kerrigan said fussing over her unexpected visitor. "Put the kettle on Essie … the poor lad must be famished … I'll boil you an egg … Essie, go out to the hen-house and get Phil a nice, big fresh brown one …"

"No. Thank you very much Mrs Kerrigan, you're very kind all the same. I've just finished a big tea in Bamma's. I'm as full as a tic and that's the God's honest truth. I couldn't manage another morsel. You're very kind to offer."

"You'll have a sup of tea anyway to settle your nerves. You've had a terrible shock. "

"One of Macready's 'authorised reprisals', no doubt. He'll learn all about our unauthorised reply before he's very much older."

"There'll be time enough to go into all that in due course. There's no point of going out again tonight. The Tans are all over the place and the curfew begins shortly." Then addressing her other visitor she said, "What do you think of our Irish soldier boy? Isn't he the darkest, handsomest patriot you ever came across?"

"He's a funny sort of a fella, Mrs Kerrigan. Every time I see him, he has a gun in his hand. I think we'll have to take him down to the hospital and have it amputated."

"You met before?"

"A long story … tell you sometime when you've a weekend to spare. Speaking of which," Lizzie said, getting up to go. "It's well for Essie, she's on her weekend's leave but I have to be back inside the nurse's home before nine thirty. So I'll love you and leave you all. Thanks very much for the lovely spread Mrs Kerrigan."

"I'll walk you back. You shouldn't be out on your own in these troubled times," said Phil, raising eyebrows on both Essie and her grandmother.

"The Black and Tans aren't a patch on our RMS … sure they're not Essie? Besides, I'd be safer with the Tans than with the likes of you … you'd get the pair of us shot if you go out again this night."

Lizzie's brave talk hid her great desire to walk with him but she knew he would be in serious danger if he so much as stepped out on the road. She was also concerned about how it would go down with Essie and her grandmother. She knew where he was now and was happy enough with that for the moment. She would visit Cabra Lodge more often in future.

Phil was rapidly being incorporated into her grand plan, though he didn't know it. She had got the job in Jacob's and become a nurse all before her time. Perhaps she would become Mrs McNeill before her time as well and why not?

"I'll walk you back to Grangegorman," said Mrs Kerrigan, putting on her coat and hat. "Whatever about young men and women, they'll hardly do anything to an old fogey like me." Before leaving, she turned to Phil. "Wait until dark then slip across Mooney's Field to Cabra Cottage. I'll drop into number 46 on the way back so as your Aunt Gypsy won't be worrying."

"Will Dunny be in tonight? I have to see him."

"Who knows these days when a mother will see her son? Sure you'll be seeing him in the morning. Won't that be soon enough for you?"

He shook hands with Lizzie and thanked her for coming to his rescue once again and hoped she would have a safe journey back to the lunatic asylum. Lizzie knew he was only prattling to delay the moment when he would have to let go of her hand. She colluded by telling him it would be nice to see him without a gun for once and that she hoped they wouldn't have to wait another four years before meeting again. While they were talking she slipped the gun back into his hand, barrel first.

"We'll all end up being shot if we don't get back home before curfew," said Mrs Kerrigan.

161

Going out the door she looked back at her daughter, sitting on the settle across from Phil and said, "Don't you two get up to anything in my absence."

"Oh granny! For God's sake," Essie said giving Phil a tiny, embarrassed smile.

But her coyness was lost on Phil who stood there transfixed, holding the barrel of his Webley 45, still warm from Lizzie Nolan.

Chapter 31

Ebony and Ivory

Dunny Kerrigan placed the barrel of his Smith and Wesson against Phil McNeill's ear and shouted, "Let him go or I'll blow your fecken head off."

Sonny's flaxen curls, his mother's pride and her main source of joy, were only inches from the whirring circular saw. His face was held fast against the smooth, steel cutting table by the powerful grip of his cousin.

"Not before I cut his bloody head off ... nobody is going to talk to me like that!"

"He's your best friend, for Christ sake, and a comrade ... nothing is worth this."

"He's a stupid cur that's what he is. Who the hell does he think he is, calling me a labourer?"

"But you are the labourer!"

"I only said we couldn't cut the big cedar against the grain and he says, 'What would you know about it anyway, you're only the labourer.' I'll cut the stupid head off him ... I will, so I will."

"Release him this instant and that's an order."

Dunny had found the magic words. As a member of the army of the Republic, Phil had sworn to obey orders from superior officers. Dunny was not only his uncle and employer, he was also the Officer Commanding B Company, First Battalion, Dublin Brigade, Irish Republican Army.

It was such a relief. The explosive eruption that had given him the strength to up-end Sonny onto the saw bench had soon burnt itself out, leaving him at a loss for what to do next. He let him go with mock reluctance.

Dunny made them shake hands and promise to work together for the sake of Ireland, the family and for the good of the sawmill.

"And do something about that bloody temper of yours. There won't always be people around to save you from yourself, yeh tempestuous hoor — yer as briary as yer granny. How the hell did I ever get involved with the Berfords? That was me downfall sure enoughsky. Shower of mad Viking feckers! If it wasn't for your Aunt Nelly, I'd sack you on the spot. Now get on with your work, the pair of yous, and don't let me hear any more nonsense out of either of yeh or so help me ..."

"Sorry uncle Dunny."

"Sorry me arse. Yous have me late for me meeting in town with your bloody codology. Now get that big cedar cut into planed, half-inch planks before I get back. They're for coffins, mind, so best quality only. I promised the joiners they'd have them in the morning. Now get a move for the love of the Divine."

Dunny hid his revolver behind loose masonry in the boundary wall, took his trilby hat off its usual nail and fussed about getting it at exactly the right angle before heading for the big wooden entrance doors. Leaving through the wicket-gate he ducked back in again almost immediately and shouted to his son, "And don't cut it against the grain or I'll cut your wooly head off meself. What were you thinking about you stupid hoor?"

He was no sooner out of sight, than the two young men looked at each other for a moment, then burst into uncontrollable laughter.

"Hey, Phil, now that me aul fella's gone, let's get up on the shed and click a few of the nurses in the Gorman. There's a new one there now and she couldn't fall on her face if she tried. The size of her diddies, and the price of melons ..."

The two boys, giggling with excitement, shimmied up the poles supporting the roof of the lean-to. Then, swinging their legs up onto its corrugated roof they walked gingerly, estimating where the rafters might be beneath the surface until reaching the back wall dividing the sawmills from the Richmond Lunatic Asylum.

Directly below them were the sports grounds, bounded on all sides by elm-lined avenues where nurses strolled or sat on the lathed benches watching patients at recreation.

Sonny was beaming with delight now that he and Phil had made up. In Stoneybatter, they said they were like the keys of a piano — always seen together, one dark and the other light. They nicknamed them 'Ebony and Ivory' because Sonny, whose cherub face was framed in loose blond curls, was constantly seen at the side of his cousin Phil with his mop of uncontrollable, black ones.

Phil was not only his best friend but also the older cousin that Sonny looked up to. Born a year and a bit earlier, wherever Phil went, his younger pal followed in his wake. The only problem being that Phil made a big wake and was often unaware of the turbulence he left behind for Sonny to travel in.

When Phil joined the Fianna, Sonny put on the green uniform a year and a bit later. By that time, Phil had already made squad leader, and Sonny found taking orders from him the most natural thing in the world. Before the War of Independence got properly underway Phil transferred to the IRA. True to form, a little over a year later Sonny joined B Company, slipping easily into the habit of a lifetime by learning the ropes from his cousin.

The contrasts extended beyond the colour of their hair. By the time Sonny reached sixteen, he was the taller of the two but Phil had the greater strength. He could pick up a blacksmith's anvil by the horn in his left hand and raise it over his head. That was good for tru'ppence on most Saturdays outside Harry Head's in Smithfield. It was the entrance price to the Phoenix picture house for the two of them.

Phil was quick to lose his temper but just as quick to forget the offence. Sonny, on the other hand, was more calculating. He never lost his rag but harboured hurt forever.

"Tempestuous hoor ... that was a good one ... he had you there all right ... lucky bastard too when all is said and done."

"What are you prattling about? And not so much of the bastard, I had a father the same as everybody else."

Conscious of Phil's sensitivity on that particular question, Sonny decided to proceed with caution but proceed he would. He wanted Phil to understand something of the difficulties under which he lived so that he might excuse his over-reaching himself in the yard that morning. He wanted to let him know that it wasn't just because Phil had become an employee ... to make him understand that that wouldn't change anything between them.

"It's like this. The two of us have to put up with him as the boss in this kip of a sawmill and as commanding officer in this heap of shite they call a war. How would you like to have him for a father — he's only your uncle, he's my father — that's what I call a lucky ba-- bugger."

"If you grew up in a house with Bamma, you wouldn't be so quick with the 'lucky' nonsense."

"Yeh, but you escaped to Aunty Gypsy when you left high babies. How lucky can you get!"

"How bad you are with Aunty Nelly for a ma? Sure everybody knows she's as soft as butter."

"Too soft … for him anyhow. I swear to God, one day I'll … Wow! I haven't seen her before, look Phil, the tall, dark one over there by the poplars. Jaysus, she'd make a great long-body ride, wouldn't she? I'd love to bang the arse off of that."

In a flash, Sonny dangled inches above the tin roof, lifted at the lapels by a steel talon, a huge right fist hanging precipitously at the side of his face.

"Don't you ever talk about her like that, yeh foul-mouthed little gobshite. That's Lizzie Nolan and if you ever so much as look at her again, I'll cut your balls off and leave your head where it is … for all the bloody use it is to you on top of your neck."

Released again, Sonny rubbed his neck until a fit of giggling overtook him.

"Phil McNeill is in love. Bejaysus, I never thought I'd see the day. You've gone crackers on nursie, nursie. Whatever will Bamma say?"

Temper subsided, it was time for a diversion. Looking over the wall again, he said: "Quick, quick, Sonny. Your one with the big bosom has just come out of the building, quick."

Sonny scrambled so fast he missed an underpinning rafter, causing the corrugated iron to sag dangerously towards the whirring machinery below.

Lazily anchored to the masonry by bent elbows, the two boys spent a delightful morning ogling the young nurses who passed on the other side of the sawmill wall. Now and then, one of the younger ones would wink back causing Sonny to jump up and down on the tin roof, thinking he nearly had his first ride. It was like heaven with the sun on their backs, beautiful young nurses in well-tended grounds at their front and the boss missing for the day.

The pealing of church bells carried on a chill wind blowing up from the sea. Nurses wrapped cardigans around the shoulders of their charges and hugged themselves inside dark, blue cloaks. Soon, men in football togs ran onto the soccer pitches passing a ball one to the other. Their appearance caused nurses to flurry about the avenues, gathering patients into buildings before sweeping in after them, leaving the grounds to wind and football.

"Soldiers!" Phil hissed through clenched teeth, lowering his head and pulling Sonny's down at the same time. "Black-enamelled, bastards … couldn't leave the playing fields to the poor demented who live in the place. That's Macready for you."

"Jaysus, and they were great gas to watch … the inmates, I mean," Sonny enthused in a low voice. "You wouldn't know where some of them would kick the ball or who they would tackle next. Do you remember the time when yer man took the two legs from under his own keeper before nodding the ball into the back of the net? I thought I'd break me bollix laughing."

"They have little enough, the poor unfortunates without a crowd of Tommies taking away their only bit of recreation. We'd better report this. There might be an opportunity here. That would put manners on the Commander-in-Chief of Crown Forces … using his special powers in Grangegorman. *Defence of the Realm* how are you!"

"Now yer talking, Phil! They'd be sitting ducks out there in their little knickers, yards away from their weapons. We'll tell me da when he comes back from the meeting … what's it about anyway?"

"I'd say it's about the Tans murdering the young fella up at the Deaf and Dumb last night."

"Macready is saying it was an authorised reprisal."

"He'll soon find out that unauthorised ones stay just as dead."

"Was it terrible Phil … up at the Deaf and Dumb?"

"Heartless … he was younger than you Sonny."

"They say he wants to bring in martial law for the whole country."

"It looks to me like he has the next best thing. And now he's brought in the Auxiliaries."

And so the two boys spent what was left of the morning, discussing the worsening political and military situation while taking down mental notes on the disposition of soldiers. They memorised their number, the means by which they entered and left the grounds, guards and pickets posted, paying particular attention to the stacking of weaponry.

The noon Angelus rang and Sonny said, "Holy Mother of Divine Jaysus, it's twelve o'clock and not a plank cut. C'mon for God's sake. Me da will be back and there'll be blue murder if we haven't got that job finished."

"I'll line up the big cedar, to be sure we're going with the grain," said Phil as the two young men dropped from the roof down onto the sawmill yard.

"We'll cut it whatever way it comes and fuck him," Sonny replied.

As they worked, Sonny sang a parody of *Marie's Wedding* over the high-pitch of the saw.

"Step we gaily as we go
Heel for heel and toe for toe
Arm-in-arm and row-in-row
Off to Lizzie's wedding...."

But Phil wasn't bothered. His pal was right. He was in love with the tall, dark girl from Mount Brown and was preoccupied with planning his next move. He wondered if the best thing to do would be to approach Essie Kerrigan to ask her pal if he could go walking out with her. Or perhaps get Sonny to ask his mother to ask Essie. It was a hell of a conundrum.

The two boys worked at a dangerously fast pace to try and get the work finished before the boss came back. By two o'clock, however, they were famished with the hunger.

The two boys ate ravenously and in silence until the last piece of burnt crust was washed down with hot tea.

"Phil, when do you think it will end?"

"When the British have had enough and pack off home."

"Jaysus! And when will that be?"

"There has to be a limit, even to the British Empire — 65,000 troops at the moment and they still can't keep a lid on it ... getting worse if anything."

"And they must be fairly bollixed after the war, mustn't they Phil?"

"Commandant McNeill says that Lloyd George will eventually offer a truce, but he'll want the IRA to hand in its weapons first."

"Collins will never go for that."

"Nor will anybody else ... it's all only talk still."

"There you have it! Eh, em, Sonny ... could I ask you to do me a big favour?"

"What?"

"The next time you're over in Cabra Lodge, would you ask your cousin Essie to ask her pal if she would be interested in going on an excursion to Mullingar — Sunday week? It's being organised out of the Broadstone by the 'Total Abstinence' ... very respectable crowd ... young ... ask her to tell Lizzie it will be great fun ... sure you could come yourself ... if you can get a girl to go with you."

"Mullin-fucken-gar! Holy Mother of Divine ... this is getting very serious. Of course I will Phil, I'd be only too delighted ... but em, eh, if she takes you up on it, would you be willing to return the favour?"

"I would indeed. What do you want me to do?"

"Would you ask her about the one with the big diddies for me?"

Chapter 32

The Richmond Lunatic Asylum

"Do you like Phil McNeill?" Essie Kerrigan asked Lizzie Nolan, as she soaped up a patient's massive posterior with a flannel.

Lizzie didn't know what to say, so she went quiet knowing that Essie would not be able to bear it for long. When she did speak, she ignored the question entirely. "We're only a few weeks away from our finals ... and there'll be no second chance, remember."

Conversation petered out as they both became engrossed in what might befall if they failed their 'finals'. It would mean instant dismissal and the shame of telling their families they had lost their good Government jobs with legions of young women begging for any kind of work.

"We might get some idea about what's involved from some of the qualified girls?" said Essie breaking the silence.

"I was reading the parchment on the matron's wall. It says: 'This is to certify that so-and-so, having been duly trained, and after examination by the Medico Psychological Association of Great Britain and Ireland, has shown that she has obtained proficiency in nursing and attendance on insane persons ...'"

"Did it say anything about spooning food into the mouths of 150 women all week long, just to wash it off their other ends all day Saturday? Will they be testing us on slapping a straitjacket on a demented patient when there is restraining to be done or laying them out when they finally give up the ghost? Because if that's proficiency, we'll be dripping in parchments."

"All the same, Essie, won't it be marvellous if we become 'grade threes'? We'll be presented with our medals ... we'll be permanent and everything."

"The extra few bob will be grand,"

"Here, clean out the bath and fill it up again before Charge sends in the next one. I'll get fresh towels and the thermometer."

"Well, did you hear what I said?"

"What about?"

"Jesus spare me, are you going to try me patience or what? Do you like him?"

"Who?"

"Phil Mc-bloomin-Neill. Who else?"

"He's alright, I suppose … Why are you asking me?"

"Alright, me eye! The way you two were looking at each other up in the house … who do you think you're coddin'?" Essie became emphatic. "He wants to know if you'll go out with him?"

"Oh! And how did that come about?" Lizzie said, trying to sound as off-handed as she could.

"Oh! And how did that come about?" Essie repeated in a snooty burlesque impersonation. "He sent that blondie little cherub of a cousin of mine over to the house to ask me if you will go with him on an excursion to Mullingar. Sunday week?"

"Oh! Well, it is my day off."

"That's the most peculiar reason I've ever heard for going out with a fella."

"Tell Phil I'd be delighted."

The patient in all her massive nudity gathered every ounce of dignity remaining. "You're only a pair of probationers," she said. Snapping her shift out of Essie's hands, she pulled it over her head, leaving the two young nurses speechless as she walked back into the ward, head held high, shift caught up at the back, arse exposed.

Lizzie found the Resident Medical Superintendent a bit frightening with his sardonic grin permanently planted on a bony face. Only one step away from God, he'd put nurses on punishment for having a watch out of time with the big clock on the annex tower. His office was above the cells where unfortunate girls and women were once locked away, some for just absconding from their mistresses. Big iron rings dangling from their walls spoke of floggings and miseries untold. Lizzie knew that many of the women in Unit 22 were as sane as her — put out of sight by families down the country because they fell pregnant as girls.

"Late pass. And what is the purpose of this request?" the RMS asked without even looking up from the paper in his hand.

"We are all off to Mullingar on an excursion from the Broadstone, sir."

"And who are the 'we', in this circumstance?"

172

"A crowd of friends, sir … very respectable … organised by the Total Abstinence Society."

"Ah! Total Abstinence … very laudable … just what the country needs these days with the self-indulgent running amok all over the place. Will it be supervised?"

"To be sure, sir."

"Very good child," he said signing the precious piece of paper. Handing it to her, he looked up for the first time saying, "Enjoy your trip to 'the interior'."

The day of the excursion broke bright and sunny. After breakfast, Lizzie went back up to her room and settled on wearing the outfit she had decided upon from the first, despite all the chopping and changing right up to the very last minute. Essie was very generous with her approval, saying she would be the envy of the whole train. "Do you have your late pass?" she asked.

"Yes. I don't have to be back inside this place till curfew. Isn't it grand? Look at me Essie. Will I do?"

"You'll do the fella you have this year," Essie said picking up on an old routine. Then added, "You're only gorgeous. You'd be any man's fancy in that outfit. Go on now and have a great time. Just do me one favour, will you?"

"Anything Essie, what is it?"

"Don't hurt him."

"I wouldn't dream … sure you know well I'm not like that."

The two girls embraced warmly, managing not to disturb the preparations Lizzie had taken hours to complete.

She was all of a flutter stepping out of the grand, granite entrance of the 'Lower House' with the odd, two-horned unicorn looking down on her and Phil waiting at the end of the path. She was sure that all the off-duty nurses would be looking out behind the shutters to see what he was like. She was just as sure they'd be mad jealous.

She couldn't believe the style of him with his baggy pants at half-mast, brown shoes so highly polished you'd see halfway up the leg of his trousers in the reflection, white cricket gansey and a floppy cloth cap of grey Donegal tweed. Lizzie thought he looked like a film star. Her heart was pounding and her head was in a spin over what she might say to him.

He took her hand, placed it on his arm and led the way down Morning Star Avenue.

"I can't tell you how happy I am that you came ... you look lovely."

"Thank you kind sir," she said giving a comical little courtesy with one knee and a slight tug at the side of her skirt. "My pleasure, I'm sure. You're quite the gent yourself." Then folding her hand snugly into the cusp of his arm to link him properly, they walked arm-in-arm down the lane towards Brunswick Street, heedless of the congregating drunks and down-and-outs all around.

In the relative respectability of North Church Street, she leaned across Phil and said, "Here, I'll straighten your tie for you." Continuing to link him with her left arm, she used her right hand to adjust the knot, all the time resting her arm across his chest. She could feel his heart racing at her touch.

"There you are now. You're a right little toff," she said, looking into his face wondering, and not for the first time, what his kiss would be like.

Approaching the Broadstone Station, she nearly died of embarrassment. His pals were all lined-up on the steps and, when they saw them coming, broke into four-part harmony, singing: 'The bells are ringing for Phil and his gal.'

Chapter 33

The Loved

"The best thing about train excursions is always the train journey itself," said John McEnroy as the locomotive steamed under the North Circular Road.

"It's like going to the Aran Islands," his brother James agreed. "Getting to the island is the thing. When you get there, what's there to do?"

Lizzie was delighted that they were all travelling together in the dining car rather than separated in those little compartments strung out along long, dreary corridors. Eight people squeezed together for the two-hour journey to Mullingar — what would they be saying to each other? The dining carriage was so much better — everybody together playing 'Forty Five's', joking, flirting with each other or just looking out the window.

Phil asked her to come with him to the little passage between carriages for a few minutes.

"Let's wave to my Uncle Philip. He'll be on the gates at Cardiff's Bridge," he said, lowering the window down on its thick leather strap.

The two of them were leaning out the little opening as the train chugged up the line towards the level crossing. Lizzie could feel the warmth of his broad chest against her back as she followed the course of the Ratoath Road across the railway line, past the still wheel-race on the deserted mill and the ruin of a great house by the Tolka.

"That's him! That's my Uncle Philip. Give him a big wave," Phil said and she fluttered her handkerchief to a lone man guarding the gates to the dying village. He looked completely abstracted, leaning there, drawing pensively on his pipe.

Phil shouted, "Uncle Philip … this is my girl."

Looking up, he seemed bemused for a moment until recognition caused a brightness to pass across his dark features. As the train took the curve towards Ashtown, she could see him waving his arm backwards and forwards, his hand still clutching the pipe.

"Your girl!" Lizzie said as he pulled the window shut again. "Full of yourself, aren't you?" she chided, then linked her arm into his to re-enter the dining car.

Sitting in the window seat beside Phil, Lizzie was enthralled at how railway and canal followed each other every inch of the way. She had never seen anything so lush and flourishing as the land around and between them. Canal banks and railway embankments were covered by berry-bearing thicket. Wild rhubarb grew as tall as trees and the trees were so ponderous with leaf they arched heavily towards each other to form luxuriant arbours. At the eleventh lock gates she watched two of the whitest, white swans, gathering their signets against the hiss and puff of the train.

In Mullingar, they hired ponies and traps and set off clip-clopping in a long procession for the Lakelands. The sun shone the day long and so windless, there wasn't even a stir in the trees.

Phil said Lough Derravaragh was so lovely, the children of Lir had rested happily on its waters for three hundred years after they were changed into swans by a poisonous stepmother.

There were swans on Lough Ennell too, all swimming around in pairs. She was mesmerised by birds swooping down on fish that broke the surface of the still water to carry them back to their young.

She thought Lough Ennell better than Killarney. Phil McNeill was in Westmeath and she didn't give a tu'penny damn as to who might be in Kerry. He was such a gentleman: entertaining her; wrapping a protective arm around every time the trap threatened to go off the bumpy gravel pathways; taking her hand as she alighted from the train; pulling back her seat in the hotel dining-room and sliding it under her when she was ready to sit. He hung on every word that escaped her mouth, even the most foolish of them.

Everything about the day was wonderful but the journey home on the train was the best fun of all. They took over the dining car again and elected poor Jimmy Wildman master of ceremonies, despite all his protestations. She would never forget the memory of him till her dying day. Standing there with his coat hanging off his shoulders like a cloak, and the smoke from his slender cigarette holder curling around his long hair, he called on each in their turn to do their party piece. Some did comical recitations, others said a poem, but the majority gave a song. Of the latter, only the real singers were called upon and they obliged with a minimum of fuss. She nearly wet herself laughing at the McEnroy brothers doing their party piece, complete with all the risqué actions you might see at a good night in the music hall.

The most amazing thing she found about it was the plummy, English accent James McEnroy affected as he launched into *Cock-a-doodle-do*. Putting Jimmy Wildman's walking stick under his arm like a swagger cane, he marched stiffly up and down the carriage like an officer on parade. His toff's accent juxtaposed with the comical, *double entendre* of the lyrics made for a hilarious turn.

Eventually the MC called on Phil to sing "his own and everybody's favourite." You could hear a pin drop as he stood up, placed a thumb into each side of his waistband, closed his eyes, then poured his heart into *The Rose of Mooncoin:*

"Flow on lovely river, flow gently along … "

He was such a powerful baritone, she was sure he could be heard in the next carriage.

"… I'll dream of you sweetheart, by sun and moonshine …"

Holy God tonight, he was looking straight into her eyes … and in front of everyone.

"On the banks of the Suir that flows down by Mooncoin …"

She was mortified, thrilled, pleased and confused all at the same time.

Thankfully, she was rescued when, by popular acclaim, Jimmy Wildman sang *The Sunshine of Your Smile*. He delivered it so sweetly, the words soothed like balm.

"Dear face that holds so sweet a smile for me …"

Phil was looking into her eyes now and she didn't feel so self-conscious as before, so she smiled back at him, allowing herself to dwell a while on his dark, handsome features.

"Shadows may fall upon the land and sea

Were you not mine, how dark the world would be …"

It was so romantic: they all joined in on the chorus line, couples gazing fondly at each other, including herself and Phil, who were becoming less discreet by the minute.

"My love forever, the sunshine of your smile."

Coming in through Liffey Junction the mood changed completely as the whole excursion party burst into *A Nation Once Again.*

It sounded like a sheet of corrugated iron had blown off an outhouse roof and landed on the pavement in front of them. It gave her a terrible start but she felt so safe on Phil's arm, she just took a sharp breath, held on to him more tightly and picked up the pace. That was before James McEnroy shouted, "Tans!" And everyone scattered in all directions.

All the way from the Broadstone, he and his brother had been singing one risqué music hall ditty after the other. At the corner of Morning Star Avenue she'd remarked on the absence of down-and-outs. There was a deadly silence before that most chilling of alarms: "Tans!"

Turning on their heels, the McEnroys darted back up Brunswick Street, lumps of masonry flying off the walls behind them as they went until they gained the corner at Church Street.

Running past the Regina Coeli with rifle fire coming in bursts and Phil dragging her along by the arm, she realised their own lives were in danger.

"Let go of my arm for God's sake and I'll show you." He did as he was bid and she led him by the hand around to the left of the 'Lower House'. The lights from the Crossley tender were dancing all around the double-horned horse and unicorn over the main entrance as they scrambled over the side gate and into the grounds. She took him past the nurses' home and into the tunnel under Grangegorman Road that led to the 'Upper House' and the male side of the asylum.

"This is as far as I can take you. On the other side of the tunnel you'll see two churches — Catholic and Protestant — and beyond them the playing fields. They're the ones you and your blondie friend are so fond of when there's nurses about. If you can get over the wall on the far side of the fields, you're into the back yards of Prussia Street and on the pig's back. I can't go with you. I'd be sacked if I were found on the male side of the house at night without permission."

He didn't know what to do with his hands. He wanted to take all of her into his palms but only allowed himself the joy of placing them on her forearms. "Will you get into trouble for this?" he asked earnestly.

Her knees were turning to jelly but she tried to hide all indications of the turmoil he was creating. "If they found out, I wouldn't get a day's leave until this time next year, but don't worry about me, you are in much greater trouble. Off with you now ... safe as you go."

Their lips were together for a few delicious seconds, there in the dark as the vaulted walls reverberated with the sound of throbbing engines and boots crunching on gravel. She could hardly hear the dissonance for the heartbeat pounding in her ears. She feared they were racing out of control, so she pushed him away with, "Go on with you now, before you get the pair of us shot."

"Can I see you again?"

"Yes."

"Magnificent! When?"

"I have a day's leave on August Bank Holiday Sunday."

"Where would you like to go?"

"Dancing ... we could go to the Mansion House."

"Why not make a day of it? We could take the train out to the Hill of Howth."

"That would be lovely."

"I'll wait for you at the end of the lane. Is ten o'clock in the morning too early?"

"That's fine, but I'm going home that weekend. Could you pick me up at the top of Mount Brown Hill?"

"Fair enough. Mount Brown Hill it is ... ten o'clock, Bank Holiday Sunday," she heard him say and he was gone, dancing across the playing fields, shoving his clenched fist up at the moon.

Climbing up the wall at the back of Mother Kennedy's, Phil didn't care very much if he was shot or not. He had kissed Lizzie Nolan and it felt like the crowning achievement of his entire life. He hoped the Black and Tans hadn't spoiled things between them. He didn't know a lot about girls but was fairly sure they didn't very much like being shot at.

He dropped down into the back yard of number 46 Prussia Street and crouched in silence among the disused cattle pens until he was sure that the Black and Tan raid was over. Going through it in his mind, it became clear to him that it had been nothing more or less

179

than an attempt to assassinate the McEnroy brothers. All the lads in B Company believed them to be members of Mick Collins's Squad. That was confirmed by the night's events and they rose immeasurably in his esteem.

When he considered it safe he threw a couple of pebbles up at Móna's window. Within seconds his cousin was at the door, opening it so quietly he didn't know it was happening until he saw her standing there in her night shift.

"Come in Phil, quick," she whispered. "I was terrified with all the shooting going on and you out. I imagined all sorts of things happening to you. Are you all right?"

He took her elbow and said in a low voice, "There's no need to worry Móna, I don't want to die for Ireland anymore. I've met the girl I'm going to marry."

Essie was a real trooper, sneaking Lizzie in by the side door without anybody noticing. They were no sooner in the room when the rest of the girls trooped in. They pestered her on the shooting, about every stitch of clothes the other girls wore on the excursion, what they had to eat, how much they had to drink and how far she had let her fella go.

"How did you manage to get a boyfriend as good looking as him?" said a voice above the hubbub.

Phil may well be handsomer than she, Lizzie thought, but he was the more smitten. She had a theory called 'The Loved'. She had noticed that no two couples were exactly equal — that in all cases, one was more loved than the other. She and Essie had whiled away many an evening going through all the couples they knew, married and courting, deciding which one was 'The Loved'.

Before she dozed off that night, Essie put her head around the door again and whispered, "Which of you is it?"

"Which of us is what?"

"Which of you is 'The Loved'?"

"Oh! It's me Essie. I'm almost certain. Isn't it amazing?"

Bath day on August Bank Holiday Saturday had Lizzie Nolan completely worn out. By the time her duty was finished at nine o'clock that evening and she had walked across town to McCaffrey's

Estate, she was only fit for bed. She didn't wake up until her mother called her for the last mass on the following day.

Washing her face in the basin, she was vaguely aware of her mother rinsing the blood out of calves' hearts in the kitchen sink and her father complaining, "We never have herrin' any more. God, you can't beat Howth herrin'."

"We can't have fish for Sunday dinner," her mother was saying in her placatory way. "Roast hearts are lovely. You could have had your Howth herrings on Friday only you weren't here to eat them."

Herrings were no match for O'Malley's on a Friday night, Lizzie thought. Then, it hit her like the slap of a wet fish — Howth!

"Holy Mother of God. What time of day is it at all?"

"The angelus went ages ago. You'll be late for the first offertory in High Street if you don't get a move on. Disgraceful, a young lady going to the drunkard's mass of a Sunday."

"Mother of Mercy, I was supposed to meet someone at ten this morning."

"He'll be well gone by now," her father ventured. "Yeh may settle yer mind on roast hearts today ..."

But Lizzie was already out in the hallway giving a quick swipe to her hair with a brush before dashing out the door and down the estate to Mount Brown Hill.

And there he was, shining in his freshly washed trench coat and a trilby hat that was steamed to newness. She was three hours late and still he waited, anxiously pacing the pavement in his Sunday best. Before he saw her coming, she had slowed down to a casual stroll.

"Are you waiting long?"

"A bit, but never mind. You're here now," he said, relief breaking out all over his smiling face.

She knew then for sure. She was indeed 'The Loved.'

Chapter 34

Hanlon's Corner

James McNeill watched the early setting sun beam its final streams of light through the window of Hanlon's licensed premises. He saw it glint off the rows of bottles lined up along the mirrored shelves. He marvelled at all the colours of the rainbow breaking out on the bevelled edges surrounding the gilded and silvered Powers whiskey sign. Slowly, he turned his attention to the pint glass of McArdle's ale settling on the bar counter in front of him. Holding the glass up against the light he watched the swirls of sediment ever falling towards the bottom of the tumbler like a continuation of the dust particles in the shafts of sunlight.

"Should we all be on our knees, Mr McNeill?" Jimmy Keogh, the bar foreman, asked. "Is it mass you're saying?"

"A bit cloudy, Jimmy. Don't you think?"

"What do you expect for tu'ppence — a bloody thunderstorm?"

"Draw him a pint of Bass from a new barrel, and none of your aul fecken guff, Jimmy. That muck must have been in the cellar since old God's time."

"Oh! Anything you say, I'll swear, Mr Kerrigan. Sean, pull Mr McNeill a nice, clear pint of ale from the barrel we just put on this morning."

The young grocer's curate stopped serving the customer he had been dealing with and immediately began pulling a pint of Bass for Mr Kerrigan's friend. For although Mr Kerrigan was nearly as old as his own father, he was known to be 'one of the boys', and as such, got preferential treatment in Hanlon's.

The young curate slid sideways past the foreman, holding the freshly pulled pint firmly between his forefinger and a thumb that went halfway down along the inside the glass. As he passed the foreman, Jimmy Keogh whispered under his breath, "Have you checked it for precipitation and low cloud amounts? The hoorin meteorological office is in tonight."

"So what's the good word?" said Dunny quietly, once the pint had a moment to settle.

"The general outline of your plan is acceptable enough downtown but the word is 'no' for the moment nonetheless. So hold your fire for now. You've no authorisation to proceed as of yet."

"Why? Everything is in place … we're ready to go at a minute's notice."

"I told you … the Big Fella won't even contemplate it right now. Save it."

"Save it for fecken what? I can't leave a crowd of young fellas on stand-to forever. The two brats in the sawmill have the ground well reckied as it is and the rest are rearing to go. What are we shaggin waiting for?"

"I've said it once but I'll say it once more, so that there can be no confusion about it afterwards. If young Barry swings in Mountjoy, you can plug your Lancaster Rifles. Two mind you — no massacres. The Big Fella is adamant. Two for one. For every one of ours they hang like a dog, we'll bump off two of theirs. That will soon put a stop to it. It's not to be done by ambushing convoys of Crossley tenders, placing mines under culverts or attacks on barracks. They can be playing football, watching the pictures or up a laneway with a quare one, for all he cares, just so long as it is clearly an execution rather than a shoot-out. He wants Macready to get the point. Remember he's English, so keep it simple. No heroic battles, just plain, honest-to-Jaysus reprisals."

"Right enoughsky. We'll wait on further orders so."

"You'll wait for sweet feck all. Kevin Barry's execution will be the signal. If he swings, it's full steam ahead. But two-for-one … remember. And, by the way, keep our two young fellas out of it — 'Ebony and Ivory' — as they're called. They'd stand out like a snot on a hob. Give this job to the two boyos."

"Ebony and Ivory is it? Dixie Minstrels would be nearer the mark, if you saw the pair of them fecken around up in my place."

James enjoyed a moment of quiet pleasure at partaking in what he considered a bit of affable banter between one long-suffering father and another rather than any serious criticism of either son.

Returning to the business at hand, he said, "We're in agreement so. You're better leaving that class of work to the two turf merchants. They have the experience and the cover to go with it."

"Fair enoughsky."

"Does Phil ever say anything about finishing his education?" Commandant McNeill said, as much out of genuine interest as to signal that the business part off the evening had been concluded.

"What is he now — eighteen or something?"

"At Easter."

"The only thing he seems to be interested in studying at the moment is a young nurse from the Gorman. Spends enough time gawking over the asylum wall at her anyway. I've a pain in me arse catching himself and that eejit of mine up on the roof of the shed. Brains to burn all the same … if he ever gets around to using them … me own fella's the self-same."

"They're like two peas in a pod, the pair of them. Sure I know it. I've watched them this long and many a day."

The flow of conversation was interrupted by the appearance of Philip Berford who came in, walked straight up to the counter without giving any sign of recognition, and called for two pints of stout. As was his habit of late, he ordered a glass of Power's Gold Label to drink while waiting for the pints to settle. He took the first sip of whiskey from the tumbler, swallowed it, then sucked in a deep breath across his teeth and tongue to get maximum benefit from the vaporising liquid. From the expression on his face an onlooker would be forgiven for thinking he had just taken bitter alum.

Jimmy Keogh brought the pints to him and threw a glance in the direction of James and Dunny. As Philip polished off the rest of the whiskey a barely perceptible exchange of nods passed between him and his two brothers-in-law. He placed the empty whiskey tumbler on the counter, paid the foreman and carried his drinks to an empty table by the window.

A short while later James and Dunny moved from their secluded spot at the far corner of the bar to join him.

"Are you with someone?" Dunny asked, placing his pint of porter on the table beside Philip's two of stout.

"No. The service around here has gone to the dogs lately. You have to order two at a time if you want any sort of comfort."

"We'll join you so," Dunny said, pulling up a chair. James followed suit.

"Please do."

"How's Bamma?" asked Dunny in a perfunctory way.

185

"As well as can be expected, I suppose. She's getting a grand innings — nearly seventy-four now. And how is my little sister Nelly?" came Philip's more searching rejoinder.

"Still on the baker's list."

"Haven't seen much of her this past while. Bamma was wondering whether she's let out at all or not these days?"

"Doesn't want to leave the confines of the house anymore — afraid of open spaces … a martyr to the aul nerves, you know."

"She could come over at night. It's not as though Cabra Cottage was a million miles from Prussia Street … Gypsy could take her."

"Funny enough, Felim said something similar. But you know Nelly as well as meself … the nerves do be bad … hard to know what to do for the best."

Philip had pushed his point as far as he was prepared to and so moved to change the subject. Addressing his other brother-in-law, he said, "And how's the cattle trade treating you James?"

"Don't see a lot of it anymore … had to ease off … doctor's orders you know … I have this new pressure disease that's going around."

"Me too. The whole country seems to be coming down with it … maybe it's the 'Troubles'. Anyhow, here's to us — first time in years we've been together, apart from funerals, of course," said Philip, taking a slug out of his pint that drained the glass below the halfway mark.

"*Sláinte*," James said as he raised his glass. He took a tiny sip and continued, "There's nothing like death for bringing people together."

"*Sláinte go foil,*" Dunny replied. "And there's nothing like marriage for keeping them apart, wha?"

"Begob, James, what's driven you to the gargle? You were always the one for the pin."

"Doctor's orders, Philip. Felim Mooney says I'm to take a sup at night."

"The perversity of the man all the same. He's putting you on the drink against your will and he's forever trying to get me off it against mine! It's a funny, blinking business this pressure disease, and no mistake."

"It would take the whole of the College of Surgeons to get you off it, me boy," a new voice interjected. The three men looked up with palpable delight at the sight of Felim Mooney coming to join them.

"Begob, if it isn't the body snatcher himself," said Philip.

"Pull up a pew and make up the quorum," said James.

"It's my call. What can I get you?" said Dunny.

"You're very kind, Dunny. Can I have a ball of malt please?"

Catching the curate's eye, Dunny shouted across the bar: "Sean, a ball of malt for Doctor Mooney ... and keep your shaggin thumbs out of the glass."

"Will they hang this young student chap, do you think?" Felim asked when he had settled into his chair.

"Hard to say. There's a lot of diplomatic activity coming from America and a big build-up of political pressure in England itself," said James.

"Then there's the reaction in Ireland. They're going to have to consider that. Especially after making such a bollix of the Rebellion and everything," said Dunny.

"He is as good as in the quicklime," said Philip.

"Depressing thought. What makes you so sure?" asked Felim.

"Superior force. No matter how nicely they dress it up. English rule in Ireland has always been based on superior force — the mailed fist in the velvet glove. For all their talk of constitutionalism and civilisation."

"But he's only eighteen! How do they think that's going to look ... hanging a lad after he's been captured a - a - prisoner of war?" Dunny demanded.

"Doesn't matter a damn. They will not be challenged militarily or politically in Ireland. That's why they have reactivated the *Defence of the Realm Act*. It's why martial law has been declared in Cork and everywhere else they've been stood up to. It allows them do what they are best at — deploying superior force — rule-fucken-Britannia ... that's what it's all about."

"Getting a little carried away, aren't we?" Felim said.

"Carried away, is it? Then explain to me why it is that a disproportionate percentage of the home army has always been based in Ireland ... even when there were no 'Troubles'?" Face flushed, Philip finished the rest of his first pint with a series of long, slow gulps without taking the glass away from his mouth. Placing it back on the table, he took hold of the second pint and moved it around in circles on the table before saying more quietly, "Superior force, that's all it ever was and all it will ever be."

"I'm glad we found a topic on which you have no strong opinions," said Felim to the great amusement of the company. Then returning to the question in hand said, "This young fella and his gang did shoot two soldiers, you know. We ought to bear that in mind."

"There were no gangs involved ... no gangs," said Dunny emphatically. "It was a military engagement. Those Tommies died in battle between two armies. It's no more nor less than soldiers expect in war." He lowered his voice in an attempt to control an old animosity that was beginning to reassert itself. "They weren't trussed up like a couple of chickens and hanged with a bag over their heads."

Felim was about to ask whether an ambush by boys in plain clothes in King Street fell within any recognised definition of military engagement. But he sensed he was again placing himself at the margins of the company, just as his coming from the 'Big House' had done during their childhood. He had spent too much of his life on the periphery ever to want to return to it.

Changing the subject, he said, "I saw young Phil on the Howth tram last Sunday ... with a very nice looking girl, I must say. Introduced her to me ... formally, if you don't mind. He's become a proper gentleman, hasn't he?"

"And did he come over to you or did you approach him?" asked James, positively beaming with surprise and pride at the news of Phil's manly behaviour.

"No, no. He came over to my wife and I as we got off the tram at Howth station. I was quite surprised. 'Dr Felim Mooney, allow me to introduce you to Lizzie something or other,' says he. 'Lizzie ... eh ... Nolan ... that's it ... Lizzie Nolan, I'd like you to meet my uncle, Dr Felim Mooney and his wife, Margaret etc., etc. Fine, tall girl ... very lively too ... a real spark about her ... in the medical business like myself, I believe."

"A mental nurse up in the Gorman," said Dunny. "I hope walking out with her stops him from spending half the day looking over the asylum wall with the tongue hanging all the way down to his boots. Him and that other gobshite of mine."

"You mean an asylum nurse?"

"No. I mean a mental nurse. She'd have to be fecken mental to have anything to do with that fiery fecker."

"And why does he call you uncle? You're not really his uncle," James asked rhetorically, a little hurt at the long denial of his own rightful title by the same young man.

"'Courtesy Uncle'. You know the way it is ... known him since a baby ... calling me uncle all his life ... hardly break the habit now."

Felim felt it unwise to overstay and so left after finishing his drink but not before buying a round for the table. He was hardly out of the door when James said, "Decent chap that. Very ordinary for a doctor, isn't he? There's no nonsense about him."

Philip swallowed the guts of a whole pint at one go and wiped the froth away from his mouth before answering. "Sure didn't we all grow up together around Mooney's Field? The Kerrigans in the lodge at one side, the Berfords in the cottage at the other; and the Mooneys in 'Springfield', back behind the trees."

"Aul Mooney was a great neighbour too, wasn't he Philip? Got you your job in the GMW. Had a nod or a word for everyone on his estate. Very good to the servants, especially the young ones that came up from the country."

"A real flunky," interjected Philip. "Couldn't get his tongue far enough up the arses of the ascendancy. I'll never forget the Gordon Bennett Race ..."

Philip suddenly went quite. He knew he would be far better off forgetting all about the Gordon Bennett Race, Molly Wilson, Columbanus Mooney and all that went with them. "Sean, can I have the same again?" he shouted across the bar.

"No, no. Thank you all the same Philip. I've had me quota for this evening," James said with a finality that left no room for further coaxing.

"I'll just have one more for the ditch," said Dunny.

Philip walked over to the bar and gave his order to the grocer's curate in a low voice. "Just a pint of porter for Mr Kerrigan so, and give me two pints of stout and a large Gold Label while you're at it. Bring the whiskey first. I'll have it while I'm waiting for the pints to cook."

Chapter 35

All in the game

Lizzie Nolan looked out the window of the Nurse's Home just in time to see the big turf lorry approaching the boilerhouse. There was no novelty about the high-backed truck with 'McEnroy & Sons' lettered in white across its blue retaining laths. It was a regular feature in an institution with over two thousand inmates to keep warm, washed and fed especially in winter months. She did wonder for a brief moment why it had parked nearer to the tunnel than the boilerhouse. Her wonderment ended, however, when she saw the two McEnroy brothers alighting from the vehicle.

They'll be up to some devilment or other that pair, she thought. Probably a 'ready-up' with the boilerman. Something like the racket over in Saint Kevin's — same old load checked in, week-in-week-out without so much as a shovel of fuel ever going into the boilers. McEnroy deliveries were usually announced by sods of hairy turf bouncing off the back of the truck and hopping all over the road for the kids of Kirwan Street and Stoneybatter to scurry after. Not on this occasion.

Sergeant William Cuthbert was even more surprised when the young lieutenant with the plumby accent swaggered up to him and gave the order for Private Allen to be called off the pitch in the middle of the game. Coming smartly to attention, he shouted, "Permission to speak sir. We are just ahead of C Company, sir and Private Allen is our best player — centre forward, sir. Can't it wait till after the match, sir?"

"'Fraid not, sergeant. Bad news from home, mother you know. Not my favourite detail sergeant, but someone has to break it to him."

Sergeant Cuthbert was a man well used to death after four years in the trenches and still the thought of a lad's mother dying touched him deeply. He was glad it was the officer's job rather than his own to break the news. It was only right and proper that it should be given to him away from his mates where the soldier could give full vent to his anguish without fear or embarrassment.

He felt deep sympathy for his great loss and guilty for wishing it had been one of the others. Robby Allen was such a joy to watch — more like a dancer than footballer the way he moved on and off the ball. He could put more goals away with his head than the rest of the team with their combined feet. He seemed to be able to stay in the air for ages after everyone else had fallen to earth. Sometimes, he could float up there until he was ready to plant a ball in whatever spot in the net he had chosen.

If it hadn't been for the bloody war and now this lot going mad again, young Allen might have played for West Brom, City or even one of the London clubs.

In his absence, C Company had sneaked in a couple and there was little prospect of a reply, the sub being no real substitute for a real footballer.

If Sergeant Cuthbert was surprised the first time, he was absolutely flabbergasted when the young lieutenant returned to order that Private Reynolds be called off the field as well.

"Sorry sergeant. Didn't realise they were brothers."

"Brothers ... Allen and Reynolds brothers?"

"'Fraid so sergeant. Same mother, different fathers."

"Well, who would have ... Reynolds, you're off ... Higgie, you're on," the sergeant shouted across the field without further ado. As Private Reynolds came across to the sideline, the sergeant gave him a pat on the backside, saying, "Well done lad. Now over to the lieutenant ... he wants a word with you."

When the game finally ended in a six-one defeat, Sergeant Cuthbert felt a little upset for himself also. Losing his best player and the keeper at such critical times in the game had not just cost him the match, it had delivered a humiliating defeat. He was even more upset when the two soldiers hadn't returned in time to board the trucks for Richmond Barracks with the rest of the Lancaster Rifles.

He rambled along the tree-lined avenue curving through the institution's recreational area, past the tennis courts and bowling green towards the steeples he had seen from the soccer pitch. Church would be an obvious place to break bad news, he thought. Not that he had been in many himself but the few times he had been, it was always for something solemn like funerals or weddings.

It didn't take him long to ascertain that there was no one in the sparsely decorated and furnished Protestant church so he crossed the pathway to the more elaborately adorned Catholic one. In the light shining dimly through an attempt at stain glass, he had difficulty discerning the endless number of statues from people and rambled all the way around the walls to make sure.

There was no telling these days, Sergeant Cuthbert thought. Allen and Reynolds might be Catholic ... may have come from Paddies in previous generations ... never know.

But they were not to be found in the Catholic chapel either. Not even in the big wooden confession box he'd peeked into.

He knew that going across to the women's side of the institution unescorted would get him a good kick in the arsehole but he had taken many of those in his career. He had lost many a man to enemy fire but none to the mud of Flanders. That was his proudest boast. Any member of his platoon that fell off the duckboards was pulled out of the quagmire no matter what and he was not about to lose Allen and Reynolds in an Irish bog.

He never smelled anything like the stench in the tunnel. It was worse than the trenches. Dirty friggin Irish, he thought. Using the underground passageway as a public toilet and the place full of lavies.

He walked into it before he saw it. Cold, wet and smelly, it hit him smack in the face. He got such a start, his expletive was still echoing around the vaulted walls when he looked up and saw Private Allen hanging from a meathook in the roof of the tunnel. Beside him dangled Private Reynolds, both rotating slowly in a half-arc, clockwise, then anti-clockwise. The ends of their football shorts had been tied tightly above their knees but he could feel the discharged wastes from their every orifice slowly seeping down their legs into their soccer boots.

The two young men in city suits slipped quietly into the little dairy in 23 Stoneybatter. Before the bell over the street door had stopped clanging they had passed through the door leading to the back room, the last man in closing the door behind him. They stood smartly to attention and saluted the old man with a huge frame sitting behind the kitchen table, sucking pensively on a briar pipe.

"Volunteer Sean Mac an Rí reporting," snapped the first in a mixture of English and Irish.

"Volunteer Seamus Mac an Rí reporting," said the second in a suppressed shout.

"Mac an Rí indeed," said the man behind the table in a quiet, menacing voice. "Mac an Rí — son of the king, is it?" he said, translating the literal meaning of their names back into English. "Sons of the king indeed. Sons of hoor's bastards would be nearer the truth, wouldn't it? Who the hell do you two think you are — Black-and-fucken-Tans?"

John McEnroy knew that he and his brother were in deep trouble. No one had ever heard the commandant swear before.

"We were only following orders, commandant," said James.

"Reprisals for Kevin Barry, commandant," said John.

"Two-to-one," said the one.

"Just as we were ordered," said the other.

"Did you have to hang them like crows on a fence as a warning to the rest? Could you not have done something decent and shoot them like soldiers? Do you want the people in America and Britain thinking that we're as bad as the fucken English, yeh pair of merciless hoors? Well do you?"

"We had our orders sir," said James McEnroy.

"Orders my shittin' arse. Orders from whom? Dunny-fucken-Kerrigan never ordered anyone to be strung up on meat hooks like sides of beef in a butcher's shop ... you pair of savages. I suppose we have to be grateful you didn't skin them alive first."

"Our orders were to do to theirs on the double, whatever they did to ours," said James McEnroy.

"They hanged Kevin Barry on Sunday," said his brother.

"I'm perfectly aware of that and I am also perfectly aware that it was me that gave that order. There was nothing in it about hanging. I can guarantee you that."

"We took our orders on that matter from downtown ... the squad, commandant," said John McEnroy.

"The squad?"

"Afraid so, commandant."

James McNeill could feel the tightness grip his chest until his breathing became a struggle, but he couldn't stop now. "Is that what we learned from the British Empire — how to behave like them? Have the hundreds of years of suffering only shown us how to inflict suffering?"

"We obeyed your orders too commandant," said the younger of the brothers to placate his commander who seemed to be in some sort of distress. James responded with a look of total bemusement, so he continued. "They'll soon find, if they haven't found them already … two Tans with biscuit tins over their heads in the grounds of the Deaf and Dumb."

"That was in reprisal for the young fella they shot up against the wall of the Deaf and Dumb … Mrs Trench's grandson, Brian."

"The one Phil McNeill reported, commandant," said the older of the two.

James could feel the pain coursing down his left arm while a huge weight seemed to be bearing down on his head.

"Get out," was all he could manage.

"The Grangegorman job cost us dearly too," said James McEnroy.

"Supplying the asylum was one of our biggest contracts," said John McEnroy.

"We're on the run now," said James.

"Our business is in tatters," said John

"Lost contracts … business in tatters… will you listen to yourselves? Get out of my sight the pair of you. Dismissed."

At the word of command, the McEnroy brothers did a swift about-turn and left the dairy as stealthily as they had come in.

James McNeill took a series of deep, slow breaths, as Felim had shown him, and waited for the episode to pass.

"Oh! Mary," he called out in desperation to the picture on the wall. "Is this what it's all come to?"

Chapter 36

November

November is the dreariest month, when low cloud drizzles down the grey, sedimentary rock from which much of the city is built, making courthouse, barracks and mill glisten damply and the populace feel it is living on the inside of a pewter piss pot. Crowded trams overpower with body smell and wool oil rising from saturated overcoats. The hordes of homeless huddle in their doorways, steam barely rising off their sodden sacks and rags.

Growth leaves the grass in Mooney's Field and migrant birds flee its hedgerows. Wild and cultivated fruits lie plucked and packed in boxes of dry straw or sealed in airtight jars. Behind the trees at the end of the field, Springfield makes its winter appearance through the atrophied veins of leafless branches.

The only bright spot on Phil's horizon was the arrangement he had with Lizzie to spend her next day's leave together. He was going to really impress her with the outing he had planned. He would take her to the Zoological Gardens in the afternoon, treat her to high tea on the Green in the evening and go to the pictures that night. She had so few days off, he was determined to spend every one of them with her and to make each very special. Even the damp, depressing month of November could not put a damper on the day he envisaged.

He was also conniving with Essie Kerrigan to find a way of getting Lizzie to spend Christmas Day in Cabra Cottage. He hated Christmas even more than he hated November. Lizzie's presence would crowd out even the most awful childhood memories. Essie was a great ally. She had already started dropping a word in here and there about how she would love to spend Christmas with a boyfriend if she had one. As she and Lizzie went about their daily work she would describe how cosy and convivial it would be in the cottage.

"I'll be dropping over in the afternoon, of course. I wouldn't miss it for diamonds. We'll have great gas playing twenty-fives, ludo and housie-housie. We'll eat plum pudding, mince tarts and drink elderberry wine until we're all as full as ticks."

She would think of other lures to drop into conversation as the days went by — things that she knew Lizzie could only have read about in the Liberties — cranberry sauce on the turkey and brandy sauce on the pudding.

Similar strategies occupied Phil's mind as he dug a hole for a fence post separating Mooney's Field from the kitchen garden of Cabra Lodge, when Essie Kerrigan emerged from her kitchen door.

"Hello Phil," she said in a voice as leaden as the sky above them.

"What's up Essie? You've a *smig* on you that would go down well at a Freemason's ball."

"I'm afraid I'm the bearer of bad tidings."

He saw so many things happening in vivid detail during the eternity between the flagging and delivery of her bad news. He noticed the big Rhode Island Red heading back to the hen house from the hedgerow and concluded she was laying out. He made a note that he must cut down the ragwort illegally growing past its deadline on the embankment. And all the time he worried that something terrible had happened to Lizzie or Mother Kennedy and prayed that God would spare him that. Perhaps Lizzie couldn't spend Christmas with them but all would not be lost if he could go over to McCaffrey's Estate and be with her for part of the day at least.

"Lizzie told me to tell you she doesn't want to see you anymore."

It was the last thing he expected and it took some time before its ramifications sank in.

"Why? What have I done? Has she found somebody else? Is she alright?" He would have overwhelmed Essie with the flood of questions pouring out of a mind in total turmoil had she not spoken again to stem the flow.

"She's perfectly alright and she hasn't found anybody else. You've no need to fret on that account. I'm sorry but I can't tell you anymore. You'll have to ask her yourself about the whys and the wherefores."

"How in the name of God can I do that if she won't even see me?"

"Go to her Phil. You two are a great match. Don't let it slip away over a load of political nonsense."

"What political nonsense? We hardly even discuss politics. For God's sake Essie tell me what's going on and stop giving me conundrums. They're giving me brain-fever and my head is fit to burst as it is."

"Her day off is Sunday the twenty-first. She'll be going home to Mount Brown the night before. So if you're in Morning Star Avenue after nine in the evening, you should bump into her. But don't tell her I told you so. It's as much as I can do Phil ... I'm very sorry."

She didn't seem to be at all surprised to see him waiting under the gas lamp at the top of the lane, nor did she make any overt objections to his walking along beside her, but then she hardly acknowledged his presence at all. Just looked ahead, cheeks as tight as crab apples. The sun had long since gone down and an early frost was settling on the old sacks covering the down-and-outs sleeping rough outside the locked hostels. As they crossed Brunswick Street in silence, he tried to open the conversation as casually as he could. Pointing to the spire of St Michan's in Church Street he said, "Did you know Lizzie that the Dublin soil is so dry, it has preserved bodies in the crypt under that church for centuries? Hard to believe in a place as damp as this, isn't it?"

"It would suit you and your friends better if you tried to preserve a few live bodies for a change." He had never heard such an acerbic edge to a woman's voice before, except for Bamma. He quickly came to the conclusion that going around the bushes might be the wrong approach to adopt at that moment and decided to be more direct.

"What's upsetting you Lizzie? If I've done something to hurt or insult you, just tell me what it is and I'll make it up to you. You know I will. I wouldn't do anything to hurt you."

"Can you bring those two poor Tommies back to life that were left hanging like game animals in the tunnel I so foolishly showed you?" she said and began to walk quicker as if to put distance between them.

"What Tommies are you talking about? There is a war on, or haven't you noticed? A lot of Tommies and 'Boys' are getting killed every day of the week," he replied, a little breathless for keeping up with her.

"Full well you know which soldiers I'm talking about. The two left to swing in their own excrement in the tunnel up at the asylum." The spectre drove her more quickly towards the river.

"Lizzie, you have to believe me, I had nothing to do with that."

"Don't lie to me Phil McNeill," she snapped back at him. "I won't be able to bear it if you heap lies on top of the rest of it. I know you were involved ... and to think it was I that showed you the tunnel ... may God forgive me." She was nearly running now, holding her handkerchief to her mouth so that he wouldn't hear the ugly sounds of crying.

"Lizzie, we won the general election two years ago and the British chose to disregard the result. And if we have a landslide victory in the next one they'll ignore that too if they don't like what the people vote for. So, how are we to become an independent nation unless we fight for it?"

"Fighting is one thing but what happened in that tunnel is a horse of a different colour and well you know it."

"So you accept we have to fight and I know you thought what Kevin Barry did in King Street was very brave. So why was his shooting two soldiers dead so very different from killing them by any other method?"

She stopped and faced him with blazing eyes. "Because it makes us no better than them. If you can't see anything wrong in what happened in that old tunnel, then all I can say is, I'm very sorry for you." She began to move off again, then suddenly turned and screamed at him, "It's where we had our first kiss and it's all ruined now ... ruined, everything is just ruined."

She was in full rush as he shouted after her, "I wasn't saying I agreed with what happened there. I'm just trying to talk the point through ..."

"You're just talking through your bloody hat," she said without turning and shot across Queens Street Bridge leaving him speechless and alone on the other side of the river.

Chapter 37

Bloody Sunday

"Jaysus Phil, did you hear the news?" Sonny Kerrigan said as he approached Phil near the junction of Prussia Street and the North Circular Road. "I hear they got a whole dose of them in the early hours of this morning," he continued breathless with excitement.

"Got who?"

"'G' men ... from the Castle — the 'Cairo Gang'. The 'Squad' plugged a whole bunch of them before they even got out of their beds this morning. Jaysus, the rest of them will be shitting bricks from now on. They'll be sleeping standing up like they do in Biddy Brewer's lodging house. Only it won't be Biddy Brewer that will be cutting the rope that wakes them, aye Phil?"

"Where did you get all this?"

"The commandant came in to see me da this morning. Told him we're all to keep the head down for a while ... until the fuss blows over. Jaysus, you couldn't do better than go to the All Ireland in Croker, could you Phil? Look at the thousands flocking to the game. What do you think Phil?"

"You don't see too many military at GAA games and that's for sure," Phil answered abstractedly.

Going to an All Ireland Final should have been something to look forward to, especially when Dublin was playing Tipperary, a county better known for its prowess in the game of hurling rather than football. The cup was as good as in the bag. But he had been supposed to be spending the day with Lizzie and Sonny didn't stand up much as an alternative.

Sonny, on the other hand, was delighted to be spending more time on his own with Phil. It wasn't that he disliked Lizzie, in fact he thought she was great fun. It was just that he felt excluded by her. Even when she wasn't around, he could feel her presence in the way Phil's mind was always elsewhere. He wouldn't even go clicking other girls with him anymore.

Phil, on the other hand, was not so circumspect around his cousin's sensitivities. It wasn't anything intentional, it was just that

Sonny was always there. Going to the match with him was nothing special but it was a sight better than being on his own all afternoon.

The game was as fast, skilful and dangerous as any they had ever seen. Being from Dublin, Phil and Sonny had a partisan interest in the outcome like the ten thousand shouting, clapping and arguing supporters from the capital packed all around them.

"Begob Phil, that's some going. Did you ever see anything like the way yer man goes down the wing for a run?" Just then, Michael Hogan tipped the ball from his hands to his incept, ducked and chicaned around two backs before dropping the ball to meet his swinging toe. It hung in the air in front of the goal for what seemed like an age. The Tipperary forwards crowded in to capitalise on a great scoring chance but a huge Dublin back soared out from among them, knocking most to the ground in the process. Plucking the dropping ball out of the air, he took three steps, hopped it once and then cleared it into the other half with an almighty kick.

"Jesus, Phil look at the way that hoor moves off the ball. He's always in the right position no matter what end of the field … impossible to mark the hoor."

Within minutes, Tipperary Captain Mick Hogan responded with a mighty toe from twenty yards that sent spectators at the back of the goal posts ducking for cover as the leather ball flew in among them. And so it went with attack and counter-attack, one following on the other as the athletes fought hip-to-hip for every ball.

An aeroplane circling overhead drew the crowd's attention away from the contest on the field. All eyes were upwards, watching its flight with a mixture of curiosity and foreboding. Some half expected a display of aerobatics and wondered why over Croke Park. Others reasoned it was a show of military power and wished it would soon end so that the game might continue without distraction. A few began to make their way to the wall at the railway end.

A red flare was shot from the cockpit and the trickle of people drifting towards the railway end grew into a steady stream. It became a flood as Black and Tans entered the grounds and began to take up positions. An officer on the wall fired what most thought was a blank from his revolver.

Phil was so glad he and Sonny were at the canal end when the Tans opened up in earnest. The Tipperary captain was the first man on the field to fall and the man whispering the Act of Contrition into his ear became the second. When they turned their machine guns on the spectators the current turned in full spate away from the direction of the gunfire towards the railway end. While some were firing indiscriminately into the crowds others were taking their time, picking off those scrambling to escape.

Phil and Sonny were standing with their backs against the wall at the canal end, when the gunfire started. All around them, people were falling over each other to escape while others just fell where they once stood. The young girl who had been standing in front of them with her fiancé's arm around her waist lay dying in his arms. The boy who had held his father's hand throughout looked like he had been bayoneted to death and still he held onto his father.

"Sonny, do you remember 'boxing the fox' over the convent wall?" Phil whispered to his cousin as they flattened themselves to the ground.

"Yes," he said.

"Right so, let's go on the word … NOW!" shouted the older cousin and immediately resumed his position against the wall, hands cupped in front of him.

In a flash, Sonny had his right foot in the firm stirrup of Phil's hands and was being hoisted up until he could grip the top of the wall. Then, reaching back down, he took Phil's proffered hands and pulled him up, counter-balancing the weight with the other half of his own body dangling on the safe side of the wall.

Dropping down onto the towpath, Sonny was immediately pinned to the ground by an escaping spectator who had lost part of his head to a round of 303 as he went over the top. Phil turned the mortally wounded man off his cousin and recited the Act of Contrition into his remaining ear, so that his soul might go straight to heaven. As he prayed, men poured over the wall, streaming out in several directions to meld with the surrounding city. Some went east towards the docks, others south across the muddy bed of the waterway, hoping to find safety in the surrounding streets. None went west for most knew that Mountjoy Jail lay close in that direction.

"Is he dead? … Holy Mother of Jesus he's dead … Will you look at what they did to his face … Christ will you look at your own face … pouring blood … you've been shot Phil … Sacred Mother, what's going to happen to us all?"

"We're going to be grand," Phil responded, feeling the warm sticky mess around his temple. "It's nothing. Just a flesh wound. It'll be fine once it's cleaned up."

"But what are we to do Phil?"

"Take it handy for a minute. We have to find out what's going on first. If there's a roundup, they might be waiting for us in Prussia Street or in any of our known haunts. For all we know, they might be carrying out massacres all over the place like they do in India and Africa. Uncle Philip will know the lie of the land … come on, let's go … we'll head for Cardiff's Bridge."

"Jaysus, you're not suggesting we go under the walls of the 'Joy', are you?"

"It's the only way. We'll just have to be very careful. It'll be safe enough once we get clear of Phibsboro."

All his life Sonny had given Phil the benefit of the doubt and he decided that this was no time to change the habits of a lifetime. As they set off to follow the course of the Royal Canal to Cardiff Bridge, gunfire was still coming from the sports ground. Taking a last look back, they saw a young man on top of the wall, who was gently dropping his girlfriend onto the towpath, give a sudden jerk then fall down on top of her.

It was slow going with the two boys constantly on the lookout for signs of British military activity. They also had to stop from time-to-time to clean the blood away from Phil's eye with the soft moss growing along the canal bank. A Crossley tender going over Binn's Bridge forced them to take cover in the reeds. After that, Sonny imagined he heard the distinctive sound of their engines at Cross Guns Bridge, Liffey Junction and every other junction of road and canal until both their nerves were frazzled.

By the time they reached Cardiff's Bridge they were hungry, thirsty and near exhaustion. Desperation was added to their list of woes when they left the towpath at Inspiration Bridge and found the level crossing unmanned. Sonny was close to tears. "Jesus, Mary and Joseph, Phil, what will we do now?"

"No need to worry, he's probably gone to Cosy Finnigan's for a pint."

The two boys set off down the hill towards the deserted village. The ruin of Cardiff's Bridge House stood gaunt on their right, all its windows broken by the last children to leave the hamlet. On the left lay the shell of the old iron mill, its millrace long since stalled and rusted, its spent stack leaning for a fall. Looking at the wide-eyed face of his cousin, Phil said, "Don't worry Sonny we'll get something soon. Uncle Philip is sure to be in The Jolly Toper, you can bet your life on it."

Sonny looked at the desolate little cottage that was The Jolly Toper, the only building in good standing in what was once a thriving community by the Tolka, and said, "Who'd want to be found dead in that kip?"

"There's not many trains on winter Sundays. He's probably slipped down for a couple to while away the time."

"I hope to Jaysus he has, that's all I can say."

It was easy to spot Philip Berford in the low-ceilinged bar with one eye of a window half closed by solid panes — he was the only customer there.

"What in the name of God happened to you?" he said to his ward as he tried to clean away the caked blood off the side of his face with a handkerchief dipped in his own whiskey. "That's an unmerciful gash you have on your temple."

Safe at last, Phil began to feel the pain at the side of his head for the first time. It got progressively worse as he told his guardian of their escape from Croke Park and about the many that had not been so lucky. As he talked, the older man continued to dip and dab from his tumbler to his ward's temple. The quieter Phil got, the more animated his guardian became.

"Divine Jesus, what's the world coming to at all? Shooting sportsmen and spectators ... thank God you're safe anyhow ... you're not hurt anywhere else are you son?"

"I'm fine Uncle Philip," he said softly, surprised and confused by his guardian calling him son. "It's just a graze, honestly."

"Graze me arse, they nearly shot the bloody head off of you, curses of Jesus on them, the bastards."

"I'm grand, Uncle Philip, I swear ... when you think of what happened to so many others ..."

"Well that's it for sure. You have seen the beginning of the end for British rule in Ireland. It's only a matter of time now."

"Come into the back and I'll fix you up. Come on now quick the pair of you before someone sees you and the state you're in," said the little stout woman opening the counter flap to let Phil and Sonny in behind the bar to her back kitchen.

Cosy Finnigan gave them beef tea to rebuild their strength and sweet tea to steady their nerves. Then she cleaned out Phil's wound with disinfectant, before covering it with a hot poultice.

Later, when she felt the poultice had drawn most of the poison, Cosy got her husband to stitch up the cut with a needle and cobbler's waxed-hemp. Then she placed a cold poultice of carbolic soap mixed with sugar over the laceration, and wrapped a strip of white bed linen around his head to hold the preparation in place.

"You're a real soldier now. That's the real Ally Dally," said Cosy, admiring her work.

"There's divil a fear on you with that injury ... clean as a whistle ... ne'er a round nor a ricochet ... a piece of flying masonry more like ... no lead in it anyway. You'll be better before you're twice married," Cosy's husband said.

"Lie down there on the settle and rest yourself awhile. I'll get himself to drive you back to Prussia Street in plenty of time for the curfew. You'll be home and dry before you're twice married," Cosy echoed.

As he dozed on the settle, Phil wondered why everyone wanted to get him married twice, while he only ever wanted to be wed only once — to Lizzie Nolan. The ache on his temple was as nothing compared to that great want.

Chapter 38

Little by little

Turning down beds was Lizzie's second least favourite job but its tedium was always lessened for being shared with Essie Kerrigan. Together they could keep up a constant chatter about this and that, gossip for ages about everyone they knew or conspire with seditious humour against the institution's management.

There was only one subject on which they were circumspect and that was Phil McNeill. They did talk about him. In fact, they did it all the time. It was just that Lizzie felt that telling Essie every detail of what went on between them would be like telling his sister. Maggie Smith was her best friend in Mount Brown and she told Maggie absolutely everything that went on in great detail. Essie, on the other hand, was still her best friend in Grangegorman but she was so protective of Phil, Lizzie thought it wiser to hold back.

They were turning down the starched white pane of the umpteenth bed when straight out of the blue, Essie said, "I see they published the coroner's report on the deaths in the tunnel."

The whole ward held its breath. The institution had been largely untouched by either the Troubles or the Great War except for shell-shocked soldiers cowering around the Upper House and English footballers commandeering the playing fields. Staff and inmates alike took the first in their stride and the second as not much more than an irritant. But the deed in the tunnel was so dark, it filled their talk with macabre variations.

"And where did you see that?"

"In the *Freeman's Journal* … yesterday … when I was at home. 'GRUESOME MURDER IN MADHOUSE TUNNEL,'" said Essie, drawing out the headline before her face with both hands as though it were written on an imaginary concertina. "'BIG SURPRISE AT INQUEST,'" she said with index fingers and thumb narrowing to indicate a sub-heading.

Lizzie wanted desperately to know the findings, but knew asking Essie further questions would only elicit more prevarication. She wanted to shout, "Oh come on Essie! What else did the paper say?"

But that would just let her know she was hooked and she was not in any humour to be played out on this particular subject. So she remained silent until Essie couldn't stand it anymore.

"Did you know they were shot first?"

"Shot?"

"Yes, shot. Stood up against the wall and shot through the heart, the pair of them, and then strung up be the neck for good measure."

Lizzie felt relieved, confused and guilty all at the same time. She couldn't reason out why the killings were easier to bear for knowing the two young men were dead before they were hanged. Yet it was so. Perhaps that's what helped change her mind.

Gradually the deaths in the tunnel became less and less of a talking point. Soon Privates Allen and Reynolds became just two more soldiers to join the myriad that death had taken during the six years since the great fanfares of 1914 — no more remarkable in conversation than the tens of thousands who were shot in the slaughter from Salonika to the Somme.

Every day Essie dropped something new into the equation. They were wheeling around the medicine trolley when she said casually, "I must bring home some of those painkillers and antiseptic for Phil. I'll slip over to Prussia Street with them after work. I'd be over and back again before lights out."

She said no more, just continued to dole out pills and linctus until this time Lizzie broke.

"Did he cut himself or something? Trick-acting with that Sonny in the stupid sawmill again I suppose."

"Cut! Cut isn't the word for it. Nearly killed stone dead he was … only by the mercy of Jesus is he still with us at all."

"For God's sake Essie, stop beating around the bush. What happened to him? I want you to tell me this minute."

"Didn't find out myself till I went home on my day's leave yesterday. Bloody Sunday. That's what happened to him. Nearly had his brains blown out by the Tans in Croke Park. I'm supposed to say nothing, so mum's the word."

"Sweet Mother of Divine Jesus! How bad is he? Will he be alright? What in the name of God was he doing in Croke Park in any case?"

Lizzie had given Essie the opening she had been fishing for and she played it out like a professional.

"I don't know. So far as I was aware, he was supposed to be going to the Zoo that day but sure you might know more about that than me."

"Was that the same day as we ..."

"It's not for me to say, but it's a great pity he didn't go to the monkey's tea party like he was supposed to because it very nearly cost him his life."

With her quarry now well in sight, Essie decided to drop a depth charge. "If it wasn't for Cosy Finnigan, he'd be in the clay with his poor mother, light of heaven to her, up in Glasnevin, this very day."

"WHO is this COSY FINNIGAN?" Lizzie asked with slow deliberation.

"Oh, just a lassie from the inn at Cardiff's Bridge. Washed, dressed and poulticed his wound until it was clean as a whistle. Mopped his brow for hours on end, I believe. Saved his life, she did."

With so many of the inmates committed to Grangegorman because of the drink, it didn't take too much time to establish that Cosy Finnigan was a stout lassie of sixty who still sported a healthy husband. Essie hadn't exactly lied, but Lizzie was quick enough telling her that it came as near as damn it was to swearing.

But the seed had been well sown. Lizzie began experiencing jealousy for the first time but about what she was not sure. It came with a vague feeling of guilt and a growing fear that her eye might be wiped.

Essies's daily reports on his slow recovery did nothing to lessen any of these emotions. "You never saw anything like it in all your born days. I nearly broke the scissors trying to remove the stitches. Cobbler's waxed-hemp, as thick as bailing twine. He'll be marked for life."

As the days moved on towards Christmas, the worry began to gnaw at her that she was being replaced. Since their first meeting during the insurrection, she had dreamed about dressing his wounds and mopping his brow and now other women were doing it. Not alone that, but he was likely to get into even worse trouble with her not around to watch out for him.

Perhaps it was that that did it!

*****

All five of the nursing staff on duty were up to their ears serving dinner with 'due regard to order and decorum' to the 150 patients in Unit 22. For even eating was prescribed in the Regulation Book. Lizzie and Essie were running out of breath getting food to everyone while it was still hot when Staff Nurse knocked the wind out of them entirely.

"Miss Nolan and Miss Kerrigan, you are to report to the RMS's office immediately."

Seeing the scarified look on their faces, she moved to assure them that there was no need to fret, that it was good news but they were not to let on to the RMS that they knew.

"Just look worried," she said as they left the dining hall.

"Well, that's a new one on me," said Lizzie who had never heard of anyone being sent for, just to hear good news. Many a nurse went up there to be queried in minute detail about some incident they had written into the Report Book, or to answer why they had not performed a particular duty according to the 1913 Regulation Manual — Grangegorman's bible.

On the way up the stairs Essie said, "Lizzie do you remember that misfortunate attendant who wished Johnny a good morning, only to find himself suspended for being drunk on duty — on the grounds that no one had ever said good morning to him before?"

"Stop it Essie, will you? I'm nearly wetting myself as it is."

At the top of the stairway the great mahogany door was wide open and the RMS standing by his desk waiting, sardonic grin firmly plastered across a funereal face.

"Come in, come in … my two star pupils," Dr John O'Connor-Donnellon said through clenched teeth. Essie and Lizzie nearly fell out of their standing.

"My heartiest congratulations," he continued, shaking each of them by the hand in turn. "You both got top marks in your finals … best in your year. I have also noted that you are exemplary in the humane way you administer to the insane persons and idiots in your unit. Well done, well done."

His perpetual grin grew so wide they wondered if he was sneering, if his words were to be taken as humorous, serious, cynical or malicious. Whatever it was the whole experience grew more unnatural by the second. Taking two medals off his great oak desk, he told the girls of his insistence on presenting them personally.

"You are now Grade Three nurses and permanent employees of the Crown. Your parents will be proud of you, I am sure. I've had these certificates framed in the carpenter's shop. Hang them on the wall in your rooms. They will act as a reminder of the high standards you have achieved today. Do your best to maintain them."

Lizzie and Essie sat on the hard bed in Lizzie's little room reading their parchments over and over.

It was grand having Essie there but it wasn't enough. She wanted to share her great moment with someone who meant even more to her.

Perhaps that's what did it.

Or perhaps the decisive influence was the pen pictures of Christmas in Cabra Cottage that Essie drew. "All of them: the Berfords, Kennedys, Kerrigans and, of course, the one and only McNeill in the family will all go off to midnight mass in Aughrim Street to keep Christmas Day clear for feasting and fun. There'll be turkey and ham, trifle, Christmas cake and Christmas pudding, tarts, sweets and elderberry wine. In the afternoon, everybody will gather in Cabra Cottage for cards, housie-housie and maybe even a few songs."

Through the middle days of December, Essie transformed Cabra Cottage into Dingley Dell, until Lizzie could almost see the light glowing across Mooney's Field from snow-framed windows.

As the month wore on she missed Phil more and more. It was as though some part of her had been amputated, leaving a place that itched and pained though it could not be seen or touched.

The note was the last straw. Essie stuck it in her apron pocket as she stood on the bed banging a nail into the wall with the heel of her good 11s/6d boots, to hang up her certificate.

"Phil asked me to give you this," she said, pausing to admire her friend's handiwork. "It suits you." Then she left as quickly as she came in.

A cool composure settled on Lizzie as she opened the velum paper envelope. It stayed with her until she reached the end of the message. Then she burst out crying.

46 Prussia Street
2ⁿᵈ December 1920

My dearest Lizzie

I beg you to believe I have never spent a single moment of our time together for any purpose other than to love and cherish you. You are far and away the best thing that has ever happened to me, the only sweetheart I will ever know.

I had often thought that going through the world without either mother or father was lonely but hadn't realised what loneliness was until you walked away from me that night on Queens Street Bridge. The world has been a desolate place ever since. I go to bed each night in dread of the morning. Every time I look in the mirror to shave, I see you there beside me. All day long in the sawmill, I am tortured by the knowledge that you are just on the other side of the wall. My head is full of the smell of your hair, my daydreams full of the life we promised to each other.

Please give me some hope. Please let me believe that there is something I can do to close the rift that has come between us.

Even if you cannot bear to be my girl again, would you please come to Cabra Cottage for Christmas for I have filled my family with expectations of you?

Please send a note through Essie to say that you will spend Christmas with us. Without you it will be more like a black fast than a feast day.

I live for your word.

Yours forever.

Phil McNeill

Perhaps, that's what did it.

Chapter 39

The Parson's Nose

Phil McNeill was plucking the last of the small feathers from under the turkey's wing when she walked in the door with Essie. Tall, dark and attractive, she held the attention of everyone in the room. Addressing herself immediately to Bamma, she said, "Mrs Berford, you must think me awful, arriving on top of you with one hand longer than the other. Can I at least take that beast from your grandson and draw it for you?"

"You're expected young lady and welcome. Do you know where the scullery is outside?" asked Bamma, giving Lizzie one of her rare smiles. "Sure, never mind. I'll go out with you; I've a mountain of spuds to peel. Phil, will you milk the cow like a good lad, after you've cleared the feathers off your good clothes and the floor? You look like a bursted eiderdown ... and dig another few potatoes out of the clamp ... we're going to have a big table today, thank God."

"I'm off to me mother's, I'll see you all in the afternoon," said Essie, kissing Lizzie and winking at Phil as she went out.

Lizzie hung her overcoat on the back of the door, rolled up the sleeves of her new dress and put on the wrap-around apron Bamma handed her, all the time observing Phil through the corner of her eye. She was greatly relieved to see that his wound wasn't so serious as she had feared. It hadn't spoiled his looks in any event. He was still the handsomest man in Dublin.

She walked jauntily over to him, closed his mouth by gliding her fingers gently under his jaw before taking the turkey from his hands. The tingling was still running up and down his jaw, long after she disappeared out to the scullery to help Bamma.

Phil had never seen such harmony and contentment in Cabra Cottage as he did that Christmas. Something told him he might never see it again. He had often heard the McEnroys say that you can't get out of life alive. But what did eventuality matter with everybody chatting happily and Lizzie sparkling beside him? It was enough.

Bamma too rejoiced in having a full house with all her surviving children and grandchildren around her. She was delighted with Lizzie and was sure she was just the sort of girl to make a man out of her grandson.

Móna and Dido couldn't get enough of her either, asking all sorts of questions about the other side of the city, where she bought her clothes and how she met their cousin. Even Nelly, who had overcome her fears sufficient to get there before dark, sat taking it all in contentedly.

Lizzie placed steaming tureens of spuds, sprouts and cabbage on the table while Mother Kennedy put out the knives, forks and spoons.

"Dunny, will you carve?" Bamma asked her son-in-law, as she placed a massive hen turkey on the table, still sizzling on its salver.

"Fair enoughsky," came the familiar reply as Dunny took up two carving knives and began swiping their cutting edges across each other. The movement got quicker and quicker until it looked like he was duelling with himself. After several minutes, he tested the new edge by slicing a sliver off the ham and dropping it into his mouth.

"Chef's privilege," he said. Then, having pronounced it delicious, he turned to the diners.

"Some prefer the leg while others go for the breast. What's your choice, young Phil?" he said sending a ripple of embarrassed titters around the table.

"I'll have a leg, if that's all right with everyone, Uncle Dunny."

"Good enoughsky. A sure sign of maturity that — a man going for the leg instead of the breast."

"Isn't he a terrible man altogether," said Aunt Nelly above the giggling.

Bamma's voice was low, slow and deliberate. "That will be enough of that, thank you very much Donal. Carry on with the carving before we all fall down with the hunger."

"You will have the 'parson's nose' so," said Dunny cutting away the snout of gristle hanging over the beast's rectum. A serious bout of laughter broke out as all the family wondered who would end up with the disgusting object this year. It was one of Dunny's regular Christmas jokes to secrete it in someone's handbag before the day was out. He always managed it in the end, no matter how they watched or hid them.

When Bamma had said 'Grace' she looked around the table with satisfaction. All of the wider Berford clan had come to pay tribute. All looked happy and healthy, tucking into the feast she had prepared for them except Lizzie. She took particular note that Phil's girl had table manners enough to wait until the host began eating before beginning herself and added that virtue to her willingness to carry her share of the day's work.

She might not be a teacher but a nurse would do well enough for her grandson who didn't even bother to finish his schooling. She took great comfort too in observing that Lizzie was a very strong character —the sort of woman that makes a man out of a boy — just what Phil needed.

Uncle Philip limited himself to a couple of glasses of elderberry wine and spent most of the dinner positively beaming at the young couple. They reminded him so much of himself and Molly Wilson, especially when Lizzie put her hair up with the silver combs Phil had bought her for a Christmas present. His nephew took his eyes off her only for as long as it took to admire the pearl-handled pocket knife she had given him. He announced that he would give Phil his gold watch and chain for his twenty-first birthday, or his wedding, depending on which came first.

Gypsy was also pleased that Phil had met such a bright, attractive girl and she too felt that Lizzie would be very good for him. She had no doubts about his being good to her. He was as steadfast as his father was and loyal as a Wicklow collie. Instinct breaking through the eyes of a cat, she thought, and smiled at her mixed metaphor.

She thought how pleased and proud his mother would be and said a silent prayer for the soul of her long-departed sister.

The only damper on the day, as far as Gypsy was concerned, was the pointed absence of James McNeill. She always felt he had as much right to be at family gatherings as Nelly's husband or her own, for that matter. His exclusion seemed particularly wrong with Phil formally introducing Lizzie to the family.

And while they ate, pulled the wish-bone, drank, played games and sang, on the other side of the earth, a high-ranking British official was asking a bishop to start the first moves to end the centuries of conflict between Ireland and her powerful neighbour. De Valera was arriving back after his long absence in America and J.J. Clune, Archbishop of Perth, was dispatched to sound out the Irish leadership on the matter of a truce.

The irony of it all was not lost on the emissary. Only weeks earlier, the British had murdered his nephew Conor along with two companions — Peadar Clancy and Dick McKee — while they were being questioned in Dublin Castle, three more of Bloody Sunday's casualties.

After November's carnage, the authorities brought the curfew forward from midnight to ten o'clock. The Dublin lamplighters responded in kind by turning off the street lights at half-past nine so that they could to be home before the curfew. When the twenty-four hour clock on the mantle-piece chimed nine times, it caused a great disassembly in Cabra Cottage along with a hurried putting on of heavy coats, hats and scarves.

Lizzie unclasped her handbag and absentmindedly rummaged around for her kid gloves while she and Phil made tentative arrangements for St Stephen's Day.

Suddenly, she let out an unmerciful shriek.

Lizzie had found the 'Parson's Nose'.

Chapter 40

The Balance of Terror

There were harder jobs in the last summer of the War of Independence than cutting roads but Phil McNeill would have much preferred any one of them. While his comrades were gathering intelligence, ambushing Tans, Auxiliaries and the regular army, enforcing the rulings of the underground Republican Courts or serving terms in jail for Ireland, he was digging trenches across minor roadways in North County Dublin.

Guerrilla warfare was all about gathering intelligence and waiting, especially waiting. He had often lain in a ditch of cold, stagnant water for hours on end waiting for a Crossley tender that had been observed to pass the same spot at the same time, day-in-day-out; except, of course, on the day of the ambush. So they would pull back, lay low, and then move up again for some more waiting until the cold cut through to the bone.

Betimes, a tender would come by, unleashing a duel of blazing rifles for a few terrifying, exhilarating, never-to-be-forgotten minutes before another breathless dash across fields under a hail of fire.

And when they weren't engaged in waiting for or carrying out an ambush, they were gathering intelligence on the movement of British military so that they could start the cycle all over again. Phil McNeill's war had, until then, been mostly about long hours of anticipation punctuated by minutes of sheer terror.

Cutting roads that were soon enough re-opened was just pointless hard work as far as he and Sonny were concerned. They wanted to get back to the real business of liberating Ireland and they were determined to tell their commanding officer in so many words. Or at least Phil was. Sonny had his own view on who was to blame.

"Sure what's the point of seeing the commandant? It's me aul fella I tell you. Thinks it's a fecken howl having us sawing wood all day and digging out mud all night. Fecken humiliating that's what it is. 'Sawyers of wood with drawers full of water,' that's what he says we are. I've a pain in me taws with it … so I have."

But Phil wasn't so sure the intent was either mischievous or malevolent and would go to higher authority to make his case. As Commandant McNeill had been too ill of late to go to B Company HQ in the Deaf and Dumb, he would go to the dairy in Stoneybatter. Sonny tagged along as always but he waited outside.

"Disrupting the lines of communication is essential to our military strategy," the commandant told him as he made a cup of tea for them both. "It keeps the enemy off balance. They never know what roads are open to them when they set out of an evening and they don't know what to expect when they do come across one that's been cut — landmines, ambuscade or just a hole in the ground — they haven't a breeze. Think of it as a bloodless battle. Remember your ancestor Owen Roe. He won most of his famous victories without shedding a drop of blood — at Annahoe, the Southern Blackwater and countless other places up and down the country."

He was breathless now, and warmed his chest with the pressure of his massive right hand as if he were trying to crack a belch.

"Well it's like this sir. When me and Sonny think of Owen Roe O'Neill, it's the Battle of Benburb we think of, where he beat the hell out of Munro's great army ... and we don't think he managed that by digging holes in the road ... and anyway, sir, wasn't he an O'Neill?"

James was struggling for oxygen but was enjoying himself immensely nevertheless. "Here, have another biscuit. Put a few in your pocket for later. Where were we? Oh yes ... Benburb. O'Neill, McNeill, it's all the one Clann Úi Neill you know. And funny you should mention it: he did cut the roads at Benburb. Did you know that? Did you know that his engineers dammed the Northern Blackwater then released it to flood the valley at Kinard and cut Munro off from his supply wagons? Oh, yes! Owen Roe knew, like every great general knew since the days of the Romans, great victories are as much about great engineering as they are about the fighting spirit of men. It's the self-same way that Julius Caesar defeated the Gauls."

Then, gathering himself together, he removed his right hand from his breastbone and raised it in a fist to coin a phrase by which he might be remembered: "The spade is mightier than the gun. Remember that— the spade is mightier than the gun." He leaned back into the chair exhausted.

Phil went over to the trough, poured water from the brass tap into a cup and brought it over to his commandant. James took a few sips before reaching into his waistcoat pocket with two fingers to fish out a piece of paper.

"Will you read this for me? It was brought up this morning from Brigade HQ ... I can't find me specks."

"It just says, 'meet you at the Jolly Toper. Regards Frank.'"

"Ah! That'll be the Ratoath Road ... out be Cardiff's Bridge. That's your next job. Be careful boy. All this will be over soon enough. We'll need steady people then."

"How soon do you think?"

"The end will be in sight when they start talking through go-betweens."

"What happens then, Commandant?"

"Once the talking starts, the heart will go out of the fighting."

"And we'll have the Republic?"

"I'm afraid that's when the real trouble starts. We all know what we're against but there's a big difference of opinion about what we're for. Some think Home Rule is good enough. Others would be delighted to stay in the empire like Canada. The bulk of the 'boys' will accept nothing short of a sovereign republic and there are even a few who want a workers' state ... like over in Russia."

"Janey Mack! It would be easier to keep fighting."

Cutting the nation's arteries had its good side. It didn't take up a lot of his time and it allowed him to see Lizzie on most of her nights off — except Mondays. For some reason or another, she always spent Mondays with Maggie Smith, her best friend in Mount Brown. In a way that suited him too. They usually got only one road to cut in a week and Monday was as good a day for doing it as any other.

The main complications were the curfew and the local inhabitants. The ten o'clock curfew had been difficult enough but following the burning of the Custom House in May 1921, the authorities moved it to seven in the evening. That was bitterly resented by the entire populace of Dublin. Whole families were prisoners in their homes all through the long, bright summer evenings. It caused nearly as big a flood of volunteers as the threat of conscription during the Great War.

The curfew also made getting to and from an operation more dangerous. The Tans and Auxiliaries shot on sight anybody caught out and about after seven. It was still bright until almost eleven o'clock in mid-summer.

"Let's go down to Stoneybatter again and tell the commandant what's happening. He'll put a stop to this carry-on once he hears what's going on ... people older than himself working shovels in the middle of the night ... not bloomin' good enough." Phil said to Sonny.

At the dairy they got two surprises — the shop was shut and bolted and their knock on the house door was answered by Mother Kennedy.

"Auntie Gypsy! What in the name of God are you doing here? We came to see Mr McNeill," said Sonny.

"Well, you'll have to go and see somebody else, won't you? He's not up to dealing with a couple of scallywags this fine summer's evening."

"What's the matter with him ... is it serious?" asked Phil.

Gypsy lowered her voice to a whisper, mouthing the word with exaggerated lip movements: "Complications," she said and gently closed over the door.

Phil was determined. "There's nothing for it. We'll have to go down to Brigade HQ in Blackhall Place and report what's going on. This engineering is causing too much hardship all round."

That's when they heard about the 'Balance of Terror'. It came courtesy of a tall, gangly young man with loose-fitting dentures and flailing arms who chain-smoked as he spoke through a cubic yard of catarrh. He was not a whole lot older than they were but his non-stop movement fascinated the boys. Arms and legs flew out in all directions as he spoke, and when he smoked, his actions reminded them of the string puppet shows in Smithfield.

"It's like this men," said the officer as he struggled to keep his false-teeth from falling out by using his tongue as a lever while at the same time holding a cigarette aloft on the end of a very long right arm. "The Tans say to a crowd of villagers in Mulhuddart, or some such place, 'fill in that trench or we'll shoot you.'"

He paused to fling his right hand out as far as it would go. Then arced it around the back of his head to the left side of his mouth to take a deep drag from the cigarette held there. Removing it, he repeated the same action in reverse order.

"Shoot you," he said, repeating the key words of his last sentence before continuing. "What we have to do is go to those same villagers and say, 'If you do fill in that trench, we'll shoot you just as dead. We're both equal now, so who are you going to listen to, us or the British?'"

The arm flew out again, as though controlled by an errant puppeteer with the palsy. The boys watched enthralled as it travelled on its haphazard way to allow him drag deeply once more on his cigarette.

"Us or the British?" came the repeated kernel of his previous sentence. "That's the 'Balance of Terror'. If we're to buckle before brute force, we'll never win because the English will always have the advantage ... English advantage. The 'Balance of Terror' levels the playing field."

Phil didn't think much of the 'Balance of Terror' as a way of going about things. Neither did Cosy Finnigan and her husband when he and Sonny cut the Ratoath Road for the second time in a week. They were the only family left in Cardiff's Bridge when the Black and Tans came to round up a press gang to fill it in again.

They were awakened once more in the dead of the night by the sound of the front door being smashed in with rifle butts. When the Tans tramped up the stairs and kicked in the bedroom door, they found Cosy and her husband sitting up in bed in their night attire, holding tightly to each other.

"Carm on ... rise and shine ... piss-pots in a line ... 'ands orf 'is cock and on to yer socks. Look lively there ... cop 'old of these 'ere — call 'em spades — French jobbies ... never mind ... one each ...we 'ave a little bit of work for you two."

All through the night as the sweat pasted their night clothes to their bodies and the mud made its way up their legs, Cosy shovelled past exhaustion, past fear. She knew she had to keep her husband from weakening or the Tans might shoot him and she would be left alone in the Jolly Toper.

As they toiled in the beam of the Crossley's headlights, they could hear the Tans loading crates of stout and ale from their meagre storeroom onto the back of the open truck. The noise coming from the bar grew more boisterous by the minute. The line in civilised behaviour had been crossed and Cosy had no idea how far they were likely to go. She was terrified about how the night might end but never let on to her husband.

A patrol from the Norfolk Regiment came by and the Tans shot out of the pub like a snot off a hob. The commander of the Norfolks was known locally as 'Haw-Haw' because of his aristocratic English laugh. He also had the reputation for being fair-minded compared to the rest of the military and his soldiers were disciplined, unlike the Auxiliaries and Tans. People said that the Norfolk Regiment was like that because the Duke of Norfolk was Catholic.

They stopped momentarily in front of the Jolly Toper before driving on over the filled-in part of the trench. It was enough to disrupt the escalating rampage. The Tans decided to take their party elsewhere, but not before leaving the chilling warning that the road had better be open when they returned.

Even in the barren darkness of the deserted village, Cosy kept digging and filling, digging and filling for fear they would sneak back and find them idling. She was so tired, she wouldn't have minded if they shot the two of them but she was in sheer terror that one would be left to pine away in their forsaken village by the Tolka.

By daybreak, the trench was filled and they went back to the Jolly Toper to lay down in all their muck and dishevelment.

Phil and Sonny were left with a dilemma. They had spent several hours digging out the trench with pick and shovel and found it hard going, but Cosy and her husband were old enough to be their grandparents. Superior officer or no, they were not putting the 'Balance of Terror' into practice with the owners of the Jolly Toper, not after the kindness they had been shown on Bloody Sunday. At the same time, they had both taken an oath to obey the orders of their superior officers. Breaking that particular oath could be dangerous as well as sinful.

"Just go back and explain that you are closing an artery of critical importance to British military operations and that the IRA takes a dim view of those co-operating with the enemy," said the superior officer as he shattered a gas mantle with a gesticulating hand.

"IRA takes a dim view. Off with you now … and drop into the Deaf and Dumb on the way and pick up the McEnroys. Tell them I said no weapons. They're just to be there when you are talking to the villagers. That's all."

"Artery me arse," said Phil as they walked up Stoneybatter. "The only transport that goes up or down that stretch of the road is Cosy's pony and trap and the odd cartload of stardust for the four-eyed feckers up in the observatory at Dunsink. Who does he think he's fecken coddin'?"

"It wasn't him that gave us this duty in the first place. We're being kept out of harm's way ... that's the why and where of it all. It's as plain as the nose on your face. We always get the latrine detail. Them McEnroys get all the exciting jobs. I'm telling you for nothing, it's me aul fella that's at the back of it all."

But Phil wasn't so sure the order came from Dunny nor was he certain that the intention was malevolent. "As far as my memory serves me, it was the commandant that gave the original orders on this one."

"Will I boil you an egg?" said Cosy, her face lighting up when the two boys walked into the bar of the Jolly Toper.

"Come into the back, the pair of you and I'll make you something. Is the scar healing at all? Let's have a look at you? Well, it hasn't spoiled your good looks anyway. You're still dark and dangerous like all the Berfords, isn't he Mr Finnigan? And young Kerrigan — a blond version of the self-same breed. You'd be any girl's choice. Whoever named you 'Ebony and Ivory' got it right. Come here till I have a look at you."

Phil turned his head sideways to let Cosy examine the Finnigan handiwork.

"Well isn't he the great seamstress, that man of mine, all the same? Mr Finnigan, you could get a great job in Pims or the Mater. Sure, you could hang your shingle out on the front wall and give Dr Mooney a bit of competition."

"Mrs Finnigan, I don't want to upset you, especially after all you've done for us, but I've been ordered to tell you that you and your husband will have to stop co-operating with the British military in re-opening the road outside. I am also to inform you that the Ratoath Road is an artery of vital military importance to Crown forces."

"Ah Jesus son! Vital artery — the Ratoath Road? Are you joking me or what? Would you ever have a look around you? The shovel foundry shut down at the end of the Napoleonic Wars and hasn't re-opened since. The Kerdiff family closed up the big house and shifted back to England before I was even born. Vital artery!"

"Cosy, I mean Mrs Finnigan, you have to listen to me. That road is going to be cut again and you are not to co-operate with them in re-opening it for all that you say may be true."

"Re-opening! Is that what you call shovelling muck in the dead of night and me in me shift at my age? It'll be the death of poor Mr Finnigan."

Her tone changed suddenly and turning around, Phil observed James and John McEnroy sidle in. One stood silently against the wall near the door. The other took up a position at the far end of the bar.

Phil continued to reason with Cosy but she wasn't listening anymore. She was watching the McEnroys whose reputation as gunmen was well established in all the parishes around.

"So you see Mrs Finnigan, if you'll just bear with us … till we make this last push."

"Ah don't worry about it son! I know it's not your fault. Sure the Berfords and Finnigans have known each other since Old God's time. We were Fenians when the 'go-be-the-walls' we see personifying themselves today were no more than flunkies and gombeenmen. When your people and mine were out in '67, they were making a tidy shilling supplying good Irish fuel for the British military to warm their arses in every barracks from here to Ticknock. I know them well — seed, breed and generation."

The McEnroy brothers went white-faced but Cosy was not to be deterred.

"Cardiff's Bridge wasn't always the dead place it is today, son. I remember when I was only a girl, they came here in their thousands with banners and bands to demand an amnesty for Fenian prisoners and the conspirators still on the run. Both of your grandmothers were there — Bamma and poor Mrs McNeill, God be good to her poor, immortal soul. Bamma was just a bit of a girl like meself at the time and Mrs McNeill still doing her best to support the cause and she after losing her young husband to the snowdrifts of the Dublin Mountains after the Tallaght debacle. Pitiful, she looked with all the children clinging on to her — the whole lot of them famished with the hunger and cold. Your own father was there trying to mind them all like a little maneen and he only twelve or thirteen … though a fine, strapping lad even then."

"My father … you knew my father?" Phil asked anxiously.

But Cosy was watching the McEnroys again. "There in their thousands they were, to support the felons of our land. But there was ne'er a one from Kirwan Street."

Then, turning to her husband, she said softly, "Come on Mr Finnigan … we might as well close the kip down … sure there wasn't much of a future in it anyway. Cardiff's Bridge died a long time ago. I don't know why we held on so long."

"Mrs Finnigan, you knew my father?" Phil said in a low and earnest voice.

"*Sinn sceal eile,*" Cosy said and turned into the back kitchen to join her husband.

"Uncle Philip won't think much of the 'Balance of Terror' next time he slips away from work and finds his watering hole closed," said Phil as they walked back towards the level crossing.

"Balance me taws. I don't want to even think about it or those poor misfortunate hoors below there in that fecken ghost town. Some bloody republic this is going to be, that's all I can say."

"Are you coming on the charabanc excursion to Enniskerry on the eleventh?"

"No. I don't think so. Won't everybody be bringing a mot?"

"Essie tells me that Myria Mack wants to come and she'll go with you if she's asked. Why don't you ask Essie to ask her for you?"

"Did she say that really? I mean about going out with me."

"That's what Essie says. You can go and ask her yourself."

"No. I believe you … though there's thousands wouldn't … will you ask Essie to ask her for me?"

"Do you know what it is Sonny? I'm better than a mother to you!"

"You will so?"

"Don't worry me aul son. It's in the bag. It will be a marvellous outing. There's going to be a big crowd of us this time — Lizzie is bringing Maggie Smith and her German fella … yourself and Myria

Mack and who knows, even the McEnroys might bring along a bit of fluff."

"Japers! Even the DMP wouldn't take those two. And they used to be such gas."

While they chatted Phil agonised over what would happen to Cosy and her husband — whether they had grown-up children with whom they might stay and what might become of them if they hadn't. She knew a lot about his father and grandfather … all Fenians whatever it was that happened to them all … or maybe she was just saying all that to upset the McEnroys … she certainly had them raging.

He was bursting with pride at the thought of Fenian blood flowing in his veins from both sides of his family. He had long known about the Berfords but Cosy had just confirmed that the McNeills were Fenians too. And though that gave him great satisfaction, he knew not to pursue it too openly. His mind had been trained from infancy never to be seen wandering into that territory.

Everything was changing too fast: the McEnroys were becoming humourless ogres; the great stand at the GPO had descended to threatening an old Fenian couple; Commandant McNeill no longer looked so indestructible.

Turning to Sonny he said, "Now don't let me down with this young one. I want you to be on your best behaviour and none of your aul tomfoolery. Not with this mot … It wasn't only Essie and me, Lizzie and all were involved in setting up this arrangement for you. Do you hear me?"

"Stop being such a worrier. I'll be the perfect gentleman. I … eh … I suppose it'll be all right if I ask her to show me her big diddies … if I say please first … do you think?" he said and ducked.

Phil and Sonny took a fit of laughing that lasted long after they crossed over the Royal Canal. It continued episodically as they passed the little graveyard at Riverston Abbey and there were still outbreaks right up to the moment they parted at the junction with the Old Cabra Road.

Chapter 41

Under the waterfall

Lunch in the Powerscourt Arms Hotel did the trick even if the roast lamb was a bit overdone and the service slow to get started. The drinkers pronounced the porter to be on the flat side yet managed to lower more pints than was strictly necessary for washing down the meal.

Sitting around the quaint dining room with only flowers on the gingham tablecloths, and not a soul asking if they had a mouth on them, tried Phil's patience to breaking point. It didn't improve when he eventually went out to the reception desk to enquire as to what time they might expect lunch only to be met with an imperious: "The staff have to go to Mass you know."

After another hour of small talk, the kitchen doors flew open and four waiters burst into the dining-room, one after the other, each carrying several plates piled high with steaming food. They tore around the room, plonking one before each of their guests with a bump. It wasn't until the material began to crinkle under the heat that Phil realised it was only printed oilcloth.

Lizzie looked at the mountains of food stacked in front of her and said to a waiter as he whisked past, "Excuse me but I didn't order yet."

"Set lunch ma'am ... roast lamb with mint sauce, two veg and potatoes. If it's not to madam's taste, the next hotel is in Bray," and he disappeared through the swinging doors to join the returned Mass-goers in the kitchen.

It was done so snootily, the whole dining room was silenced for a fraction of a second before erupting into laughter. It was all great fun but not quite what Phil wanted, so as soon as the meal was over, he and the other non-drinkers went out to the foyer to await the return of the charabanc.

While the big, motorised coach tried to negotiate its way around the Enniskerry Diamond, Phil became fascinated, entertained and eventually incensed by the huge, framed photograph in the foyer. The caption proclaimed: 'MAJORITY OF HON. MERVYN

RICHARD WINGFIELD. PRESENTATION AND ADDRESS BY A GRATEFUL TENANTRY 1901.'

A large body of bulky men stood hats in hand either side of the Viscount and his heir. The rest of the Wingfield gentlemen sat on the sun-warmed, paved and terraced gardens to witness the tribute while Wingfield ladies, reclining on wicker chairs, looked suitably detached.

"Didn't the clothes look really lovely in the old days?" said Maggie Smith. "Look at all the lacework on the dresses ... and those hats ... My God, they're only beautiful."

And even though she was Lizzie's best friend in Mount Brown, Phil couldn't stop himself from saying, "They were lovely enough for the blood-sucking landlords and their pasty-faced women anyway."

"Oh! Don't be such a grouch. She's only admiring the fashions. We don't have to have a speech from the dock at every hand's turn, now do we?" Lizzie said, linking Phil with a cajoling arm. "Don't mind him Maggie. He's too green for the Hill of Tara sometimes."

"It vas remodel by German architect, name Richart Castle," said Maggie Smith's German man friend, pointing to the Palladian mansion forming the backdrop to the photographer's composition.

"He laid out zie formal gardens as vell. Zie house vas castle before he remodel."

"It's a pity someone didn't remodel his lordship's head," Sonny said as he passed.

"He's bad enough on his own without you making him any worse," Lizzie said, giving Sonny a little swipe of her hand.

"Come on now lads," interjected poor Jimmy Wildman. "We're all Irish and the ship's name is Murphy ... our charabanc awaits ... to the waterfall."

They set off in high spirits from the hill village of Enniskerry along the tree-lined road to Powerscourt Demesne. Fortified by roast lamb and porter, they cared little for the royal land grants held by the Viscount and made a point of displaying their feelings on the matter. The group entered his grounds by the gate on the Roundwood Road talking at the top of their voices. The gatekeeper remained inside his gate lodge. It was probably as well.

But the avenue was so long, winding and verdant, it soon mellowed the most rebellious spirits. They strolled leisurely, linking arms in the summer sunshine, one couple behind the other at a safe distance. Phil and Lizzie in the middle, Sonny Kerrigan with Myria Mack behind and Maggie Smith with Willie Stumpf in front, they made their way slowly along the Dargle River towards Ireland's greatest cascade.

"Well, opposites attract and no mistake," Phil said to Lizzie.

"I see what you mean. You're tall, dark and broad as barn and I'm tall, dark and skinny ... very nice, I must say."

"No! I don't mean us ... I mean you are of course ... I was referring to them ... in front ... your friend Maggie and her German fella. She's young, buxom and Irish and there she is, doing a steady line with a middle-aged man who is thin as a rake and as foreign as a three-shilling bit."

"They could do a whole lot worse. He's very nice and gentle and he's very good to her ... that means a lot you know. Everyone doesn't get the sweetheart of their dreams ... Maggie's doing alright, thank you very much and so is Willie ... and what makes you so pass-remarkable, anyway? What about your friend with his goo-goo eyes rambling all over the place, aye?"

The McEnroy brothers caught up with the courting group and suggested a diversion towards Powerscourt House to see the suggestive statues in the Italian gardens. Phil knew that stately homes also meant hunting rifles and boxes of ammunition but declined nevertheless. He had other business on his mind for this day. Sonny and Myria Mack agreed to go part of the way so that Sonny could show Myria the big maze of high hedges in the formal gardens. Maggie and Willie (he pronounced it Villie) chose to continue their stroll to the waterfall with her best friend.

They could hear it before they could see it — a dull hum gradually building to a great, continuous roar. It made its first appearance as they came out of a tunnel of interlocking sessile oaks. Bursting through a crevice in the rocky coum, it crashed in a torrent of white water, smashing off worn granite and sending a spray into the air through which a rainbow scribed its multi-coloured arc.

Sitting on flat stones at the side of the cascade, the two couples watched the primordial rush of water breaking its strength before becoming a brackish stream again, flowing towards Bray and the sea. They felt part of a continuum watching a wonder that people had gazed on for thousands of years before them and would for thousands of years after they were gone.

"Zie rifer is valling 400 veet from a blanket bog on top of zie mountain — highest vasservall in Irelandt. Alvays bigger after rain."

"Willie, what are the names of those huge trees over there?" Maggie questioned to divert.

"Vell, zare is oak, beech, birch and rowan but zie biggest vun is zie great redvood."

"Didn't I tell you, that man knows everything. Oh Willie, let's go over and you can show me which is which," Maggie said, winking at Lizzie.

Phil waited until they were completely out of sight. He wanted everything to be just right but the roar of the waterfall continued to hinder his purpose. So they strolled arm-in-arm down the sloping pathway to the bend in the river away from the pounding waters.

It was so tranquil on the grassy bank with the gentle Dargle burbling as it passed. They sat silently for the longest while, listening to blackbird, thrush and linnet, dancing their melody along the top of the lapping water and drone of the distant falls. Phil saw a tree creeper entering his nest in the smooth, round arse formed in the cleft of a dividing trunk. He had a worm wriggling in his beak, big enough to feed a small clutch. Seconds later, he was off to forage once more in the teeming valley at the base of the roaring water.

They let the sounds of the mountains wash over them, feeling the sun gently tan their upturned faces until he felt his moment arrive.

He took her hand, and looking into her eyes he said, "Lizzie, I have something I want to ask you. Don't get offended or angry ... or run off again ... will you?"

"Don't be silly," she said and waited for him to continue, her calm demeanour a flat contradiction of the wild expectations rushing in gushes from her stomach to her brain, driving her heartbeat on a thundering course.

"Will you marry me?"

"Yes!"

"You will?

"You only had to ask."

The suddenness of her answer left him hovering in mid-flight. He had prepared a long speech to convince her of his love and devotion. He wanted to let her know that he would work hard and give up every penny he ever earned so that they would have a decent home. He wanted to tell her that he would protect her all the days of her life and that he would never raise a hand to her no matter what passed between them. Above all else, he wanted to reassure her that he would adore her until the day he died.

But she said yes so soon and stalled his great speech before it had even begun. So he told her that she had made him the happiest man in the world and kissed her hands, cheeks and lips over and over. And as the long speech proclaiming his devotion was in his head, he delivered it anyway.

Lizzie committed every last word to memory, along with the way he said it, the scene as it was set and everything leading up to and away from it. The waterfall was behind him in the distance, the mist maintaining its tiny rainbow. The other side of the riverbank was covered in ferns and around them were all manner of trees laden with leaves of every shade of green under the sun. In between were wild flowers of all hues and above them, the air hummed — was it bees or the sound of distant water ever falling?

She was fixing the moment in her mind so that she could put it away carefully to take out again whenever she felt the need during the rest of her life. She also knew that Maggie Smith would expect a word-for-word account of the proposal and what the whole world around them was doing at the time.

Lizzie did put one condition on the actual marriage and it was one with which he readily agreed. They would wait until the 'Troubles' were over and not tell anyone about their plans except Maggie, Sonny and Essie.

After the 'Troubles', he would go back to school at night and qualify as a railway surveyor, like his Uncle Philip. Uncle Felim would surely get him a place in the Midland Great Western Railway, once he had qualified.

She would have to give up her nursing job and didn't mind too much. After more than three years working all the hours that God sent for a meagre reward, she was ready for the change.

The sun was still high in the sky when Willie Stumpf's shadow brought them back to reality.

"Ve better go now to zie automobile if ve are to get back before zie curfew."

Maggie immediately latched on to Lizzie, linking her so tightly all the way back to the charabanc, squeezing every last drop out of the proposal she knew had taken place. She didn't have to wring too hard for Lizzie was full of the excitement of it all and desperately needed to pour it all out just to confirm that it had actually taken place.

"You're not the only one with news, Lizzie Nolan."

"Go on … tell me … what happened?"

"Take a look at that," Maggie said, flashing a silver ring with a single diamond on the middle finger of her left hand.

"Mother of God, that was quick — ring and all. When did all that take place?"

"Well, when your fella was getting all poetic over by the waterfall, Willie was presenting me with an engagement ring over by the trees. Isn't it marvellous? We'll both be married together just like the way we made our Holy Communion and Confirmation. Wouldn't a double wedding be grand?"

"Oh, congratulations Maggie. I'm so pleased for you. Oh God yes. After the 'Troubles'. A double wedding in John's Lane … I don't like that St James's — very plain … suppose we'll have to get a dispensation for moving out of the parish but it'll be well worth it."

"I'll have to get a dispensation anyway. Willie is Lutheran … side altar and side door, I suppose. He wants us to marry before the winter sets in so the three of us can go over to Stuttgart to see his family. A funny honeymoon with three but little Willie is a real dote and sure that's the way it has to be. His family lives in the Black Forest … it's supposed to be very beautiful. Will you do bridesmaid?"

"I thought you'd never ask. Will you be mine?"

"Of course. But if you two are going to wait till after the 'Troubles', I'll be well married by then — bridesmaids are supposed to be virgins, you know … hope to God I'm not still one by then."

After they got over their fit of giggling, Lizzie said, "You can be matron of honour then … with my sister Agnes … she's getting married this year as well … Essie Kerrigan can be bridesmaid … you'll love her. Whenever the 'Troubles' are over," she added wistfully.

"Willie asked me to ask you if you'd ask Phil to do best man for him."

"Doesn't he have anybody close?"

"No, God love him, they're all in Germany. Isn't it sad?"

Lizzie gave her life-long friend the warmest hug and said, "He'll do it, of course he'll do it, and be honoured to."

"I wonder how his blondie friend is getting on with that big country girl?"

As they came near to the gate lodge, a big-bosomed girl emerged from the trees followed by a youth whose blond curls flopped about his face as he tried to catch up with her. Both were giggling.

"Don't vorry, it's okay ven everybody is laughing," Willie said to calm Phil whose hands had turned to fists.

"Did you hear Maggie's news?" said Lizzie. "Go on, tell her."

"We both have news," Maggie said. "We're both getting married!"

They went through every last detail again with Myria without ever getting bored by the repetition, each finding a new detail or nuance to explore.

Finally Lizzie said, "And how did you get on with Sonny?"

"More hands than an octopus that one … give him an inch and he takes a mile …"

"Go on tell us," said Lizzie.

"A bit of a go-boy then, is he?" asked Maggie.

"What did he do?" they asked almost in unison.

"What did he not do?" Myria replied with upcast eyes.

The charabanc almost freewheeled down the mountains back to Enniskerry, engine still idling as it glided through the Scalp, passengers lying back into their seats, arms around shoulders, hands resting in hands. The motor hummed easily past the walled gardens of Kilternan, Foxrock and Blackrock. It began to chug along by the artisan dwellings lining the flat land at Irishtown and Ringsend where people stood around in animated knots.

As it crossed Butt Bridge, even the courting couples became aware that something unusual was happening. The city streets were filled with milling people as though Fairyhouse or the Donnybrook Fair had moved to town. Beresford Place was so crowded it brought the charabanc to a complete stop.

Everyone on the coach was glued to the windows speculating on the cause of the clamour until the driver opened the cab door and shouted to a passers-by, "What's all the excitement about?"

"It's all over," said a woman pulling the veil up off her face and fixing it on top of her broad-brimmed model with a long hatpin.

"The British have called a truce," said a young man propping his bicycle against his hip.

"They're all getting out of jail," said another.

"We've won ... we've shaggin' well won ... saving your presence ma'am ... we've beaten the almighty, British shaggin' empire to a shaggin' standstill ... saving your presence again ma'am."

Lizzie turned to Phil to ask what it all meant only to find him cupping his mouth in both hands, tears rolling silently down his cheeks.

She put her arms around him, uninhibited by the crowds. As she stroked the side of his face he began to murmur.

"My poor, sweet country ... my poor, sweet country ..." over and over again.

In Lees shop window, a huge poster proclaimed, 'NO TRUCE WITH BAD VALUE.'

Chapter 42

Harry Head

Harry Head sat in the doctor's waiting room feeling very let down. Since getting the pressure disease, Dr Mooney was forever telling him that the heavy lifting and hammering would be the death of him. But Harry had been left to run his smithy alone for all the sons and brothers he once had.

He was cracking on to James McNeill about such matters while he waited his turn to be called. He found him a great listener; a rare talent in Stoneybatter and its environs.

"I'm the last of the Heads in Head Brothers. Did you know that James? I'm working out of that bloody forge in Smithfield for over forty years now, just as me father and me father's father did before me. The brothers all left one-by-one … saw no future in the place once I took over all those years ago. I had four fine sons then … all dead and buried now … God rest them. The brothers all went off to Africa, England, the Tramsheds in Inchicore … never see them anymore … terrible to think of letting the place go. We've been the smithies of Smithfield for over a hundred years. Did you know that?"

"That would be an ogeious shame? Head Brothers is as much a part of the neighbourhood as the cobblestones in the square." Then to cheer things up a little, he said, "You're getting to be the image of each other — you and Smithfield — both nearly as broad as you're long."

He was delighted to have James for company, though he would have wished for a more original greeting than: "Hello Head." James was straight as a die and a good pay and that made him A1 in Harry Head's book. You couldn't get a better rating.

"Do you know when you're beating a curve into a white-hot bar of steel, going hammer and tongs, so to speak, as you shape it around the horn of the anvil and you racing against time to get it done before the metal cools and loses its malleability?"

"Bejasus I do, and nobody knows it better."

"And you get them pains across your chest that go tracking down your left arm?"

"I do by Christ but I do work through it. I don't let them best me."

"That's where you're going wrong. No one should ever work through that class of thing. A fella could fall down on the flat of his back, stone dead just from working through a tightening in the chest."

"Jaysus, James, don't be telling me things like that. You'll frighten the shite out of me … sure I have to earn a living."

"Now Harry, you know it as well as the next fella — a man should work for a living, not die for it. Those pains are your heart telling you it's running out of oxygen. If the man on the bellows doesn't blow enough oxygen on the fire, what happens?"

"It dies of course and isn't worth the full of your arse of roasted snow … ends up as a knot of useless bloody clinker in the end."

"That's precisely what will happen to you. One day you'll be hammering away at a hasp for a gate or a chassis for a cart and the next thing you know, *bang*," James said, loudly slapping his two hands together to make his point and lifting poor Harry nearly out of his trousers in the process. "Working through them pains is the quickest way to a heart attack … there's nothing surer."

It was time for a diversion before a heart attack occurred in the doctor's waiting room.

"What do you think of this deal they're offering? Will the boys go for it, I don't suppose?"

"Hard to say. A lot of the TDs up in the Mansion House are buying it … not because they particularly like it or anything like that. It's more because they believe it's the best we'll be offered."

"What about Dev? I hear he's spitting fire."

"Dunno. He's telling the Dail that it isn't Ireland that's being offered dominion status but two broken bits of Ireland. Takes the North being separated very badly. The pogroms aren't helping matters … neither is the oath … that's sticking in everybody's craw."

"What's a fecken pogrom when it's at home?"

"The killings and burnings going on every night of the week up in the nationalist areas of Belfast."

"Oh, is that what it fecken is? And what about the Big Fella? Collins will hardly go for it either then. Will he?"

"Hard to say. He's over in London at the minute seeing what he can get out of them. I don't know so much about the rest of the delegation but I do know this. If Mick Collins makes a bargain, he'll stick by it."

"They say he's given the nod to Frank Aiken to shoot two Protestants for every Catholic — two-to-one ... thinks that'll put a stop to them fecken pogroms, if that's what they're called — the quintessence of a *sleeveen* that fella."

"I haven't heard that one. Where did you get that?"

"That's the word at the moment. It'd be true to form ... pugnacious Cork hoor ... like the rest of them down there," said Harry Head. "He'll have less chance over in London. The Welsh Wizard will dance rings around him ... mark my words. I'd put me money on Lloyd George in that contest, if you have a couple of bob to spare?"

"Mick Collins is not so green as he's cabbage-looking. He got us this far and that's a sight further than anybody has done since the fall of the O'Neills."

"Fall of me fecken arches. Wouldn't you think him and Dev would go well together — a Limerick ham and a Cork cabbage-eater — a right couple of 'country mugs' the two of them? What about Charlie Burgess? There's a real Dubliner for you."

But James couldn't tell his old friend that the Irish Republican Brotherhood had first call on his loyalty as it has on that of its President Michael Collins. Neither could he tell him that Cathal Brugha and De Valera are not IRB though one is a Minister and the other President of the Republic. It was the way with secret societies.

"I don't know, Harry. I've been out of things this while back ... what with being laid up and all ... and by the look of it, I think I'm well off out of it."

"You out of it! Sure you can't have a show without Punch. There's been a Fenian McNeill in this parish since the longest day I can remember."

"The aul ticker Harry ... Have to take things very easy these days. Even the walk up Manor Street to this bloomin surgery has me banjaxed."

"Do you miss it, James?"

"Mixed feelings, Harry ... mixed feelings. Truth to be told, the Truce is causing a lot of tension ... endless wrangling up in the Dail ... 'Truceliers' swelling the ranks since the war ended ... causing a lot of resentment. I miss the cattle business ... I'll tell you that ... being around animals ... a great life ... loved every minute of it. Wouldn't care much for the way things are going now with the other thing. No end of argument and cross-talk ... and it's going to get worse. I was over in Dunny Kerrigan's place this morning and himself and the son were at it hammer and tongs, saving your presence Harry. Dangerous talk. Dunny's going to follow the chief come what may and Sonny says he's only a Spanish onion — right to his father's face."

"Youth of today!"

"Oh, there's a pair of them in it. If it wasn't for young Phil McNeill working his heart out, that mill would be in a right fix."

"Is that the same young fella with the jet-black hair that lifts anvils up be the horn in his left hand?"

"The very same."

"Jaysus, he was always hanging around the forge of a Saturday ... watching everything. Seemed to be fascinated by the shapes that could be made on hot metal with a hammer and a dolly. Used to get picture-money be lifting the damn thing over his head and he only about sixteen years of age. Terrible strong hoor altogether ... handsome fecker as well."

"And strong as an ox. Never stops working according to Kerrigan. Just as well Dunny hasn't the pressure disease like the pair of us because he's certainly going to miss him."

"Why? Where's he going?"

"No idea. Don't think he knows himself yet. Keen on a young one you know ... nurse out of the Gorman ... think they're making plans ... only the labourer down in the sawmill ... wants to better himself ... you know the way it is."

"Eh, wouldn't be interested in learning the blacksmith game would he? Wouldn't be a proper apprenticeship or anything. He's too old for that and in any case his father or uncle would have had to be in the game for him to be let into 'The Society'. But I'd teach him all he needs to know and the pay would be better than labouring in a sawmill ... healthier too. A blacksmith's helper ... semi-skilled ... it'd be a leg-up from being just a fecken labourer and you'd never know what chances might come up. God only knows I could do with a strong lad that doesn't have too much to say for himself. It's either that or let the business go. And to think I had four sons — all lost to the consumption, God rest them and their poor unfortunate mother."

"Light of heaven shine on them all," said James, blessing himself.

"We have to soldier on as best we can. Sure no one knows that better than yourself, James and you after burying two lovely wives. Jaysus, I remember Mary Berford, God be good to her immortal soul. People used to stop and turn whenever she walked down Smithfield to the fruit and vegetable market. A fine-looking woman. You made a great job of rearing them all on your own. They're a credit to you."

"Thank you Harry. I was as good as I was let."

"Will you send him around to me so?"

"I will to be sure."

"Isn't he your own lad by that same Berford girl? Lord have mercy on her?"

"He is, but mum's the word."

"Jesus, Mary and Holy Saint Joseph, don't tell me that aul nonsense is going on yet?"

"Harry my old friend, it's been going on so long, it's taken on a life of its own by this stage. I'll send him around but say nothing to him about the other matter."

"That Bamma is the quintessence of a *targer* and no mistake. Her bile would burn through tempered steel."

And then it was James's turn to adapt diversionary tactics.

"You know, according to Dunny, no matter what they do up in the Mansion House, the 'boys' won't go for anything that falls short of a thirty-two-county republic. Says they're talking of shooting anyone who swears an oath to the king."

"Bejasus, there'll be trouble in this country yet," said Harry Head as Felim called him into his surgery.

Chapter 43

The Smithy of Smithfield

Smithfield is a broad, cobbled, rattle and clatter of a square. Through the arched door of the forge, Phil watches carts on iron-rimmed wheels grinding over the worn granite sets loaded down with produce from the rich soils of North County Dublin. They come with hay and straw to Christopher Dodds and Sons, or corn for John O'Neill's bruising and grinding mills. Above the din of the smithy he can hear flocks go bleating, squealing and snorting to O'Brien's Pig & Sheep Factors and drovers driving herds down the skittery stones to R & J Wilkinson, Cattle Salesmen; Laurence Cuffe & Sons, Salesmen and Auctioneers; or to the cattle lairs of Dreaper and Finlay.

Every day he jostles with the bread-and-tea terriers that shuffle out of their tumbledown tenements onto the crowded thoroughfare in search of a casual shilling. They push sacks of potatoes on barrows for Edward Carton, potato factors, haul bags of barley on scrawny shoulders into John Jameson's or H. H. Bishop, the square's two distillers, or hang around J. Sheridan Carriers in the hope of a day's pay loading.

Michael Furlong is the farrier and Louis Lemass the automobile mechanic. But Phil works for Head Brothers Blacksmiths, and that premises holds pride of place among all the traders of Smithfield.

This is his new world and he loves every single thing about it.

Toasting his lunchtime sandwiches by the forge fire he is never envious of the stall-fed cattle dealers going into Edward Boggies dinning rooms in number 32 to get their ribs further tightened on mutton and potatoes. At any minute or hour of the day he is likely to observe prosperous Salesmasters from Hanbury & Potterton Seed Merchants adjourning to W.J. Egan, Grocer and Wine Merchant in number 30 to chase balls of malt with large bottles of stout and he isn't even tempted. As he douses the last of the embers and hangs up the tools for the evening, strong farmers, heavy from their patronage of both establishments, would be heading for Michael Dogget's lodging house in number 28 to make arrangements for staying overnight.

This is not the way for small farmers. Day after day, Phil sees them arriving at Smithfield so loaded down with hay or straw, there is rarely room on the carts for the drivers who lead their horses by the harness from places as far away as Ashbourne, Mulhuddart and even Swords.

Lodging houses are not for them. They never sell all their produce but keep back a few sops to scatter a soft bed on the floor of the wagon. As he heads up Prussia Street, they are already asleep, leaving their animals to find the long road home.

But heavy burdens are not just hard on draft animals. They cause leaf-suspensions to warp, brake-springs to snap and shoes to be thrown. The shoeing goes to Furlong the Farrier, the rest of the misfortunes come to the smithy shop for rectification.

Phil laps it all up. He virtually inhales the atmosphere in Smithfield and thrives on the peculiar coke and hot metal air of the smithy. He can't get enough of the work. He opens up in the early morning and has the fire going long before Harry Head comes near the place. He won't let his craftsman work the bellows or carry anything heavier than a hammer and is happy to take even that out of his hand when allowed.

Every day brings something new. There is always some tool or farm implement needing fixing or transformation into something else at the end of its useful first life. One day he helps Harry transform a worn shovel into a *sleán*; the next it might be a broken scythe that has to be turned into a useful sickle. It seems to him that everything entering the fire in Head Brothers emerges renewed or refashioned into something else entirely.

The smithy is a great stop-off shop for the local craftsmen — for even a paint scraper with a bent blade can be either straightened or ground into a putty-knife that in its turn might become a one-inch filling tool as time wears on. Phil wants to know it all and Harry is only too delighted to teach him. He is a highly charged magnet picking up every little knack and trick of his ferrous trade. He can't wait for the day when he will be able to perform such wonders on his own.

With generations of experience linked once more to great physical strength, the smithy in Smithfield begins to prosper once more. Harry loves the way Phil applies himself to the task without ever whinging or giving back-answers, though he would never tell him to his face.

Enjoying a few pre-Christmas drinks in Hanlons, with the boy's natural father James McNeill and his guardian Philip Berford, he confides: "If I had a son ... and I had four sons once ... I would want him to be like Phil McNeill. A hard-working fecker without so much as an ounce of aul lip on him. Those that say least do most. It was only the God's honest truth for whoever said it on the first day."

James, almost exploding with pride, orders and drinks the first whiskey in his life. It makes him feel so good; he calls a second round out of turn.

Philip was so pleased by the behaviour of his ward; he neglects to sneak an extra drink for himself as he passes the counter on the way to the 'gents'.

"He's as strong as an ox — built just like yourself James," Harry says in Philip's absence. "Mary would be very proud of him too, God be good to her."

The festive season brings a few quieter moments to the forge with people putting off all but the most essential jobs until the trouble and expense of the holiday are done. During such times, Harry talks about the old days when his own father showed him and his brothers all the skills of the blacksmithing trade just as he is doing for Phil.

"Would you like to know how to make a pike?" he says one day when they have little else to do.

"I would to be sure ... but there can't be much of a call for pikes theses days ... can there?"

"You'd be surprised Phil ... get orders betimes for ornamental purposes ... graves, flagpoles and all that class of thing. A monumental weapon in their day, you know. A great man for cutting through reins and rider all in one go. Stuck in the ground, they'd break up a cavalry charge ... monumental weapon. But your grandmother told you all about that I don't suppose?"

"Bamma's great on the history, Mr Head."

"God be good to your own lovely mother, Mary Berford. Bejasus, she campaigned with great gusto against the stupid, bloody Boer War and your father too for all the good it did gobshites the likes of me poor brother. Lord 'a mercy on him."

243

And as he blows up the fire on the bar of two-inch, dark-mild steel that Harry has chosen for the pike-head, Phil tells him about Lizzie and their great plans for getting married and living in Islandbridge beside the park.

Phil knows how to keep the fire in, how to work the bellows until the metal gets white hot and when to remove it before it begins to burn. Then Harry takes over, turning then hammering, turning and hammering until the spearhead appears between the flat of the anvil and the four-pound hammer.

Phil blows up the fire on the piece for the hook and Harry hammers it as sharp as a sickle, and then shows Phil the art of forge welding. When the job is finished he is allowed to do the burnishing all on his own and to temper it with fire and water. He loves the acrid smell and the boiling surge when the white hot metal pierces the cold, still liquid. He loves the way streams of sparks fly from the grinding wheel as he smoothes down the joint and puts a fine cutting-edge on the hardened steel.

Later, Harry lets him forge-weld chain links by hammering the heated metals back over themselves. Every bit of work in the forge is an excitement to Phil but the thing that transfixes him most is the oxyacetylene. Through the smoked glass in the welder's mask he watches in wonderment, holding both pieces of a broken implement as Harry floods molten metal into the fissure until all three elements are melded into one.

Every day he learns more and more of the blacksmith's craft while, bit by bit, Harry drops in little pieces he hopes will one day come together and give him a picture of his parents. Phil has long known not to ask questions on the matter, but Harry just allows them their place in everyday conversation.

His mother emerges as a beautiful, educated and patriotic woman from Harry's daily monologue. His father's image remains trapped within layers of talk that cannot hide the shape entirely. If he remains patient that too might become more defined.

"He'd be a bit older than her but a fine cut of a man for all that and well got with all that dealt with him … showered her with gifts he did … campaigned side-by-side with her against the African war."

"And where is he now?" Phil asked as casually as he could between ringing hammer-blows.

"Those that are dear to us are never far away," hammer and turn, hammer and turn. Harry never stayed on that topic for long no matter if Phil cajoled or kept his lip buttoned but he was always more forthcoming about his mother.

"Died of a Good Friday … did you know that? Neglect … bloody doctors … the quintessence of … hold back on that bellows for the sweet love of Jesus. Yer burning the bollix out of that crucifix … won't last pissing time on the top of Art's Cross the way yer going and the last one was there for donkey's …"

"I made a half-inch hasp on the anvil today and Harry let me forge-weld it onto a gate-chain for Hanbury & Potterton down the square. Harry inspected it when it was done and said, 'That's blacksmithing.'"

They were walking around the rose-beds in the Flower Gardens — the only flowers still in blossom in the weak, wintry sun.

"Do you know what it is? I think you are just marvellous the way you're able to pick up all those things … and so fast!"

"And Harry himself nearly burned a two-inch bar of dark-mild steel only I grabbed it out of the fire with the tongs in time."

"Did you say anything to him yet about the half-day?"

"No, I didn't get the chance. We made a pike-head with the steel I was telling you about and Harry showed me how to forge-weld the hook onto it."

"Are we still talking about metal?"

"Ok, ok, I'm sorry. What do you want to talk about then?"

"Do you think it will last … the Truce I mean?" she asks then stops to hold a rosebud between her up-turned fingers, taking in its scent with a deep breath, her eyes closing out the rest of the world. "So beautiful," she says.

"It's hard to imagine it starting up again. Sure they know who everybody is at this stage. Even Collins's picture is all over the place."

They walk in silence for a while around the rest of the gardens, barely noticing the flower-less shrubs cut well back in late autumn. They are alone, hand-in-hand and that seems enough for the moment. Phil breaks the silence.

"In a short while the English will leave and we'll surely sort something out among ourselves."

245

"I hope to God you're right ... the way we're saving since you got into the forge ... we'd have enough to get married by the time I'm twenty-one."

He slips his arm around her waist, leans his head under the rim of her hat and whispers, "Lizzie Nolan, you're the loveliest-looking girl I've ever laid eyes upon."

"I won't be so lovely if you don't get me back to the hospital before lights out," she says, giving him a gentle kiss on the mouth.

The thrill he feels at the touch of her lips is greatly accentuated by the boldness of her kissing him in a public place.

"Will you kiss me in the Park when we're married?"

"I'll kiss you anywhere you like," she replies and blushes.

They leave by the park gates on the Infirmary Road and walk along the tree-lined North Circular Road doing what all the latest songs called 'canoodling'. At the four-cross roads where Aughrim Street and Blackhorse Avenue meet, they stop to watch a company of Volunteers march past with flags flying, openly shouldering weapons on their new green uniforms.

"There's your best friend. 'Sonny ... Sonny Kerrigan'", she shouts waving to the young officer with the blonde curls still visible under his slouch hat.

But Sonny stares more rigidly in front than before.

"He doesn't see us," she says with disappointment.

"It's hard to get him to see anything at all these days," says Phil as he gently steers her towards Grangegorman and the hospital.

They stop to admire the clusters of flowers holding their buds firm against the crisp winter air. Phil says suddenly, "Would you like to spend Christmas with us in Cabra Cottage again this year?"

"I will if you'll come and do the Christmas shopping in town with me."

"Oh Lizzie, not shopping. I'll do anything else you care to ask but don't drag me around the blooming shops again."

"I'll drop your presents over on Christmas Eve so."

"Alright! Alright! I'll go then."

"Lovely ... that's settled so. I have a day off Saturday week. Saturday is your half-day too, so all you have to do is ask Mr Head if you can have the morning off and we can spend the whole day together. Won't that be lovely? We'll start off in McBirneys. They have grand cardigans there that would suit Bamma down to the ground. Then we'll go over to Clery's. We had great fun last Christmas … didn't we? I won't be caught out with the parson's nose again, I'm telling you that much. I suppose Sonny will be there too … like last time."

"So long as you are there, that's all that matters. You just have to walk in the door and it will be as if someone turned up all the lights."

"Phil McNeill. You're a tonic on a winter's day. Do you know that? I love the big, black head of you."

As Phil made his way home he can hear the newspaper boys call out their familiar, "Heraldie-mail, Heraldie-mail," but they were saying something else that was a little more difficult to decipher. Soon, it began to sound like "trees are sighing in Downing Street."

Buying the paper, he hurriedly opens it. The *Dublin Evening Mail* had a two-page report headed, 'Peace Treaty issued at Downing Street at 6.45 on December 6 1921." The subhead declares:

Conference on Ireland 11 October to 6 December Concluded

He mouths the words as he reads: signatories, Lloyd George, Chamberlain, Birkenhead, Churchill, etc. for the British … no surprises there … for the Irish: Arthur Griffith, Robert Barton, E.J. Duggan and M. Collins. He doesn't read any further.

They leave their shopping 'til Christmas Eve's final bargains and still find their desires exceeded their budget and then some.

Relaxed at last in Bewley's of Westmoreland Street sipping his *café au lait* and reading the complimentary copy of the *Irish Weekly Independent*, Phil waits while Lizzie gets a few 'personal' bits and pieces for herself.

The report on Dail proceedings in the National University in Earlsfort Terrace appears under ominous headlines:

Collins Confident that Nation will Vindicate Him
De Valera Says Instructions were not Carried Out

"They'll be squaring up to each other before we're all very much older. Mark my words," said Lizzie with a quiver in her voice as she reads over his shoulder.

"Divil a fear of it. They'll have the whole of the Christmas holiday to think better on it. You'll see — 1922 will be a better year all round."

As they run to catch the tram, Lizzie points to the *Irish Times* vans swerving into Westmoreland Street from their Fleet Street dispatch gates. Monster posters, plastered all over the sides of the vehicles, carry a chilling Christmas message:

Huge Casualties in Belfast

Ferocious Outbreaks by Orange Gunmen

Phil squeezes her hand and moves her gently towards the stationary tram. When they are settled in their seats, he speaks to her soft and low in his base baritone voice.

"You're too lovely to be putting furrows in your forehead over matters you can do damn all about. It will all be settled soon enough … wait and see. Sure you and I will make a great Christmas out of it anyway, and have a grand life together come what may."

She knows he is still young, yet she feels so safe, almost indestructible, in his presence. "We will to be sure and we'll let the New Year look after itself," she replies. She snuggles up beside him in the steaming air, finding in his clean carbolic smell a protection against the 'malodorous effluvia' of the enclosed tram.

"Talk to me Phil."

"About what?"

"About anything you like. I just want to hear your voice."

As the tram rattles across the points of the festive streets, he recites again the details of the cosy ground floor rooms that will open out into a garden that they will rent in Islandbridge when they are married. This time he leaves out the condition about the 'Troubles' being over first. If Lizzie notices, she does not protest its absence.

Chapter 44

The ghosts of war

James McNeill observed the evening shadows shorten across the ceiling of his Stoneybatter bedroom; saw the dust swirling through the ebbing light on the other side of mid-summer's cusp; spoke to the gentle phantoms forming and transforming in the ghostly whirlpool; felt the pain in his chest slowly squeeze his life's breath away; heard the whispered blandishments of his two pallid women; smelled the sour air of unscalded urns wafting up from the shop below; walked to the landing only to collapse before the picture of the Saviour. He lay there transfixed by the burning heart crushed with thorns and lit by the barely flickering flame of a votive lamp.

The taste of unleavened Eucharist remained on his palate since the young curate from Aughrim Street brought it to him — was it yesterday or the day before? His dead wives came close and closer still. The first to ease his surrender to the Holy Will; the second tilted the brim of her hat and urged him to stay in the light just a little longer. And while the senses he had lived by and sinned by failed and fooled him, his country slipped into civil war.

Somewhere in the mid-summer city, an anti-Treaty raiding party captured the Deputy Chief of Staff of the pro-Treaty Army. Somewhere in London an old Englishman lifted the phone to tell a young Irish hero to take a hold of his new state or it would be taken from him. And while the rest of the city continued with its daily business, young men in generals' uniforms readied boys for battle.

In Smithfield, the oxyacetylene torch and grinding wheel were on the go from morning to night, removing crowns and broad arrows from military equipment surplus to the requirements of a withdrawing imperial army. Harps were welded onto things retained by the inheriting forces.

In Grangegorman, Lizzie, Essie and all the doctors, nurses and staff stopped being British civil servants at the stroke of a particular midnight and awoke on its morrow as employees of the Irish Free State. Most were glad, some disconcerted, but all continued working the same long hours caring for the same patients for the same pittance as before.

Out in Cardiff's Bridge, Philip Berford manned the gates to his desolate village as he had done for the previous six years, only now there was no Jolly Toper to slip into for a quick one or two. All day long he flipped the lid of his pocket-watch as the Great Midland Western trains flew past to the same old schedule.

In 46 Prussia Street, Gypsy noticed the first white streaks in her jet-black hair, wrapped them into a circular bun with the rest and caught an early tram to the spectacular summer sales in McBirney's of Aston Quay.

By afternoon, Bamma was near to exhaustion. Since Findlaters sacked her grandson for buttering a customer's face, she resolutely refused to darken any one of the multiples many doorsteps. Her inflexibility on the matter gave her a fine walk all the way to Haffners in Mary's Abbey for the makings of the big fry for tea.

The Kennedys and Kerrigans were coming as was Phil and his girl. Together with herself and Philip, it made for a table of nine. Two sausages per person and two for the pot, made twenty, plus a pound-and-a-half of narrow-back rashers along with two rings of mixed pudding — a tidy weight for a seventy-five year old lady to carry.

The butcher's parcel didn't get any lighter at the bottom of her big patchwork leather shopping bag when she added tomatoes, onions and mushrooms as she passed through the fruit and vegetable market in East Arran Street.

Cutting through Smithfield, she considered asking Phil to take a few things but quickly dismissed the notion of approaching him at his place of business in favour of stopping at Gypsy's for a cup of tea and a little sit down. But there was no answer at number 46, so she continued the long drag up the Old Cabra Road to home.

Being a bright summer's day, Lizzie decided to walk from Mount Brown to Cabra and save the price of the tram fares. As she turned under the arch at Christ's Church Cathedral, soldiers marched past on the double, hurrying down Winetavern carrying their rifles at the slope until they faced 'Gandon's Masterpiece' on the North Bank of the Liffey. Looking back from the other bank, she thought their guns were aimed at the Four Courts' top-heavy dome.

In the afternoon, Queenie went down to Stoneybatter and found her father lying on the landing floor, his face as cold and grey as slate. She hauled the dead weight of him back into bed, washed his face and feet and made him as comfortable as she could before dashing off to Aughrim Street.

Her first port of call was to the rectory beside the Church of the Holy Family to get Father Carroll; her second was to the surgery at 62 Marlborough Terrace for Dr Mooney. She hoped with all her heart that his surgery wasn't over. For while Doctor Mooney was renowned for answering sick calls at all hours of the day and night, Springfield was a long walk from Stoneybatter.

She was not disappointed. Felim immediately suspended his surgery with hurried apologies to his waiting patients, quickly shoved stethoscope, sphygmomanometer and nitro-glycerine tablets into his bag and drove down to 23 Stoneybatter. Queenie sat rigid beside him twisting the ends of her auburn curls, oblivious to the fact that it was her first time in a motorcar.

"They'll ease his distress for a while," he said to the still distraught young woman when he finally emerged from her father's bedroom. "Pop one under his tongue when the pain gets too bad."

Then he followed her into the parlour where Jimmy McNeill sat with his brother and other sister. He addressed the family, his low, gentle voice softening the edges of the dreaded news. "I'm afraid his heart muscle is badly damaged. There's nothing more I can do for him. It's all in God's hands now … we can only pray." He shook each hand and excused himself to go back and attend to his surgery.

At the end of another day, Phil doused the forge fire, hung up the tools and locked the gates on Head Brothers Blacksmiths. He was no sooner in the door of number 46 than he was out across the yard to the scullery to wash and shave by the huge earthenware trough. He was meticulous about his ablutions. He was going to Cabra Cottage for tea and, even though he was twenty, Bamma was not beyond carrying out an inspection.

He lathered the soap good and proper all over his face and around the back of his neck; got well into the inside and around the back of his ears; scrubbed under his nails with the short, stubby brush; then washed his hands way up to the shoulder. As Lizzie would be there too, he washed under his armpits.

In the newly re-named McKee Barracks in Blackhorse Avenue, a brass-pipped Lieutenant General Frank Lee summoned Lieutenant Kerrigan into his office. Sucking his loose upper plate to a more secure position and clearing some of the catarrh from his air passages with a couple of muffled snorts, he flung his right arm out to its furthest extent. "Kerrigan, get a detachment together immediately. We are going to take some die-hards hostage before the day is out — reprisals for General J.J. O'Connell. We are going to give these bastards a taste of the 'Balance of Terror'. A bunch of Irregulars are reported to be personifying themselves up in the Old Cabra Road. If we move quick, we'll nab the lot."

Sticking one calf-high leather boot on the desk, he took his cigarette from its cradle on the cut-glass ashtray and, swinging his right hand around the back of his head to the left side of his mouth, took a deep drag that went all the way down to his toenails. Exhaling slowly, he said thorough the smoke, "A certain Dunny Kerrigan is reported to be among them. I am given to understand that he is family … you can excuse yourself from this detail if you so wish."

"I'll gather together some of our best men, sir."

"Good man Kerrigan," said the General too forcefully for his teeth, but a well-practised hand caught them before they exited his mouth completely.

Bamma stood over the hob, clothed in black from the collar of her frock to the polished uppers of her high-buttoned boots, when the soldiers kicked in the door. Shrunken in her old age and camouflaged against the dark background of the cavernous inglenook, she continued cooking unobserved. The other ranks pointed their rifles at Dunny and Phil while the two officers stood legs well apart, hands on the butts of their side arms. The more senior of them removed his hat and spat on his fingers to flatten down hyena tufts on the ridge of his head.

"Up on yer feet the pair of you. We're taking you to Marlborough … McKee Barracks where you'll be held until your Irregular friends release 'Ginger'… eh … General O'Connell. Up

252

before we change our minds and shoot you where you sit," he continued with much gesticulation. "You've been on one end of the Balance of Terror," he said looking at Phil. "Well now you're going to be on the receiving end. Yeah chose the wrong side, so get used to it."

"Oh Sonny! Sonny! Don't let them harm your father," Nelly screamed, clinging onto her husband's sleeve.

"If he doesn't get outside that door this very minute, I'll shoot him meself. Now keep out of this mother … you're out of your depth on this one."

"Well I'm honoured. Fully commissioned officers of His Majesty's Irish Army in the kitchen and a lorry load of newly-signed up Truceliers waiting in Mooney's Field — all to arrest two Volunteers. Speaks volumes right enoughsky … doesn't it? Orders come from Beggar's Bush Barracks or straight from London, I don't suppose?"

"Very funny. Very funny indeed," said General Lee, his loose dentures marking time like castanets. "Well, they love comedians down in the Castle … down in the Castle. Perhaps that's where we should be taking you. But let me tell you this in case you don't know. We have our own Irish state now for the first time in history … with an Irish Government elected by the Irish people and we've no intention of allowing die-hards the likes of you destroy it. You're both under arrest. So move yourself … outside and up on the lorry,"

Gypsy was on her feet, nostrils flaring, eyes glaring with schoolmarm disapproval honed to razor sharpness during years of teaching in the Loreto Convent.

"How dare you talk to anyone in this house in that manner! I'll have you know that my father died for the cause in '67 … my brother was the hero of the Athlone train in Easter Week … thank God neither of them are here to see this." Then, pointing to Phil, she said with trembling voice, "My nephew over there has been doing his bit since he was only a gosún and his poor mother, God rest her soul, was working for the separatist cause when you and your likes were little better than 'Castle Catholics'. Hasn't this family done enough for Ireland? Have we not suffered enough? What right have you to be coming into a house like this and threatening the Berfords? Take yourself out to hell wherever you came from … make yourselves useful for a change … take your trucks and guns to the

North and do something to stop the murders up there, why don't you?"

While Gypsy fumed and fulminated, Nelly held onto her husband's sleeve, whimpering. "Oh Sonny, not your father, you won't let them shoot your father?"

"I'll shoot him meself if I have to," he repeated, drawing his weapon from its leather holster.

Over at the coal range, Bamma worked slowly, methodically, sharing out the Saturday fry from her big cast-iron pan onto the warmed and waiting plates. She carried the first big, blue plate from her cherished willow-pattern dinner set to the table. She held it in both hands because it was heavy with the still sizzling sausages, rashers, black and white pudding, mushrooms and tomatoes, all floating in rich gravy. Gaining the table, she cracked it across the side of Sonny's face. His revolver slid across the table as he hit the floor, strips of fried bacon and sausage balancing on the crown and peak of his officer's cap while the gravy dripped down his nose and chin to pool on his newly starched officer's shirt.

The soldiers were fixed to the spot like lamped rabbits, staring blankly at Sonny's buckled body, the black and white pudding stuck in his epaulets making a good accompaniment to the rashers balancing on his hat. General Lee levelled his revolver at Bamma as she slumped ashen-faced onto a kitchen chair.

In a split second, Phil had him off the floor and against the wall. Holding him by the throat with his left hand, he poked him in the chest with the index finger of his right, practically spitting the words into his ex-leader's face. "You're a fecken professor. Do you know that? With your theories on this, that and every curse of God thing under the sun. All I've ever seen come out of them are good Irish women frightened out of their homes. Did no one ever teach you that you should never raise a hand to a woman, aye? Only a coward does that … do you know that you ill-reared …"

The general was doubly unlucky. For one thing, Phil, not being the loquacious kind, was soon done with talking. For another, being held by the lad's left hand, meant the stronger one was free. Consequently, the short right jab to the general's mouth sent a long spurt of blood into the air and dentures scattering in shards across the flagged floor.

"You've done it now for certain, you hot-headed hoor," said Dunny, picking up his son's revolver and training it on the soldiers standing agog. "You had better go on the run now for certain. Out the back with you now … you know where to go. Stay low until we organise something for you. Don't go near any of your old haunts. They'll be watching everywhere … they're not like the English … they know us and everything about us … Jaysus, the more I come to think of it, the feckers used to be us. Go off with you now … I'll take these two to the Four Courts."

"You'll never get them past the Army and DMG. You'd better go on the run as well Dunny. Tie them up quick and let's get out of here."

Nelly sat on the floor whimpering over the head of her dazed son, cleaning his soiled locks with her handkerchief and wailing: "What's to become of me? Oh Lord, God Almighty, what's to become of us all? My only son is lying in his gore and my husband is off to the hills to live like a wild raparee?"

"Pull yourself together woman. I've no fecken intention of living up in the fecken mountains because of that spoiled brat of yours. I'm off to join Rory O'Connor in the Four Courts. That'll be as near to the mountains as I want to be. Will you leave that little gobshite where he is and look after your mother, for the sweet love of Jesus? And another thing, that's not gore on his golden locks, it's gravy."

"Mother Kennedy, will you please stay with Bamma? I don't like the look of her at all," Phil said as he tried to get his grandmother to take a sip of tea. "Someone better get the doctor to come over … get him to give you all the once over. I'm sure Aunt Nelly could do with a little something to settle her nerves as well. Uncle Dunny, we best move before the rest start coming in the door … you can't take those two to the Four Courts … they're unconscious … you'd have to carry them. Come on. Let's get out of here while the going's good."

Outside, in Mooney's Field, the cottage shielding them from view of the soldiers on the truck at the front of the house, Dunny said, "We had better split up. Go to Springfield … Felim will look after you. Get him to come over to the house and see to Sonny and Bamma, and another thing, ask him to bring something to quieten your Aunt Nelly. Will you do that?"

"Don't worry Dunny. I'll look after it."

Chapter 45

On the run

Phil looked out of Mooney's barn at June's long twilight sprinkling brass filings through the leaf-thick trees around Springfield. It was as though time had back-peddled. Again, he was incarcerated in its decaying timbers where rats rustled straw all night long. And yet, the place gave him a strange sense of security. He always had sanctuary there from further interdict, the barn itself being the punishment. Again, he awaited the action of others to determine his future.

Listening to the aftermath of skirmish blowing ever more intermittent on the warm night air, he began rationalising his position. Soldiers wouldn't lightly raid the property of someone as important as the Chairman of the Great Midland Western Railway. And in any event, civil war had turned out to be not much more than a row in a kitchen. Everyone would get over it and soon enough.

Nevertheless, he was relieved that Lizzie hadn't arrived before all the fuss and bother began. Her seeing that class of 'kafuffle' could easily spoil things between them. He'd get a message to her first thing in the morning. Pass it on through Essie so she wouldn't be worrying. He could slip across the field to Cabra Lodge when it was good and dark. He knew the lie of the land so well, he had few doubts that he could get there and back without difficulty.

But doubts sprouted like mushrooms in the warm darkness. He worried how Bamma fared, how Sonny recovered and whether Dunny had made it safely to the Four Courts. The realisation that he couldn't stay long in Mooney's barn soon came to him. When Sonny started talking he would be bunched. He wondered if Willie Stumpf might give him a temporary job in his pork shop and maybe even put him up for a while in their place in Inchicore.

He put it to Felim when he called over with tea and sandwiches. "That'd be the ticket … never dream of looking for me in a German pork butchers on the other side of the city. He can tell everybody I'm his German cousin — one foreign-looking fella looks much the same as the next to the people in this town."

"I'll certainly pass the word along and see if your German friend can put you up. I think getting away from the environment around here an excellent idea in any event. But how would you like to continue with the blacksmith trade?"

"God, I'd love nothing better but I can't go back to Smithfield in the circumstances … you know what I mean."

"Quite, but I wasn't thinking of Head Brothers. If you're interested, I could give you a letter to Mr Johnston. He's the manager of the Spa Road works. I believe Mr Head's brother is the shop steward. If he can square it with the union, I don't see any problem in you starting with the Tramway Company."

"That would be grand if it can be managed. I don't know how to thank you Uncle Felim … for everything."

"It's time to stop the fighting Phil. The British have left … time to stop now."

"Sure we might if we're let."

As the net closed, Felim moved him to the relative safety of Springfield House proper. Through the skylight of his attic room, he looked towards the Wicklow Mountains and considered how it might be living the life of the outlaw up there like Michael Dwyer. Spotting the chimney of Jameson's Distillery in Smithfield, he wished he could walk freely through the rush and bustle of the square to Head Brothers and blow up the fire for Harry. Mostly, he looked longingly towards Grangegorman, lost in imaginings of what his girl might be doing at each exact moment of his long vigil.

And as the days were moped and pined away, courtesy uncle, foster-mother and all the rest of his surrogate protectors fired off a blunderbuss of correspondence in the hope that something might hit the desired target and bring their charge to safety.

Philip Berford broke a twenty-year silence and wrote to Molly Wilson begging her to sponsor him to America. His plea, notwithstanding all that had passed between them, was for her to save the liberty, and perhaps even the life, of the child they once pushed in a bassinet along the banks of the Royal Canal.

From her sick bed in Cabra Cottage, Bamma sent a note to James McNeill's equally sick one above the dairy in Stoneybatter. Reading it out, Queenie's sweet voice told him of Bamma's deep desire that they should set aside their differences for the sake of the boy's future. She watched the colour return to his cheeks as she conveyed the estranged plea that he use his influence and secure his son's safe conduct out of the country.

In the large study, three stories below the fugitive's feet, Felim Mooney admired the Italian plasterwork on the ceiling, just as he had done every day of his life. Cherubs smiled as Persephone rose from the underworld, sheaves of wheat springing incongruously from her nipples. He marvelled again at the relief, so three-dimensional, it almost qualified as sculpture. Picking up a sheaf of Dublin Tramway Company headed notepaper, bearing its chairman's monogram, he penned a letter to the Spa Road Works Manager requesting he find a position in the forge for Phil McNeill.

As those who loved him sought to save him, in his crow's nest at the top of Springfield, Phil heard British artillery boom once more across the River Liffey, reducing another bit of the capital's civic pride to shell and ember.

Only this time he knew that both the gunners and the gunned were native born.

Chapter 46

End of the road

And while Phil passed the time as best he could in his loft above the big house, in the mountains overlooking Dublin, shepherds minding their scattered flocks found Dunny's body, eyes blindfolded, hands tied behind his back.

Before the week was over, word came through that Sonny had been shot dead in an ambush in County Kerry.

Even in the bitterness of civil war, Phil knelt at the side of his bed to recite the rosary in all its five sorrowful mysteries, tears streaming uncontrollably down his cheeks. There was no more 'Ebony and Ivory,' just the dark notes were left in a discordant world.

And the blows kept coming. Felim informed him during one of his frequent visits that Bamma was failing fast and that Nelly wanted to sign herself into Grangegorman.

Philip Berford arrived after mass one Sunday, anxious with steamer tickets, an address in Philadelphia and twenty silver dollars.

"I always wanted you to have this," he said taking off the double-Albert gold chain with the gold watch on one end and the gold matchbox on the other that had enthralled Phil since childhood. "I intended you to have it for a wedding present but ... but who knows where or when?" He broke off and disappeared down the stairs before Phil could see the tears welling in his eyes. He shouted back, "God keep you son wherever you may be," and was gone.

Mother Kennedy came in the afternoon with Móna and Dido to say their hurried farewells. Before leaving, she kissed him on the lips for the first time in his life, and said, "It's all arranged now and it's all for the best. Don't look back ... you're going to where there is a good life and a future for everyone. It's a republic, son. There's no ascendancy in America. Molly Wilson will look after you ... We'll be praying for you constantly."

Then she took his breath away: "Don't worry about Lizzie. We'll get word to her after you're safely out of the country. It's the best we can do. Otherwise you'd both be at risk. You can send for her later." Then she left.

But the day wasn't done with him. Before it reached noon, Felim came up the stairs and announced that a young lady awaited the pleasure of Phil McNeill in the drawing room. Phil entered the biggest, most ornate room he had ever seen, bursting with expectations of Lizzie's tall dark form.

He was taken aback when confronted by a beautiful red-haired young woman who ran to him sobbing, "Phil, oh, Phil. Thank God I found you. Daddy's asking for you … We didn't know where you were and we nearly lost him so many times. He talks about you all the time. You must have known it was him."

"Of course. Things unsaid so long are sometimes better left unsaid. But I'm sorry Queenie … I truly am … I can't go … there's a difficulty …"

"We heard all about it. Here, you'll need this if you're to get as far as Kingsbridge never mind Cobh or America. He's been watching out for you all the time you know."

"I know."

He took the harp-embossed paper from her hand and read: "Please afford safe conduct and render all reasonable assistance to Phil McNeill wherever he travels in the Irish Free State." His eyes dart to the signature, 'Richard Mulcahy, Chief of Staff.'

Later that day, Queenie nearly dropped out of her standing on hearing footsteps on the stairs. Charging out to the hall, she couldn't believe her eyes. Her father stood there fully dressed, taking his best trilby off the hallstand.

"And where do you think you're going father?"

"Take it easy Queenie, child, take it easy. I've been cooped up in this place since I don't know when. I'm only going as far as Oxmantown Green to watch the cattle sales for a while, with the help of God. Give me a hand with me coat." Then, conspiratorially, "I'm feeling much better today sweetheart but don't tell Dr Mooney, sure you won't? Just get me a couple of those tablets he brought like a good girl. I'll be back in an hour. I promise."

After many stops to catch his breath or to slip a tablet under his tongue, James finally reached Blackhall Place. The square in front of the Bluecoat School teamed with farmers and animals, here a cattle jobber, there a costermonger and everywhere balladeers selling their song sheets on the latest sporting hero or martyr for the cause.

James stood on the low plinth of the Bluecoat School linking his arms around the paling for support. From this vantage point, he observed all the buying and selling, the feints and closures, sleight-of-hand and the downright thievery.

"Twang, twang, a penny a lump. The more you eat the more you jump."

"Get the last of your Irish bananas."

"How up! How up! Finesht baste from the lush meadows of Meath."

At Watling Street Bridge, Phil stopped to watch boys fishing for eels by dangling lengths of bailing twine weighted with iron bolts into the flowing water. Fish coiled their bodies around the lines and were hauled up to have their heads bashed off the parapet until the wriggling stopped.

At Croppies' Acre he pulled the peak of his cap almost down to his nose as a truckload of Free State soldiers approached from the direction of Parkgate Street. They turned left and disappeared into the barracks. Phil punched the air with the sudden realisation.

"I have a safe conduct pass in me pocket. I can go anywhere I damn well please," he shouted to the buried lamplighters on the other side of the Esplanade railings.

In Cabra Cottage, Bamma stopped talking to her dead children long enough to say, "What's keeping me?"

Then closed her eyes and sent her soul to join them.

Felim and Philip walked in what was left of Sallcock's Wood, mourning the loss of Bamma, Dunny, Sonny, Nelly and Phil. All gone from them in their different ways. But there was nothing to be done, so they retired to Hanlon's for a pint and a small one.

In Philadelphia, Molly Wilson, childless wife of Police Captain Rory O'Donnell, prepared a room for the ward of the only man she ever loved.

*****

263

In Grangegorman, Lizzie and Essie hung a picture of 'Our Lady of Perpetual Succour' on the wall of a cubicle, placed a vase of flowers on the bedside locker and let a few drops of lavender water fall on the pillow slip. In such little ways they fussed about making it as homely as possible to receive Nelly Kerrigan.

At Blackhall Place, Cosy Finnigan sat by her widow's window and began to worry about the old gentleman still standing at the railings long after the cattle and the cattle-dealers had gone.

Going over the road, she recognised James, son of the Fenian McNeill. He was not so much standing as being held up by the paling. She touched his stiffening body, then crossed herself to pray for his immortal soul.

Acknowledgements

With special thanks to my wife Lora for her unending support and encouragement; Vinny Caprani, renowned expert on all things Dublin, for ensuring historical and geographical accuracy; Professor Jason Sommer, who encouraged me to begin this journey; Kevin Stevens for his advice on early drafts; and Pádraig Hanratty for his professional job of editing.

Made in the USA
Charleston, SC
13 April 2014